⟨THE⟩

BITTER

VETCH

D.L. CALVIN

ISBN: 0988840243
ISBN 13: 9780988840249
CreateSpace Independent Publishing Platform
North Charleston, South Carolina

∽ CHAPTER 1 ∾

SALLY PRITCHARD WAS A VERY handsome woman, a great body and Hollywood face, and it didn't subtract from her allure that she owned several high-profile companies. To top it off, she was a widow with no children. Once the drift of the dream had been firmly implanted in Bradshaw's mind, he turned his overactive imagination into picturing Sally Pritchard nude, enticing him to lay her out. He fashioned himself pressing on top of her, kissing her throat, his fingers squeezing her nipples and causing her to gasp in pain and pleasure.

A crack of lightning startled Bradshaw...

Momentarily confused, the young doctor observed two things happening almost simultaneously—a driving rain suddenly hitting his office window and the lights flickering—then the room went dark. Surprised, yet thankful for the diversion, it gave him time to adjust his posture to relieve the pain caused by his erection. This Pritchard woman was really something.

Mary Nash, his administrative assistant and his "right hand," knocked twice on his door and walked in carrying a burning candle. "I'm sorry to barge in on your session, doctor, but I figured you both could use the light."

Giving his assistant a smile, Doctor Bradshaw said, "Good thinking, Mary."

"Should we continue, doctor?" Sally asked, getting up off the couch.

"No, Sally, let's call a halt to this session, and we will pick it up at our next get-together."

As she slipped back into her shoes Sally agreed, "Fine with me, doctor."

"Please see Mary on the way out so she can schedule you."

"Yes, doctor," Sally replied, slipping out of his nice, cozy office.

Watching his patient leave, Doctor Bradshaw then brought his thoughts back to the business at hand. Picking up his pen, he began writing his notes on Sally. He knew that seeing water in one's dream was symbolic of spirituality, knowledge and healing. As water is the essence of life, to dream that you hear water (as a babbling brook) denotes reflection, meditation and pondering of your thoughts and emotions. To dream water is rising up and in your house signifies your struggles and overwhelming emotions. *The dream describes Sally perfectly.* He thought.

He had finished writing his notes about Sally's session when Mary entered his office. Handing Sally's file to Mary, she in turn handed him a stack of letters to sign.

"Now, doctor, don't forget you're going to the Policeman's Banquet tonight. I already picked up your tuxedo. It's hanging in the front closet. And here is Doctor Jackson's phone number. She called while you were in session to say she is running late and will meet you at the banquet."

"Thank you, Mary," the doctor said with a smile for his organized and efficient assistant as she turned and left his office.

A big grin was on Doctor Bradshaw's face as he dressed for the banquet and thought about Alexandra, otherwise known as "Doctor AJ" or just plain "AJ." He was thinking how best to describe her—*Tall, maybe six-foot, with dark-green eyes, red hair, a band of freckles that ran across her cheeks and nose, with a dynamite smile that lit up her whole face when she was happy or delighted. In addition, she was an avid sports watcher. Especially college football and baseball. Personally, she did not care too much for basketball and professional football because she thought that blacks dominate them. It probably has something to do with an article, she once read that stated twenty-two percent of the NFL players were convicted felons.*

Though he understood nothing much would ever come of his persistent pleas for her to marry him. He, nevertheless, continued to harbor a hope that one day they would at least live together.

As he continued to prepare for the banquet, his heart wasn't in it. What he would rather do was invite AJ over to his townhouse, order a pizza, open a bottle of red wine and watch an old Charlie Chan movie, or maybe a porno film to warm AJ up—not that she needed much warming up.

However, there really wasn't an acceptable excuse to get out of the banquet since they both worked as profilers for the Washington D.C. Police Department, plus both did consulting work for the Federal Bureau of Investigation. In other words, it was politically correct they both be at the banquet, end of subject. *Besides,* he told himself, *the food was always good, and he could dance with AJ and whisper things in her ear that would make her face turn red. To say he loved the woman would be the understatement of the year...*

Doctor Bradshaw drove to the hotel, parked and then waited for Alexandra in the lobby. After a few minutes, he looked at his watch. *Where is she? Fifteen more minutes and the banquet will start. It just isn't like her to be late…* Pacing, he walked by a large mirror in the hotel foyer where he momentarily stopped, adjusted his bow tie and straightened his boutonnière.

"Oh, Doctor Bill, you're so handsome!" Came a mocking voice.

Before he turned around he recognized the voice as belonging to Raphael Gonzales. "Hi Gonzo."

"What the hell are you doing here at this respectable hotel?" Gonzo asked with a big grin. Both men laughed as they shook hands.

"I'm waiting for my date," Bill said in a very perturbed tone of voice. "By the way, Gonzo, where is your wife?"

"At home," Gonzo replied, sticking his right hand back into his pocket.

Immediately Bill knew something was wrong by the tone of Gonzo's voice that was accompanied by a very dejected look. "What is it? We men say about women? You can't live with them, and you can't live without them?" Bill said, slapping Gonzo on his massive chest.

Gonzo gave a bitter laugh, as he said, "Ain't that the truth? I bust my balls, so she can have beautiful things and drive a nice car and what does she do? She divorces my sorry black ass because she saw me with a prostitute coming out of the Best Western."

"Oh, you were working undercover on a case?" Bill asked.

"Hmmm," Bill uttered, trying to keep a straight face. He knew Gonzo had a passion for white women ever since his playing days with the National Football League. Every season Gonzo had been in the news, always with some beautiful white woman who would eventually end up dumping him because he had found another one to satisfy his lust. Having such a voracious sexual appetite, he would have sex twice maybe even three times a day, each time with a different woman. Sometimes he would have two women at the same time. Now, the once-feared and powerful middle linebacker who used to crush men into the dirt every Sunday for ten seasons, stood before him—a mere mortal. He consoled himself with the thought that at least he had AJ, while Gonzo had nobody.

Looking at his watch again, Bill saw only five minutes had ticked by since his last check. "Excuse me, Gonzo," Bill said as he walked back down the long foyer to the street. After going through the large revolving door, he first looked up and then down the street; there still was no sign of AJ. Impatient, he reached into his pocket and pulled out his cell phone, flipped the top open, scrolled down the list and hit auto dial for AJ's number.

Taking the Invitation from Bill, the sergeant exchanged it for Bill's nametag and a table number.

"I guess we're both going stag tonight, Gonzo," Bill said disappointment resonating in his voice.

"Sorry about that Doc," Gonzo said, patting the doctor on the back as he headed for his own table.

Table twenty-three was a big round table. The doctor looked at his place card, picking up each one and looking at the names that were in very small print. As he went around the table, he made a mental note that all the attendees at his table were doctors. *Boy is this going to be boring;* he thought. *I don't recognize any of the names except AJ's and mine.*

Since most of the tables were empty, he walked over to table twenty-five and looked at each of the name cards. At that table, they were either judges or lawyers. *Hmm,* he thought. He grabbed two name cards and placed them on table twenty-three. Then he picked up AJ's nametag and his own and placed them on table twenty-five. He told himself, *Well, at least it would be better than listening to a bunch of doctors talking about malpractice insurance or some other mundane illness or operation that would turn my stomach.*

He hated the sight of blood. If he saw blood from a wound or accident, it made him grow faint, nauseous, and more often than not, he would vomit and pass out. When this happened, AJ would call him, her "he-man" and kiss him on his forehead. At times like this he would feel foolish for his weakness, yet his dad had been a hemophobic as well.

It had been hell for him in medical school. Often times he would deliberately work a different rotation just to avoid the emergency room and surgery. That is why he became a psychiatrist, so he did not have to deal with people's blood and guts. He felt safer and more comfortable dealing with their minds.

Dinner without AJ was boring. Although the dinner conversation started out light and lively, it dried up when one of the judges asked him what he did for a living. When he told them, the table became quiet and subdued. He guessed they were afraid he was psychoanalyzing them. After the dessert and before the speeches began, Bill took his name card from the table, and stuck it in his pocket stood up and bowed to the ladies and gentlemen, excusing himself and walked out of the banquet room.

Upon leaving the climate-controlled atmosphere of the hotel, the warm humid night air hit Bill full in the face. It felt as if someone had thrown a bucket of warm water over him. His undershirt felt sticky, and he could feel sweat running down his chest.

A few yards in front of him, Bill spotted Detective Gonzo "Hold up a minute, will you, Gonzo" Bill yelled. Gonzo turned recognizing his friend, he stopped and waited for the doctor to catch up. When he did, Bill was sweating profusely obviously winded from too little exercise.

"Gonzo, I'm a bit concerned about Doctor Jackson. She was to have been my date this evening. About four or so she called my office and told my secretary, she would be running late and would meet me at the banquet.

I have called her, but she doesn't answer. I was wondering if you would follow me to her apartment complex, so we could check on her."

"Oh, Doc, I was on my way to see somebody. Where is her apartment complex?" Gonzo whined like a little schoolboy who did not want to eat his peas.

"She lives north of here about ten minutes depending on traffic over by Georgia and Missouri streets."

"Well then let's go. She probably layed down to take a quick nap and slept through your date. However, we'll check it out," Gonzo said as he opened his car's door and got in.

Doctor Bradshaw was in luck. His car was across the street and heading in the right direction. Hurrying towards his car, he pulled out his keys, hit the fob to unlock his BMW and within a few minutes both, he and the detective were heading north up Sixteenth Street. Bill observed the traffic was light, for some reason. At Missouri, Bill made a right-hand turn and sped down the expressway, getting off at Georgia. Two blocks later he made a quick left turn into her apartment complex and gently pulled his BMW into one of the spots designated for guests. Right behind him, Gonzo pulled into the other spot.

"Boy, this is nice," Gonzo, said walking up to the BMW.

"What's nice the car or the complex?" Bill asked with a laugh.

"Well I was talking about the apartment complex," Gonzo remarked, helping the doctor out of his car. "How much does this place cost a month?" Gonzo asked looking all around the grounds and then pointed toward the complex's rental office. "They have both surveillance cameras and a security guard." Gonzo asked.

"The apartment rents for $2500 a month plus utilities and a maintenance fee of $75 a month. The security guard works from six in the morning to six in the evening." Bill replied, turning up the sidewalk towards AJ's apartment.

"Oh, and how do you know that?" Gonzo asked.

"Well, the complex has been victimized so many times that the insurance company told the owners. They would not insure the complex unless security was beefed up. That was when the complex powers that be installed the cameras and hired a retired police detective to handle security. I know this because the rental agent told AJ and me the day we came to look at the apartment."

Arriving at AJ's front door, Bill pulled out his key ring, inserted the correct key and opened the door. With one eyebrow raised, Gonzo looked at the doctor with an unspoken question. "AJ and I are lovers, Gonzo."

As soon as both men walked into the foyer, they knew something was wrong. AJ's purse laid open and emptied on the kitchen floor. Her credit cards were strewn about the kitchen and hallway. Signaling for Bill to stay back and be quiet, Gonzo pulled out his service revolver.

"AJ, Metro Police!" Gonzo called. There was no response. Silently, Gonzo crept down the hallway, his revolver at the ready.

Not able to bear the silence any longer, Bill called out, "AJ!" Fear caused his voice to crack. Still, there was no response. Quietly Gonzo inched his way down the hallway, his training and experience telling him to be cautious. He opened the bedroom door and looked down, as he turned on the light. Spread out on the bed nude, lay Doctor Alexandra Jackson— dead!

∽ CHAPTER 2 ∽

ROCKED BY BOTH SHOCK AND grief, Bill stood silent, tears streaming down his cheeks. He had not cried like this since his mother's death when he had been a senior at the University of Georgia. AJ's death brought back memories of his parents and their deaths. His father had died only two years previous. He remembered that to the end, his father had been the same racial, maniacal bully he had always been while Bill was growing up. Per his instructions prior to his death, his father's coffin had been draped with the U.S. Flag, the flag of Georgia and the Grand Wizard robe and mask of the Ku Klux Klan!

Now once again, Doctor Bradshaw was experiencing the pain from the loss of a loved one. However, this pain was different. On some level he could accept the death of his mother. Although her death had been painful to him, he understood that untreated breast cancer could ravage the body—his mother being no exception. The disease had ravaged her small slender body, taking her once beautiful smile, soft skin and silver hair, leaving only in their place the shell of a once beautiful woman.

He had visited her every day in the hospital and witnessed the steady, daily decline of his beloved mother. She seemed so small, helpless and lost in her hospital bed. Her head was bald, her face sunken and her once bright, shiny eyes had become a dull, lifeless blue.

His father had died of old age and a broken heart. At least that's what Bill's sister, Evelyn, had told everyone. This, too, he could understand.

The police had roped off the area from the parking lot of the complex to the front door of AJ's apartment. While Crime Scene Investigators were taking pictures and taking samples, uniformed police officers were knocking on doors, asking people if they had seen or heard anything suspicious or out of the ordinary. The fingerprint team was slowly, painstakingly lifting prints from every conceivable surface.

From out of nowhere, Gonzo appeared and handed Bill a cup of hot, black coffee with sugar. Normally the doctor did not drink black coffee, but Gonzo knew he needed the stimulant.

"Gonzo, my world is rocked," Bill said between sips. "I loved her very much. In fact, I had asked her to marry me but she turned me down. My next hope was that I could at least live with her. In fact, we practically *were* living together. You will find my suits, ties and shaving stuff in the master bathroom. If you go to my place, you will find her stuff hanging in my closets.

"Who could have done this to her? If they wanted to rob her, then rob her, but they didn't have to kill her."

Out of the corner of his eye, the detective saw the EMT unit pulling the gurney into the living room. Gonzo turned, deliberately placing himself between the doctor and the gurney carrying AJ's corpse. Upon seeing the covered body on the gurney, Bill leaned his head into the detective's chest and once again broke down in tears, his body racked by emotional turmoil as he sobbed unashamedly in front of his friend.

"Let's get you home," Gonzo said, motioning to a uniformed officer.

Bill couldn't sleep. Still in his tuxedo, he sat on his bed, picked up the phone on his nightstand and dialed Alexandra's parents. As the call was traveling through the thousand miles of wire and airwaves, he happened to look at the alarm clock it said 5:30.

On the second ring, a deep, male voice said, "Hello?"

"Hello, sir, this is Bill."

"Bill who?" came a very terse reply. "And why in heaven's name are you calling somebody at this ungodly hour?"

The terseness pissed him off. "Sir, this is Doctor Bradshaw. Up until last night, I was dating your daughter. However, it is my sad duty to inform you that your daughter is dead."

He slammed down the phone, angry with a man he hardly knew. Bill fumed to himself; *Maybe it is the only way to get his attention, as he seems to care more about his sleep than his daughter! The selfish son-of-a-bitch will probably roll over and go back to sleep thinking it had just been a wrong number.*

Bill stood up, kicked off his shoes and removed his bowtie. While unbuttoning his ruffled shirt, he happened to look across the bedroom and saw a pair of black sapphire and diamond earrings lying on the other nightstand. He had bought them for a very special occasion, but he could not remember which one. What he did remember was that AJ had worn a black dress that showed lots of cleavage and the earrings went well with the dress, not to mention they went well with AJ.

As he pulled down his pants, he idly wondered: *In what dress would her parents bury her?* Then he wondered, *Would she be buried here in Washington D.C. or back in Arkansas? If buried in her home state, how many of her D.C. friends would go to the funeral?*

He turned on the shower and adjusted the spray and temperature. The last time he had showered, the two of them had showered together to conserve water. That had been yesterday morning. Stepping into the shower, again the doctor felt the onrush of guilt and loss overwhelming him. Sobbing as the water rained over him, he rubbed his burning eyes. *It's not fair*, he thought. *Nobody as talented or beautiful as Alexandra should die so young.*

As he stood in the shower thinking, he decided then and there to use his skills as a profiler to help Gonzo catch the person or persons who had committed that terrible crime. Then he had a flash of memory. *Wait a minute! AJ had been a Federal Agent. That means the FBI could be called in to help!*

His body clean, his clothes changed, Bill walked over to the bedroom phone and called Mary at home. It was now six o'clock and Mary would be getting up to walk her dog. The phone rang only once when a crisp, clear voice inquired, "Hello?"

"Hello, Mary, this is Doctor Bradshaw. I want you to cancel my appointments for today and reschedule them for late next week."

"Okay, doctor, I will do that, but may I ask why?"

"Because, Mary, last night Doctor Jackson was murdered in her apartment and I'm in no condition to see anybody. So when you have done as I ask and you have caught up with any outstanding work, you are free to take the time off with pay."

"Oh, doctor, I'm so very sorry about Doctor Jackson," Mary commiserated.

"Thank you, Mary. I will call you next week. Good-bye." The doctor placed the receiver back into its cradle and walked into the kitchen. Upon opening the refrigerator door, there staring him in the face was part of the uneaten pizza that he and AJ had had the night before. He pulled the box out, pulled two slices apart, placed them on a paper towel and slipped them into the microwave oven. Next he turned and made a pot of coffee. As he walked out of the kitchen, he set the timer on the microwave for sixty seconds then proceeded to the living room where he turned on the TV to hear the local news.

The local reporters were having a feeding frenzy with the vicious of AJ's murder. One reporter was standing in front of AJ's apartment. In the background could be seen the gurney, carrying AJ's lifeless body, being rolled down the sidewalk and then being loaded into the coroner's van. A quick pan to the right showed Bill crying, his head bowed. Then a news flash ran across the bottom of the television screen saying—The police have arrested two black youths caught while driving Doctor Jackson's stolen car—

The police have already caught the murderers! Bill stood in stunned silence, digesting this latest development as he continued to watch as the news camera showed the two killers, handcuffed, their heads bowed in shame, as they were being led to jail by uniformed police officers. Suddenly, Bill noticed that one of the killers was wearing AJ's University of Arkansas sweatshirt and the gold bracelet he had bought AJ for Christmas last year. He knew that when the police examined the bracelet, they would find it inscribed with two interlocking hearts and the inscription—Heart of my heart, light of my life, Love Bill— She never took the bracelet off except for bathing and lovemaking.

Bill soon became aware his heart felt as though it were banging against his rib cage along with his breathing becoming very labored. Then he became aware of his anger rising. He started cursing loud expletives, something he seldom did. Without conscious thought, his repressed racial hatred came to the front as he watched the two shines, (his father's pet nickname for blacks) being led like little lambs.

He supposed the news reporters would interview the killer's mommas and with big tears in their eyes, they would tell the world how good their sons were. Upon investigation, it would be found that their sons had been in and out of trouble since they were twelve. Further investigation would reveal that one of the mothers, if not both, probably had four children with four different daddies. One was probably knocked up at thirteen, the other at twelve. Neither mother could read nor write, but people would still believe these people were worth saving. *Not hardly! How can you help people who cannot help themselves? When they condemn themselves to a worthless class with every word they utter? Like beasts of burden, they are meant to work in the fields,* he thought.

The doctor picked up the remote and clicked off the TV...silence reined in the room. All that could be heard was the coffee pot gurgling in the kitchen and the beep from the microwave telling him his breakfast was ready.

On a normal morning he would have sat down, read his paper, drunk his coffee and listened for AJ. But she was no more. That chapter of his life was over. Two drug-crazed young black men had ended it. In the deepest recesses of his mind he could still hear his father ranting and raving as he taught him about the shines.

In the 1950s, seven Negroes had tried to attend an all white high school in Little Rock. His dad had organized a huge KKK march through the streets in Valdosta, just in case the shines there had similar ideas. Then in the sixties had come the outbreak of riots in Selma, Atlanta and Jackson over civil rights and voting. "Why do those damn Yankee agitators keep sticking their noses in our business?" his dad would yell. "They have no right to tell us how to treat our niggers. If they love them so much, why don't they come down here and take them up north? Then watch what happens. Neighborhoods once beautiful will become slums. Why? Because they don't know how to fix anything! They can't read or write. All they are fit for is to work in the fields and to serve whites. They are incapable of independent thought!"

Perhaps it was intuition, or maybe divine inspiration but Bill reached out for the phone that had not yet rung. "Hello?" he asked.

"Hello, sir," the voice said. It was the same voice with whom he had talked only an hour earlier. It was AJ's dad.

∽ CHAPTER 3 ∾

SINCE AJ HAD NOT BEEN affiliated with any local church, it was decided to have a two day viewing at the local funeral parlor in Washington D.C. Then her body would be transported to Little Rock where AJ could have a "decent Christian burial," her dad's exact words. The pompous son-of-a-bitch had made it quite clear to Bill that he did not have the money to pay for AJ's funeral. Bill remembered AJ had once told him, "My dad was raised during the great depression and to this day he hoards both food and money. Everything he owns he paid for with cash as he doesn't trust banks."

After his conversation with her dad, Bill called a local mortuary to make the arrangements, an appointment to pick out a casket and to make the travel arrangements for AJ. Without hesitation, he took out his check-book and paid cash for everything. Though he was not obligated to, either legally or morally for that matter, he paid AJ's final bill. He did it out of the strongest and noblest of reasons—love.

Later, as Bill left the mortuary, he looked at his watch. It was nine-thirty in the morning. A quick calculation told him he had now been awake for over thirty-six hours but there were still things that needed to be done before he could sleep. Sleep, no he wasn't ready for that yet. He decided to go to the Central Police Station, talk to Gonzo and tell him about the gold bracelet and the Arkansas sweatshirt. After that he would call AJ's folks and let them know of the arrangements he had made.

Thirty minutes later he had parked his beamer and was walking up the steps into the police station. Whenever he could, he liked to park at the rear of the building, away from the heavy downtown traffic. He walked down the hall to the last door on the left where, if he were lucky, he hoped to find Gonzo. Walking into the office he saw Gonzo was not there. Disappointed, he decided to leave him a note, asking him to call his cell phone. As he leaned over the detective's very cluttered and unorganized desk to grab a note pad, he glanced down and saw, right on top, the preliminary autopsy report on one Alexandra Jackson.

Bill's hand, seeming of its own volition, picked up the report. As he read it, he could feel the acid churning in his stomach and feel the onrush of nausea. When he flipped up the page and saw a picture of AJ's naked body lying on the bed, her beautiful red hair soaked in her own blood and flesh actually torn away from her breast where her nipple had been, he turned and puked, his coffee and pizza now at the bottom of Gonzo's trashcan.

Gonzo walked into his office just in time to see the doctor heaving his guts into his trashcan. "What the fuck are you doing?" Gonzo yelled.

Startled, Bill quickly turned his pallid face towards the disgruntled voice. Traces of vomit rested on his chin and in the corners of his mouth. The smell of vomit permeated the small office. Just as the doctor was about to speak, Gonzo turned and rushed into the men's room just across the hall. Bill could hear him retching even through the closed double doors. Wiping his mouth with his handkerchief, Bill then went to the water cooler for a long drink of water. Just then, Gonzo reappeared. He did not look well.

"God damn it, Doc, you had no fucking business looking at that file!" Gonzo said angrily.

"I'm sorry, Gonzo. I didn't mean to look at it. In truth, I was going to leave you a note telling you that the Arkansas sweatshirt and the gold bracelet belong, or should I say belonged, to AJ. However, when I looked down and saw the report I just had to read it. I'm kind of sorry I did. As you now know, I hate the sight of blood and guts. On occasion I have gotten sick and even passed out cold."

Gonzo stood silently for a few moments then asked softly, "What about the gold bracelet?"

Bill explained the inscription and even told Gonzo which jeweler had inscribed it. Then he told him about the funeral arrangements and about AJ's father and what a cheap bastard he was.

"Thanks, Doc," Gonzo said. He turned, and walked down the hall.

Now that Bill's business was finished, he turned and walked back down the hall in the opposite direction. Just as he was about to exit the police station, he glanced to his left just as one of AJ's killers was being led into interrogation room two. Room two had a one-way mirror and a listening post. Stopping, Bill looked around and saw that no one else seemed remotely interested in this case. He guessed it was what the police and district attorney called a "slam-dunk." They were correct; as far as he was concerned, it was a slam-dunk. However, the question of motivation kept nagging at Bill. He had to know so he could try to understand. Then, perhaps, he could better accept AJ's death and find closure.

Bill adjusted the volume control on the speaker so that it was barely audible but loud enough for him to hear. He watched as the interrogation officer began his questioning. Slowly, methodically, the detective began questioning the young man. Each question asked was challenged with, "Man I don't have to tell you a fuckin' thing!" Patiently, the officer repeated the same question and again came the same reply. On the third try, when the young man spit on the detective, the officer picked the young boy up and began throwing him around the room, as if he was a rubber ball. Then, when he had the young man's full attention, he pulled out his penis, pissed on the kid, grabbed him by his neck and sat him back down in the chair.

"We will try this one more time," the detective said. "What is your name?"

"Kareem Abdul Roche," the scared young man replied as tears began to stream down his cheeks.

"How old are you?" the detective continued.

"Sixteen," Kareem replied.

"You have been given your rights. Do you understand these rights?" the detective asked softly.

"Yes, I understand my rights," Kareem replied.

"Please tell me why you and your friend killed Doctor Jackson and why you singled her out to rob and murder?"

Kareem looked at the detective. "Man, I did not murder no white doctor bitch. You see dude, this white lady was stopped at the light in her shiny new car. She was one fine looking white bitch. Anyway, Mustafa was driving this old raggedy-ass Honda he copped and we was just ridin' around. You know, looking' at the female population, see in' if we could score a shot of leg. You copy?"

The detective smiled and shook his head that he understood what was said.

"Anyway, like I was saying', this fine white lady in her expensive, shiny, new car pulls up on the left of us. Mustafa smiles at the lady and she smiles back. He honks the horn and yells to her 'How about some, fine lady?' Well the lady turns and speeds down the street. Mustafa makes a left from the right lane in front of rush hour traffic and chases the lady to a bunch of apartments. She pulls through the gate and then drives around back. But man, we can't get to her because there is this old faggot-faced rent a cop standing' guard and carrying' a cannon, ya see."

Once again, the detective nodded his head, his face grim and his teeth clenched. Bill could see the visible anger on the detective's face, but still the detective said nothing, preferring instead to let the boy talk.

"So, my man Mustafa drove around the block, and found a crosswalk that led into the apartments from the rear. He pulled up and parked and we got out and walked into where the apartments was and we looked up and down the drive and we saw this lady getting out of her car. She didn't see us. So, we followed her around the front of her building and she checked her mailbox and then we walked real fast until we got behind her. As she opened her door, we pushed her into the door and knocked the bitch to the floor. I grabbed her purse and grabbed some coin. While I was robbing the rich bitch, Mustafa was tearing' off her clothes. He yelled for me to help him hold her down. I grabbed her arms and pulled them up over her head. Then he, I mean Mustafa, reached up and pulled down her panties and pushed up her dress. Then he tore her blouse wide-open sending' buttons flying everywhere. Then he yanked the white bitch's bra off and her titties kind a you know, were there. Mustafa just stopped and stared at them, then he began to suck on one of them and then he began to bite her. She screamed and Mustafa took out his gun and began hittin' her across the face and head until she was quiet. Then he stuck his dick in her."

"Why did we find her body in the bedroom if Mustafa took her in the hallway?" the detective asked.

"Well after he finished with her she was layin' there. She was still breathin', so we let the bitch be. Anyway, we found jewelry and I found some more money and Mustafa, his shirt was covered in blood so he found this sweatshirt with some school name on it. Then he flushed his shirt down the toilet. When we come downstairs, the bitch was gone. We found her in the bedroom reachin' for the phone. Mustafa went nuts, man. He began beatin' the woman, laughin', yellin' and callin' her names. Then we saw her keys, walked out the back door, grabbed her ride and left. How did we know the place had cameras?"

Kareem went silent. The detective picked up his tape recorder and told the boy to stand up. He cuffed him and sat him back down. Not speaking, he turned and walked out of the room.

The doctor was standing on the other side of the door. "Excuse me, sir," the detective said as he walked back down the hall towards Gonzo's office.

The boy was alone. Left unattended, thoughts of murder raced through Bill's mind. *It would be so easy*, he thought. *Just walk in, put my hands around the boy's throat and choke him to death.* While rage coursed through his mind, he was suddenly struck by a vision, almost a divine inspiration. *Why kill just him? Why not kill them all? Kill all the shines, just like my grandfather wanted to do years and years ago. Kill them all before they take over the country and ruin it. Kill them in one mass execution. Make them suffer slowly and fatally, so no matter what the doctors did they would die...so many in fact that the authorities could not bury them all. The authorities would be forced to burn the bodies and the fire would consume their souls and send them all to hell!*

∽ CHAPTER 4 ∽

THE FUNERAL FOR AJ HELD in Little Rock was simple, straightforward and dignified. There may have been fifty people in attendance and most of them were family. Bill did not go back to the church with the others. Instead, he got into the rental car and drove back to the airport. Basically, he wanted nothing to do with AJ's family, especially her father. Her mother had come over, shook his hand and thanked him for bringing their daughter home. That simple sentiment touched him deeply. He realized that was really the only thank you he wanted or needed; just to be acknowledged and have somebody say "Thank you" to him.

The drive back to Little Rock's airport took less than ten minutes. On the way he contemplated how best to rid the country of the Mustafa's and the Kareem's. Whatever he planned, he knew it had to be subtle, deliberate and slow. Also, it had to require the fewest people possible and they had to hate the shines as much, if not more so than he did. Plus, it was imperative they keep their mouths shut. After all, what he seriously was pondering was genocide.

Fortunately Bill's flight home was uneventful. From the time he landed at Reagan Airport until the time he threw his car keys on the kitchen counter top was less than thirty minutes. He continued to walk on through the kitchen and into the den where he made a right turn, climbed the fourteen stairs and entered his bedroom. In one fluid motion he removed the navy blue blazer AJ had bought him last fall and hung it up. Next, he kicked off his shoes, removed his tie and flopped down on the bed. Glancing at his alarm clock, Bill noted only five hours had elapsed since the funeral in the morning until that very moment, not counting the time change.

Feeling so alone, he reached over and grabbed the pillow that AJ always used. In the recesses of his mind, he vaguely noted the imprint of her head was still clearly visible and her scent still clung to the pillowcase. Once again, Bill's eyes filled with tears as he buried his face in AJ's scent and between his sobs he again, vowed to kill them all.

Bells ringing penetrated his mind. The sound crystallized into the jarring tone of his phone. In the past five days since AJ's murder, he had slept very little. His body was sleep deprived and malnourished, his mind was constantly twisting and turning, never resting, always trying to figure out the best way to commit mass murder and get away with it. He had narrowed it down to various types of poisons or some sort of biological germ such as Ebola or perhaps some nerve agent, maybe even anthrax.

Upon lifting the receiver of the intruding instrument, he heard, a sexy voice ask, "Hello, Doctor Bradshaw?"

"Yes, this is Doctor Bradshaw," he replied, still groggy from sleep.

"Doctor, this is Doctor Ruth Schwartz of the Federal Bureau of Investigation," the soft sexy voice identified.

"How may I help you, Doctor Schwartz?" Bill replied, trying to put a face and body to the soft voice that held his attention.

"Well, Doctor Bradshaw, your name came up in the rotation here at the bureau. Are you interested in doing some profiling work?"

Suddenly alert and fully awake, he sat up on the bed and asked, "What type of case?"

Doctor Schwartz paused, as if debating whether to trust the person on the other end of the line. However, the bureau had approved him, plus he was well known. "We have a serial killer," she blurted.

When only silence greeted her, she wasn't sure how to proceed. She thought to herself, *Do I dare speak…or let him decline the work offer?*

"Hmmm…where are the killings taking place?" he finally asked.

"In Georgia, around the Atlanta and Valdosta areas," she replied.

"Really," he stated. "Will I be allowed to travel to Atlanta and Valdosta?"

"Yes, you will go with me," she promptly replied.

"Okay, send me all your data by courier, along with both your office and home phone numbers. After I have reviewed the data we will compare notes and plan our trip," Bill replied. When he hung up the phone, he began to laugh and giggle, slapping his hands and yelling, "Thank you God!"

∽ CHAPTER 5 ∾

MARY WALKED INTO DOCTOR BRADSHAW'S private office and said, as she handed him a file folder, "This just arrived by special courier and is labeled, 'eyes only'."

Smiling at Mary he said, "Of course you know that anytime you want to you can read this file. But, if you do the FBI will hunt you down and kill you," Bill laughed.

"No, doctor, that is one side of this job I don't care to know about until it is over. And that is only when I type up your notes," Mary responded.

"Here you go, Mary. Please type these notes on these three patients, and can you tell me how long until my next patient?"

"Mr. Douglas is here now. As usual, he is early," Mary said as she turned to walk out.

"Send him in please," the doctor asked.

Mr. Douglas suffered from Obsessive Compulsive Disorder or OCD. Also, he was a kleptomaniac, loved to shoplift and just couldn't help himself. Part of his probation was that he go to counseling. As a man he was very small, almost diminutive, with effeminate characteristics, but definitely not gay, far from it. In fact, he loved to seduce young women in their late teens and early twenties by telling them he was gay and that he never had sex with a woman. Nine out of ten times, the young lady would oblige him with her favors in hopes of "rescuing" him from the depths and depravity of homosexuality.

Mr. Douglas's session went extremely well. He pulled out a clean, white-knotted handkerchief and spilled the contents onto the doctor's desk. Out tumbled a valuable ring, an expensive watch, a bracelet and a couple of other items he had recently stolen from local merchants. The doctor looked down and began to laugh. "I see that our therapy sessions are working, Mr. Douglas. You only have five items here. Last time you gave me about twenty."

"Yes, doctor, I do seem to be getting better. When I take my medicine, sleep and eat right, I don't want to steal as much," Mr. Douglas responded, looking small and vulnerable as he sat on his hands in the big, overstuffed, leather chair.

"Okay, Mr. Douglas, let's make a list now," the doctor said, taking out a pen and a piece of paper.

"Where did you get these items?" the doctor asked.

Mr. Douglas answered each question, describing his emotions and explaining why he took each item. When all the items were accounted for, the doctor asked Mr. Douglas to do him a favor. He wanted him to go into food stores and eat food—grapes, apples, bananas etc. Just walk around the store and eat. Thus he would be satisfying his uncontrollable urge to steal, but at least he was stealing food. The legal consequences would not be as severe nor the danger so great. With that sage advice, he stood and shook Mr. Douglas' hand, wished him luck and asked him to make an appointment with Mary.

After Mr. Douglas had gone, he buzzed Mary to come into the office. He retired the jewelry into the handkerchief, handed it to her and said, "Please call the police robbery detail and ask for detective Sergeant Matt Braden. Tell him to come and get this merchandise." This had been going on for several months and the sergeant would ask no questions, although he knew it was Mr. Douglas that had stolen the objects and given them to Doctor Bradshaw.

With Mr. Douglas being his last patient of the day, Bill was finished. He meticulously documented Mr. Douglas's activities and progress, and then closed the file folder, placing it in Mary's basket for her review and billing. Then he opened the large envelope the courier had delivered earlier and poured the contents out onto his desk.

Carefully, he reviewed each of the eleven photos. They were all of young women; some white, some Hispanic, no blacks. He then read each bio of the women whose picture lay before him. All were prostitutes. The oldest was twenty-five but looked fifteen; the youngest nineteen but looked twelve. All had lived in Georgia and had been killed with in forty-five days of each other. Though there was no DNA evidence, all the women had sexual relations with their killer. Strangulation or a means of smothering had been the cause of death in each case. Their bodies had not been desecrated; yet each body had been placed in a pose denoting prayer or submission to someone else's will. Each body had been found in either public parks or rest areas along the interstate.

According to the medical examiner's report from Atlanta, two of the young women had been sexually assaulted after they were dead.

The doctor sat in silence, his mind working different angles as he tried to come up with a reasonable hypothesis. Leaning forward, he grabbed his phone and called Doctor Schwartz at her office.

As there was no response, he left a message and asked her to call him at home that evening.

After hanging up the phone, he gathered everything up, placed it in the envelope and walked out of his office. Standing in front of Mary was a very tall, blonde, blue-eyed woman who was somewhere between beautiful and awesome.

"Doctor," Mary said, "this lady doesn't have an appointment but she wants to see you. She says she is with the FBI."

"Doctor Schwartz, I presume?" he said with a big grin.

"Correct," she replied, her smile burning a hole into the doctor's wounded heart.

"What a coincidence. I just tried to call you at your office. When you didn't answer, I left you a message to call me tonight." Doctor Bradshaw held out his hand to her.

"Well, Doctor Bradshaw, there has been another murder and this case unfortunately is heating up in the press."

Looking into her eyes, Bill found himself getting lost in them. His repressed male libido was now at full mast. He was surprised to find he wanted to take this woman—wanted to consume her, to use her for his own amusement and satisfy his burning lust. Reluctantly he let go of her hand and asked if she had time to discuss the information she had provided.

"That's why I'm here, doctor," she replied.

"Okay, then," he said as he led her back into his office.

"Mary, when you are done, just buzz me and let me know that you're leaving. I will lock up," the doctor said, walking into his office.

She was about to respond but he had already shut his office door.

Mary's intuition began working overtime. She did not like Doctor Schwartz. There was something about her, as if she were a feline predator. As though she used people and abused them for her own sick and perverse pleasure. But Mary knew Doctor Bill could handle that cold-hearted bitch.

The doctor walked over to his desk while Doctor Schwartz found the leather sofa across the room from the desk. She kicked off her high heel shoes, unbuttoned her blazer, slipped it off and placed it across the arm of the chair the doctor often used when analyzing his patients. Against the soft white light of the desk lamp, she looked like a model posing for an artist. Next, she unbuttoned the top two buttons of her white frilly blouse, exposing her more than ample cleavage.

She was then ready to hear Doctor Bradshaw's theory on the case. What she hadn't told the doctor was that the other two agents she was working with, one in Atlanta and the other in Valdosta, the two agents in Washington and she had already developed their theories. They had decided the killer was a male truck driver, a religious zealot or pretended to be and he was impotent, suffering from erectile dysfunction. Also that he was probably in a very unhappy marriage. Still, there was room for other theories and speculations and she wanted to hear Doctor Bradshaw's ideas.

Doctor Bradshaw looked across the room at the blond goddess who had peaked his curiosity.

"Are you comfortable, Ruth?" the doctor asked.

"Yes Bill, very comfortable, thank you," she replied, smiling.

Bill smiled at her, then opened the envelope, poured the contents out once again and stacked the photos to his right and the medical reports to his left, leaving the center of his desk open. He clasped both hands and began to speak.

"Ruth, I have looked at each picture and read each report. I have come up with a working theory. And mind you, it is loose but it works.

"We are looking for a mortician, I think. He probably has an established route and approximately every month and a half he is on the road. The car he drives is a company car, perhaps a Mercury Sable or Ford Taurus—I am guessing of course. Anyway, the car is nondescript, probably black or white. He likes prostitutes that look like little girls and he is a part-time necrophiliac. This is evidenced by the ME's report from Atlanta, where two of the bodies had been sexually assaulted after their deaths. He kills by strangulation or smothering his victims by luring them into a sexual position—doggie style I think—then uses his tie to strangle them. Or, he may just clamp his hand over their nose and mouth and smother them. When he has satisfied his lust, he calmly puts his tie back on and drives to a rest stop where he dispassionately and calmly carries the body to a park bench, puts it into a submissive pose and drives off. Furthermore, I think our man is in his early forties to mid-fifties."

Doctor Ruth sat in stunned silence and disbelief. The director had told her Doctor Bradshaw was good. Now she believed the director. In her estimation, Doctor Bradshaw was unbelievable!

"With such a small amount of data, how did you ever deduce what you just told me?" she asked, bewilderment causing deep furrows to appear across her forehead.

"Well, Ruth, when you break down the data into smaller segments, they begin to give you a pattern. I use this pattern as a starting point and then

I build upon it. First are the dates and places. When you look on the road map, you see that all the girls work the circuit or the truck stops. They are called 'lounge lizards.' Also, you will notice these truck stops are located at major interstate exits. It would be easy to deduce that a trucker is killing the girls. And if you have so deduced, you might be correct. However, when you look at where the bodies are being found, then one must ask how a trucker could go unnoticed. Looking at the ME's reports from both Valdosta and Atlanta, you find on three of the bodies traces of cornstarch and talcum powder. This same powder is found on surgical gloves. Also, there were small circular burn marks around the mouths caused by chloroform or ether.

"Something else: Two of the women had minute traces of formaldehyde on their clothing. Now where would a trucker come up with a chemical used in embalming? So, only a mortician who has recently embalmed a body could possibly have formaldehyde on his hands, clothes or perhaps his gloves, thus no fingerprints. Another point, perhaps he has no pubic hair as he shaves his pubic region."

"Anything else?" Doctor Schwartz asked.

"Only that our killer is left-handed," added Doctor Bradshaw.

Looking at her watch, Doctor Schwartz noted that from the time she had walked in until now, only twenty minutes had passed. However, she had learned more in those twenty minutes about profiling than she could ever hope to imagine. She acknowledged to herself she was in the presence of a genius and decided, right then and there, she wanted this man in her life. He was good-looking, well educated, made a great living and besides he was influential. Another thing she picked up on was that he was hiding something deep down inside; a dark secret. How she knew this, she could not say. Perhaps it was because there was a sadness about him.

"Bill, are you hungry?" she asked.

"Yes, Ruth, I am hungry."

"Good! Let's go get a pizza," she said taking the initiative.

"And beer?" he asked.

They laughed as they prepared to leave. Doctor Bradshaw put the contents of the envelope away and locked it in his office safe. Meanwhile, Ruth freshened her lipstick. Mary was just getting ready to close up as they walked out of his office.

"When is my first appointment in the morning, Mary?" Doctor Bradshaw asked.

"9:30," Mary answered quickly and professionally.

"Thank you, Mary. I'll see you tomorrow around eight-thirty," the doctor said, opening the door for him and Doctor Schwartz.

"Very well, doctor," Mary replied.

Ruth turned to Bill and asked, "Where to?"

"To Romano's Restaurant. They make a great pizza and besides, we will be early and the place will be quiet," Bill replied.

"I'll follow you," Ruth said, walking towards her car.

❧ CHAPTER 6 ❧

ROMANO'S WAS QUIET, JUST as Bill had predicted. They were shown to a booth in the back of the restaurant where they could have privacy and talk about the case without ordered a carafe of red house wine. He always diluted his wine by adding an ice cube because. Romano's wine was potent and if you were not used to it, it could knock you on your ass. That was exactly the effect Bill wanted. When the wine was served, he ordered a large pizza with the works. Ruth sat silent, one hand resting under her chin and her other hand holding the wine glass.

"So Ruth, where did you go to medical school?" Bill asked, taking a sip of wine.

"John Hopkins, then a fellowship at Yale," she replied. She sipped her wine, rolling it around in her mouth, savoring its taste.

"How about you? Where did you go to school?" She asked.

Bill laughed, "I am afraid my pedigree is not as good as yours, Ruth. I went to the University of Georgia and then Tulane. I interned in Waco,

Texas before coming here, as a resident at George Washington and Bethesda.

"Are you from here?" Bill asked.

"All over," she replied, and then explained her daddy had been an Ambassador to a half a dozen different countries. Her mother was an heiress to a tobacco fortune in North Carolina. An older brother was a lawyer; her younger sister was an artist. She explained further that her mother was graduated from Duke University with a degree in molecular biology and also held a PhD from Columbia in molecular engineering.

"Is your mother as beautiful as you?" Bill asked.

"Oh my yes mother is the most beautiful and intellectually gifted woman you could ever meet. She also speaks four or five languages and can curse in Spanish, French and Mandarin."

"Is your sister as beautiful as you?"

"No, she is an ugly hag. Just because she posed for Playboy a few years ago, everybody in my family thinks she's a hussy and a gold digger. The reason she did it was that she needed money for school and when she asked Daddy, and he said no. She posed to embarrass him. Daddy was mortified when the President called him on the carpet over the picture."

Bill began to laugh. He was actually beginning to loosen up and relax.

"What is so funny" Ruth asked.

"You are telling me your sister is a hag, and then telling me she posed for Playboy. Your sister is not a hag, in fact; I'm willing to bet you she is beautiful." Bill said in a serious tone of voice.

"I confess, she is gorgeous," Ruth replied.

"So let me get this straight in my head. Although you choose to call nowhere special your home, your mother is a tobacco heiress, and your dad was or still is a career politician who has served in half-dozen countries. Do I have this correct so far?" he asked.

"Correct," Ruth replied.

"You have a brother who is a lawyer, a younger sister who is an artist, a mother who is a PhD, and you're a medical doctor."

"Again correct," she replied.

"May I ask what your dad is doing now?"

"Presently, Daddy is the U.S. Ambassador to the United Nations."

Bill took a gulp of wine. He sat silent, as he had no more questions for Ruth. She was an intimidating woman, not only because of her beauty and education, but also because of her parentage.

"Now let me ask you some questions," she said, taking another sip of wine. "Are you married?"

"No Ruth, I'm not married," Bill responded.

"Are you divorced?"

"Seeing that I have never been married, I cannot be divorced."

"No girlfriend either?" she asked.

Bill felt his chest tighten, and his breathing became shallow as anger once again came to the forefront of his brain. He clenched his teeth, took a long swig of his wine and waited for the anger to pass.

"No girlfriend anymore, either," he replied.

"Ah, let me guess. You were madly in love with the woman, and she threw you over for a proctologist," Ruth said laughingly.

"No, Ruth, she was murdered."

Ruth fell silent. Her eyes began to tear, and her beautiful face began to flush red.

Bill reached across the table and grabbed her hand. "Ruth, it was seven months ago now. I thought I was over her and over her murder. I guess I'm not."

Just then, the server brought the pizza to the table where she placed small plates in front of them before dishing out two large slices of pizza. Smiling, she reminded them both if they needed anything else to let her know.

They ate their first pieces of pizza in silence. Then Ruth cleared her throat, took a small sip of wine, wiped her mouth on her napkin and asked, "Bill, what was her name?"

"Her name was Alexandra," Bill replied.

"You mean AJ!" Ruth asked.

"Yes I do! Did you know her?" Bill asked.

"Yes, I knew her," Ruth replied. I would have attended the funeral, but I was in Europe for three weeks spending time with mom and dad. I did not know of her death until I got back to work."

Once again, they ate in silence, each lost in their own thoughts. Ruth's thoughts of AJ were purely sexual. She admittedly liked girls as well as men and had made AJ a top priority some time ago, in Chicago, where they had attended a conference and afterward went out to eat. They ate very little, but drank heavily. In the hotel elevator Ruth had leaned over and kissed AJ on the lips. AJ responded. The kiss was deep and sensual. It appeared as though AJ was not adverse to sex with another woman as she obviously enjoyed it as much as Ruth. The tryst had lasted until AJ's murder. Now here she was with AJ's other lover. *What are the chances of that? Perhaps one in a million,* she thought.

"More wine?" Bill asked, pouring the last of the wine into Ruth's goblet.

"This wine is excellent," she said.

Bill was about to ask her if she wanted another carafe of wine when the waitress showed up with another. Nodding his approval, the young lady placed it on the table and once again magically disappeared around the corner, taking the empty carafe with her.

The atmosphere and wine were having the desired effect. Ruth let her shoe fall off her foot and began rubbing her foot up and down the inside of Bill's leg. Bill said nothing, as he was engrossed in visualizing Ruth naked in his arms. His manhood was so hard it was becoming painful, as it had no place to go.

Patiently Bill waited until she brought her foot up to his knee. He gently grabbed her foot and placed it between his thighs, pressing her foot against his fully extended manhood, letting her feel its immense size and the heat radiating through his cotton underwear and the silk cloth of his suit pants. Bill knew it was now or never. If she were interested in him, she would let him know. If not, she would pull her foot away, put her shoes back on and say, "Excuse me, I must use the ladies' room."

Ruth looked at her watch. Then the corners of her beautiful mouth curved upwards into a warm, soft, inviting smile. "Do you live close by, Doctor Bradshaw?" she coyly asked.

"Yes I do, Doctor Schwartz. In fact, we could walk to my condominium from here, and I insist that we walk as we have been drinking, and we must act responsibly, mustn't we?"

"Yes, we must," Ruth replied.

Bill let her foot go then slid out from behind the booth and faced Ruth, shielding her from the view of the restaurant staff and other patron's that were now starting to fill the once empty seats. The outline of his erection was clearly visible under his suit pants and when Ruth looked at it, she smiled. Saying nothing she gently reached out, grabbed its out-line, and squeezed. "Oh my Doctor Bradshaw, did I cause this to happen to you?" Ruth said, smiling as she tried to stand up.

Bill backed away and took her hand and kindly pulled her to her feet. "Yes, you did," he replied, kissing her gently.

"About one hundred yards," Bill replied.

Bill reached into his pocket and pulled out his keys. In the dim light of the street, it was hard to see the door key. He ran his finger over each key until he found the one that felt right. As he neared the front door, he held his hand out, as if aiming for the key slot. With the practiced eye of a surgeon, he turned inserted and turned the key. The rush of warm air greeted them both as they walked down the short hall into the foyer, the table lamp casting a welcoming glow.

Ruth asked in desperation, "Where is the bathroom?"

"Second door on the right," Bill said as he pulled down his zipper and raced to the master bathroom.

Finally, Bill heard the other toilet flush. In the length of time, it had taken Ruth to pee. He had gone to the bathroom and changed his clothes.

Going to the living room, he picked up a remote control, pressing the "On" button and the fireplace ignited, casting a warm, inviting glow around the room. He picked up another remote device, this one to his stereo and clicked the number four, which was his favorite CD—the one he referred to as his "seduction music.") he turned the volume setting to five. Upon experimenting with the different levels, he had found at this level you could carry on a conversation without speaking loudly.

Patiently, he waited for Ruth to appear. She did. In fact, she was already ahead of him and wearing AJ's robe. He smiled and held out his hand, pulling her into his embrace. As he nuzzled her, he could still smell AJ on the robe.

Ruth snuggled into his arms as if she always belonged there. Bill closed his eyes, imaging, she was AJ. He kissed Ruth's cheek, then her eyes and mouth. Softly, he caressed her cheek with his right hand. His left hand slowly inched its way across her chest until it found Ruth's warm, naked breast. He felt the hard, tiny nipple growing under his hand, as his finger and thumb pinched and pulled it. All the while she was moaning and whimpering in his ear. Bill flicked his tongue across Ruth's nipple before taking it into his mouth. Gently Bill massaged her other nipple between his thumb and finger; squeezing and teasing it until it stood hard and firm against the palm of his hand.

Moaning, Ruth grabbed his head and planted a soft kiss on his neck, sucking in his flesh and tasting his skin. Bill turned to Ruth for a kiss. Her eyes smoldering, he could feel her passion as she plunged her delicate soft tongue deep into his mouth. Their tongues entwined and circled each other's searching, probing and heightening their sexual hunger.

By now, Bill's penis was rock hard. Needing her, he climbed on top of her slim body, rose up on his knees, looked into her eyes and whispered, "Put it in."

Ruth reached down, aligned his manhood and whispered, "Please, put it in slowly."

Bill felt himself start to slip into her. He pushed slowly, gently, watching Ruth's face for any sign of discomfort. Ruth rested her hands on his chest and looked directly into Bill's eyes. He leaned downwards kissing her softly. Smiling up at him, Ruth brought her hands up under his armpits, pulling him on top of her. She threw her legs up and locked them around Bill's back. She moaned as Bill entered her while at the same time he kissed her neck and bit her earlobe. It was important for her to become used to him. Then he felt her muscles tighten, slowly squeezing and releasing driving him wild with passion.

Keeping up a steady pace, Bill grabbed a fistful of Ruth's hair, holding her head in place as he kissed her, gently at first and then as his passion took over, he plunged his tongue deep into her mouth, all the while pinching her nipple, causing her to moan into his mouth. Bill could feel her heart beating against his chest, her breath coming in gasps as Ruth tried to push him off of her. He rose up a little, allowing Ruth to take a much-needed breath. Sensing Ruth was close to an orgasm, Bill leaned down, kissed her gently and looked into her beautiful eyes. Pushing her closer to the edge of sexual bliss.

Ruth raked her fingernails across Bill's back and tightened her legs around his waist; squeezing him so that he could hardly get his breath. Feeling his orgasm building as it came from deep within his loins, Bill suddenly exploded once, then twice and yet again. Ruth moaned her contentment into his ear. He felt Ruth's muscles tense just before she gave a sudden gasp and then a deep sigh as her body went limp under his. Bill collapsed on top of her, drenched in sweat. Kissing her cheek, he whispered into her ear, "Are you okay?"

She kissed him, smiled and said, "I'm just fine now!"

⚭ CHAPTER 7 ⚭

D R. BRADSHAW FINALLY RECEIVED permission to visit the murder sites in Georgia. The professionals who dealt with murder everyday thought his trip nothing more than an expensive boondoggle. At best, they were skeptical about profiling criminal behavior. Murder was usually about motive—sex, money or greed. One of these was always the reason people killed. Doctor Bradshaw had heard all the reasons but had learned to ignore the skeptics and concentrate on his own theory.

Since Doctor Schwartz had flown down the day before, she picked him up at the airport, and together they drove north from Atlanta. They picked up, I-75 and headed towards Chattanooga. Bill was holding the first victim's file in his lap. As were the others, she had been a prostitute and was young, twenty-one to be exact. She was arrested on several occasions for prostitution. Her blood toxicology screen showed she had not been a drug user, nor did she have any alcohol in her system. She was a clean Jeanne.

The pitiful part of the whole mess was that her high school transcript showed she was an exceptional student and was beautiful. Why prostitution when she could be anything, she wanted to be? The lure of easy money was probably the best guess.

Doctor Schwartz began to slow down. Turning on her blinker, she eased the car off the freeway. The sign read: Exit 348 Ringgold. Bill looked over at Ruth, wondering what she was doing.

"You mean we're here already?" He asked.

"You have been reading and studying that file for an hour, maybe longer. You did not even kiss me or say hello."

Bill looked over at her, smiled and asked, "How far to the park?"

"We're here," she replied driving the car into the park and turning off the ignition. Bill leaned over and kissed her on the cheek, as he said, "Hello there."

Ruth kissed him back and smiled. "I took the liberty of booking you a suite at the hotel. That way, we can be together."

"Good thinking."

Bill got out of the car, the bitterly cold wind forcing him back into the car to put on his winter coat. This time both got out of the car, and walked around, neither really expecting to find anything of any significance. They were more interested in ascertaining how the killer got to this spot. So far, the police had no idea where the killer picked up his victim or how far he had brought her.

Bill was asking himself, *Did he kill her here and then carry her body over to the picnic table or was she killed somewhere else?*

Suddenly, a small little voice said, "Hello, are you the police?"

Both Ruth and Bill turned and looked down and behind them. A little girl of maybe five or six stood there. Her lips were blue from the cold, and she was clutching a baby doll, shielding it from the cold wind. A small, nondescript puppy was at Bill's feet, smelling his shoes.

Ruth spoke first, "No, sweetheart; we're not the police. We're the FBI."

Ruth and Bill laughed when the little girl said, "Wow, the FBI! Can I see your badge?"

Ruth reached into her handbag and pulled out her identification card. The little girl took it, looked at the picture and showed the card to her doll. She handed the card back saying, "Thank you, ma'am."

"Sweetheart, why did you want to know if we were the police?" Bill asked softly.

"Are you with the FBI also?" she asked.

Ruth began to laugh, and Bill followed suit. "Honey, this is Doctor Bradshaw of the FBI. He is helping me catch the person who killed the young girl who was found here," Ruth explained.

"I remember when that was. I found the lady. She was lying right there on that table. Muffin really found her first. When Muffin jumped up and began licking her face and the lady did not move, I knew she was dead just like when Rags and I found Grandma Wanita last Christmas. She was dead, too when I found her. Rags, was my dog before Muffin. However, Rags got run over by a car. He's in heaven you know."

"Sweetheart, what's your name?" Ruth asked

"My name is Emmy Lou Ringgold. This town is named after my great-great-grandfather."

"Emmy sweetheart where do you live?" Ruth asked.

"Why, up there on the side of that hill," Emmy Lou said, pointing to a large two-story house tucked away behind the trees.

"How did you get here without crossing the freeway?" Bill asked.

"Oh that's easy doctor. Come with me and I'll show you."

Emmy Lou took hold of Ruth's hand and started walking up the grassy knoll.   Soon, she turned and went under some low-hanging branches. From there a footpath led to a large drainage tunnel that went under the freeway. There, out of view, was a beautiful pond with two large weeping willow trees. A footbridge led up a few stone steps to the front porch of Emmy Lou's house. Both Bill and Ruth looked across the freeway right onto the small roadside park.

"Emmy Lou, how old are you?" Bill asked.

"Well, doctor, next week I will be eight-years-old."

"Going on twenty-eight," Bill whispered beneath his breath.

Hearing that last comment, Ruth laughed. Then she turned to Bill and said, "perhaps we should talk to Emmy Lou's mother or dad. Maybe they saw something?"

"Oh, no, ma'am, mother and daddy were watching television when I saw the lady get out of the car with some man."

"Can you tell me more about the lady that you and Muffin found?" Bill asked. "Emmy Lou, you saw the lady who was dead get out of the car. Is that right?" Ruth asked.

"Yes, doctor, she got out of a car-like yours…except his car was a different color."

"Emmy what color was it?" Ruth asked.

"Black. It also had writing on the doors."

"What did the writing say?" Ruth asked, softly trying to hide her excitement.

"I don't know. I don't read very well yet."

Bill began to laugh. Leaning down he took Emmy Lou's doll and kissed it. Then he picked up Muffin and kissed Muffin.

"Did you happen to see the man the lady was with? Ruth asked.

"Yes, I saw him."

"Was he white or black?" Bill asked.

"He was white."

"Was he a big man like me?" Bill asked.

"Oh, doctor, he was much bigger than you. And he had on funny colored straps that held up his pants, and he had a big belly like my daddy has," Emmy Lou said.

"Emmy, honey, what time of the day was it?" Ruth asked.

"Well, ma'am, I get home from school around a quarter to four. I had already eaten my cookies and milk, and gone upstairs to change my clothes. After I changed my clothes, I walked to the window to pick up Sally. When I looked out I saw the lady, and the man get out of the car. So I guess it would be about four, maybe a little later."

"The police are not going to believe this," Bill said.

"What do we care?" Ruth replied. She handed Emmy Lou her card with her name, telephone number and title on it. In exchange, Ruth wrote down Emmy Lou's name, address and phone number. They both thanked her for being so helpful and said they might want to talk with her again.

"Nobody is going to believe what we just heard, and we aren't going to tell a soul," Bill said, taking Ruth's hand and leading her back to the car.

They now knew what the others did not know: The murderer drove a black Ford Taurus with writing on the side; he was a big man who wore suspenders that were multi-colored and they had the approximate timeline.

Once in the car they kissed, as they waited for the car to warm up. Heading back to Valdosta, they now knew they were one step nearer to catching the murderer. In addition, Bill was one step closer to meeting up with his cousins Jimmy Ray Houghton and Billy Bob Lee.

∽ CHAPTER 8 ∽

BILL SAT ON THE SIDE of the bed, listening to Ruth as she prepared to join him. He pulled out his all-important cell phone and proceeded to dial a number that would change his life and the lives of millions, forever. The phone call lasted only a minute, more or less.

"Hello, Jimmy Ray? This is your cousin, Bill. Could you get a hold of Cousin Billy Bob? I want a sit-down meeting with both of you at your place this Thursday. How would that work out for both of you? There is something very important I wish to discuss with only the two of you..."

For seven months now, the idea of how to kill millions of shines had been on his mind. It was his intention to eradicate them like roaches. One night, while cooking supper, an idea had come to him. He was preparing a stir-fry and boiling water for rice. His reasoning was: *All God's children must eat, even shines. So why not attack the food supply? This could be accomplished by giving out free samples of rice and gelatin that had been laced with some sort of poison that was self-absorbent and slow acting when ingested.* Then he thought: *Why stop there? Why not give out free samples of poisoned body lotions and shampoos that would cause a multitude of problems when applied to the skin, such as flu-like symptoms, indigestion, asthma or even heart failure?*

He figured to go by zip codes to find cities with dense and dark populations. By using disposable cell phones and hiring people of the Muslim faith to dispense the free samples door to door, why, in a month his plan could be fully implemented. In the length of time it would take the authorities and medical communities to figure out what was happening, it was possible that one, maybe two million shines could be dead.

However, all of this was just idle speculation on his part. What he really needed was help, and the financial resources from various hate groups to implement his ideas. That was why he needed his cousins Jimmy Ray and Billy Bob. They were first cousins on his daddy's side of the family, which meant they probably had strong ties to hate groups like the Klan.

Jimmy Ray was now living in the house where Bill had grown up. After his mother's death, Bill had no further desire to live in Valdosta. Although Valdosta was a very old and beautiful city in the great state of Georgia, he figured he had outgrown it.

The history of Valdosta could be traced to two things—the railroad and the soil. Sandy loam soil allowed Valdosta to diversify when the boll weevil infestation hit the cotton crop in the early 1900s. Giving up on cotton, the farmers started growing tobacco and pecan trees and the rest is history.

Originally, Valdosta had been called Troupville and was nothing more than a whistle stop for the railroad before it became the county seat in 1860. When the Atlantic Railroad decided to move its operation four miles south, the good citizens of Troupville picked up and moved with the railroad. They moved to the Val d' Aosta plantation—thus the name Valdosta.

Great-grandfather Bradshaw had become very wealthy. In fact, he had become one of the richest and most influential men in the state of Georgia, making his fortune in real estate, land speculation, farming and tobacco. Although it was never spoken about, it was understood he had also dealt in slave trading and the breeding of slaves.

Valdosta had a population of forty thousand when Bill was a boy, making it one of the largest cities in the state. The town folk liked to remind Yankee tourists that Doc Holiday, sidekick of Wyatt Earp, had been born and raised in Valdosta and that the composer of Jingle Bells, Jimmy Pierpoint, also was from there. Another tidbit that the town folk bragged about was the Valdosta High School football team had won more games than any other high school in the nation, which is why the sign says "Winnersville" when you enter the city.

Bill was proud of being from Georgia and proud of being from Valdosta. However, as big as the city was, it still had that small town mentality. And being a psychiatrist in a town like Valdosta was difficult at best because of the underground rumor mill. In Valdosta everybody would know his client's business and diagnosis before the ink was dry on his notepad. Ethics would be violated, feelings would be hurt and the stigma of craziness would be attached to families. So he made the wise and prudent decision to follow the money.

"Whom were you talking to?" Ruth said as she stepped out of the warm moist bathroom, filling the room with moist steam.

Bill laughed. Even over the sound of running water, with the door shut and the television on, she had heard him on the phone. He made a mental note to be alone next time.

"I called my cousin Jimmy Ray in Valdosta, telling him I would be there on Thursday and we would do dinner."

Ruth said nothing, just turned and walked back into the bathroom. Soon, he could hear the hair dryer coming to life, its noise drowning out the volume of the television.

Bill became impatient. He wanted her in bed next to him; he was horny and needed relief. This time, he decided, he would let her get on top as he was tired and Ruth would probably enjoy it.

Over the past few days he had noticed she was sexually aggressive and that she displayed what he termed, "strong bi-sexual tendencies." In fact, he would bet she was bi-sexual. That afternoon of their first date at Romano's, he had watched her eyeing the very pretty young waitress. Then today at the airport, as they waited for his luggage, he watched her eye the flight attendant. She licked her lips and her eyes never left the flight attendant until she was out of sight. Now he knew for sure that he was just a boy toy to her. Ruth's true love was women.

❧❦❧

Tuesday was sunny but cool; the wind was sharp, stealing your breath when you least expected it. Ruth had driven Bill to Red Top Mountain State Park where a newlywed couple from Atlanta had found the nude body of victim number six. Although petite, the victim must have fought savagely for her life. She had been found raped and sodomized.

Bill closely examined the photos provided by the FBI, compliments of the Atlanta Police Department. They were extremely graphic. The ME had found traces of human flesh under her fingernails and traces of blood.

It made him feel pleased to know she had gotten him good. However, her efforts had not been enough to escape her murderer's size and strength. A broken condom had been found still lodged in her anus. However, strange as it may seem, there was no sperm.

The ME's report showed she was twenty-two years old and had been attending the University of Georgia. In the past year, she had been arrested two times for prostitution. Her arrests just happened to coincide with the school's terms. Otherwise, she was the girl next door.

He next picked up and studied her high school picture, which the FBI had graciously provided. She was pretty; not what you would call beautiful, but she had a look of quiet serenity about her. In the photo she seemed introspective, not bubbly or outgoing, but kind, gentle and trusting. And that trusting attitude had gotten her killed. Another thing the ME's report mentioned was that she was already dead when she had been sexually abused.

Bill was now more certain than ever that his initial assessment of the killer was accurate. Coupled with Emmy Lou's description of the black car with the writing on the side, He was sure they were looking for a mortician who was not only a rapist and murderer, but also a necrophiliac. *A real sick-o,* he thought.

As Ruth was writing her trip notes and talking on her cell phone to her mom about what she was doing, Bill read the Medical Examiner's report on victim number nine from Valdosta. Glancing down, he just happened to look at the signature of the ME. A Doctor Regina Furbish had signed it.

He had known her in medical school where she had been given the name "hot twat" because of her aggressive sexual appetite. If he remembered correctly, Regina was of Cajun decent, tall, about five feet nine, a slender build and the most beautiful smile. And those emerald green eyes of hers would light up just about any man. She liked sex and it did not matter with whom—man or woman—Regina was always game for a romp in bed.

Letting his thoughts drift, Bill idly wondered: *How would Ruth take to Doctor Furbish? That not only would be very interesting, but also very useful. Ruth could use my expense card and take Regina to dinner while I meet with Jimmy Ray and Billy Bob. In that way, Ruth would be occupied and out of my way, interviewing a material witness, so to speak.*

Back to business, he told himself: He continued to read and checkout the information on the ninth victim. She appeared to be a thin, very chesty prostitute with a criminal record that dated back to her junior year in high school. In high school she was expelled for excessive truancy. It was noted she specialized in threesomes and loved gay men or bi-sexual men and women. For a while she had also worked for an escort service out of Atlanta. There was a special note in the file—victim number nine was not a true woman. She was a she-male: In other words, a woman on the top and a man on the bottom, thus more than able to please any gay, bi-male or female. According to the Atlanta Police report, she made in excess of ten thousand dollars a month, all tax-free money. One could see her point: Why should she go to school when she could make more money than the superintendent of the Atlanta public school system?

Bill sat silently, listening to Ruth now chatting with her dad. He watched her as she applied lotion to her legs and began to smile. Just then Ruth happened to look up and see Bill's smile. She could not tell whether he was smiling because he was happy, he wanted her body again or he had found something in the report.

Then, as she watched, Bill's smile suddenly faded as a realization suddenly came to him: *Victim number nine had died because she was not a real woman. She was an imposter masquerading as a woman. Therefore, she could not satisfy her murderer's lust. The victim had been found hanging upside down with her penis cut off!*

Bill closed the folder, got up, and went into the bathroom to shower. As he showered, his thoughts turned to Ruth and Regina, causing his manhood to grow exponentially with his lewd and perverted thoughts.

"Ruth, can you come here? I need you!" he called out.

◌⊙ CHAPTER 9 ⊙◌

THE DRIVE TO VALDOSTA, GEORGIA was slow and tedious. Intermittent road construction caused traffic slow-downs along the interstate. Professional bureaucrats called Ruth with supposedly urgent questions, but all they really wanted, as far as Bill was concerned, was to flirt with Ruth. However, between all the road construction and useless telephone calls, they finally managed to make their appointments with the two Valdosta police detectives who were working on the two cases. They were to meet in the lobby of the Exedra around three.

Ruth had made the reservations the day before, being sure to ask for adjoining rooms. Though she was a stickler for decorum, last night in the shower had been nothing more than pure lust gone wild. When they had finished, they both staggered toward the bed, naked and wet. They laid in silence trying to catch their breath.

Bill was able to reach Doctor Furbish, and she was very agreeable to meeting with both Bill and Ruth. She also informed him that she had important news about the murderer.

It was almost one in the afternoon as Ruth steered the rental car into the Exedra parking lot. It had taken five hours to drive from downtown Atlanta to Valdosta. Bill opened the back passenger door and grabbed his suit coat and brief case. Ruth hit the little black button in the glove compartment, popping open trunk. Bill grabbed their luggage while Ruth picked up her shoulder bag.

The lobby was plush, even by Washington D.C. standards. Ruth walked up to the counter and told the clerk she had made reservations for two adjoining rooms. She showed the clerk her FBI identification card, so they could get the government rate. Bill found that amusing as he billed direct cost, plus he received one hundred and fifty dollars a day food and phone allowance, plus his professional fee.

With their check-in completed, they proceeded to their rooms. Bill threw his bag on the bed and went directly into his bathroom. He looked down while he peed; watching what was once a large coffee pass into the Valdosta sewer system.

When he turned to wash his hands after flushing the toilet, he glanced at the mirror and noticed he needed a shave. His usual custom was to shave at night, but he had forgotten that the night before when Ruth had distracted him. He walked into his room, stripped down to his shorts and tee shirt, retrieved his shaving kit from his bag and walked back into the bathroom, to finish what he had not done the night before.

When Bill walked out of the bathroom, Ruth was sitting on the edge of his bed reading her notes. She had freshened up and changed her clothes. As he reached for clean underwear, Ruth's eyes were level with his penis. She licked her lips and slowly raised her left hand, her index finger lightly tracing the outline of Bill's now semi-rigid erection. Not saying a word, Bill gently reached out and grabbed the back of Ruth's head and slowly pulled her towards his erection.

Ruth did not need an invitation to satisfy his lust. What she wanted to do was tell him she was falling in love with him. But didn't know how to express herself other than through sex. Furthermore, she wanted to be honest with him and tell him she was bi-sexual and loved threesomes.

Bill knew he had only teased Ruth, making her hungry for more sex. She was insatiable when it came to sex. He also knew she had a meeting with Regina on Thursday. Regina would take one look at Ruth and want her

* * *

The two detectives were prompt, courteous and open minded, something Doctor Bradshaw had not expected. Detective Sergeant Jamie Lee Buford and detective Hiram Davis were the original odd couple. Where Detective Buford was overweight by a hundred pounds, Detective Davis was small, almost petite, looking nothing like a police detective.

When Doctor Bradshaw had finished explaining his theory, Detective Buford sat silent, his deep-set brown eyes staring straight ahead while Detective Davis said a little incredulously, "So what the FBI is saying is that the police are looking for a large white man wearing multi-colored suspenders, driving a black Ford Taurus with gold lettering on the side, and the man is a mortician. A traveling mortician at that!"

"Doctor Bradshaw, that is thin," Detective Buford said, closing his notebook and putting his ink pen into his shirt pocket.

"Detectives, the description was given to us by an eyewitness who actually saw the man. The fact that the man is a mortician is based upon forensic science," Ruth said, folding her note pad and placing it in her briefcase.

Both detectives had been superstitiously eyeing Ruth. It was obvious Ruth's looks had infatuated them, and Bill happened to notice that every time Ruth crossed and uncrossed her leg's Detective Buford would begin to sweat and wipe his face with his large, blue, polka-dotted handkerchief. Detective Davis just sat and stared at her.

"Is it possible we could also be looking for a salesperson who sells mortuary supplies? And the writing on the car was not from a funeral parlor but from a supply company?" Detective Davis asked quietly, his eyes never leaving Ruth.

"Hmmm," Ruth muttered beneath her breath. *The detective might have a point. She* thought.

Ruth turned her head noticing that Bill was also considering Detective Davis' hypothesis.

"Okay, I can accept that hypothesis," Doctor Bradshaw said, standing up and shaking both the detectives' hands.

"We now have two theories that work: A mortician or a mortuary supply salesman. Let's run with it guys," Ruth said.

As they rode the elevator back up to their rooms, Ruth's eyes were downcast looking at her shoes. Both she and Bill were lost in their own thoughts. The sound of the elevator chime announcing they arrived at their floor interrupted their respective thinking. Looking up, they smiled at each other. Bill stuck out his hand for Ruth to take. Together, they walked down the hallway hand in hand. To Bill's door smiling but not speaking. Still not saying a word, Bill inserted his key card, turned the handle, and pushed the door open allowing Ruth to enter his room.

"Well, Detective Davis may be correct," Ruth announced rhetorically, not really speaking to Bill directly.

Bill was already undressing, changing into his jeans and sweatshirt. He looked back at Ruth and smiled.

"Well, he could be right," she said, shrugging her shoulders and causing her breasts to juggle for a position within the confines of her bra.

"He could be right. However, stop and ask yourself this question, Ruth. Have you ever seen a salesperson wearing multi-colored suspenders? Sales personnel are taught early on how to dress, how to speak and how to sell their product or product line. I can assure you, Ruth, the wearing of multi-colored suspenders would not be in good fashion sense. Unless of course the colors were representative of their company colors and I have never seen those colors anywhere in the state of Georgia. Or for that matter, how many sales representatives would use their product if they were selling mortuary supplies? However, if agreeing with the detectives will intensify their efforts and the efforts of the other police departments in the state of Georgia, then why not agree with them?"

Ruth stood silently, digesting Bill's logic against that of Detective Davis' hypothesis of a traveling salesman. She was torn in her thinking as both Bill's and Detective Davis' conclusions were both realistic and logical.

Bill was putting on his shoes when it finally dawned on Ruth that Bill was preparing to go somewhere.

"Are we going somewhere?" Ruth asked.

"No, *we* are not going someplace," Bill replied. "*I'm* going to meet my cousin Jimmy Ray and maybe even Billy Bob for drinks and perhaps a hamburger. Furthermore, I can tell you with a certainty that you do *not* want to be there as they are not very polite, nor do they smell nice. They are rednecks and proud of it. However, they are family, and it would be an insult not to say hello and have a beer with them and get caught up on family news."

"So I'm to stay home like a good little girl and behave myself," Ruth said, pouting her lips and searching for a kiss.

Looking at his wristwatch, Bill saw he had an hour to drive across town to the End Zone Bar and Lounge and meet Jimmy Ray. The End Zone had been a local sports bar before sports bars were fashionable. Tony Garza had opened the bar shortly after returning from the Korean War. Bill's dad and Tony served together during the Korean War. In fact, both had been drafted on the same day, gone through boot camp together, advanced to infantry training together and ended up in the same company and platoon in Korea. Bill's dad had used his considerable influence with the city of Valdosta's bureaucrats to help Tony secure his business license and his state liquor license. Otherwise, with a name like Garza, his chances of ever securing any kind of license were next to impossible in Georgia back in 1953.

"Well, Ruth, I'm sorry but I will tell you what I'll do for you. I will give you my credit card and let you take Regina to lunch tomorrow, and you may buy whatever you want and I will pay. Will that make things all right between us? "Bill asked.

"Anything Regina and I want, and you will pay for it?" Ruth asked. Walking over to Bill, she slid her arms around him and pulled him towards her.

Bill kissed her gently, feeling her body, as it moved against his. "That's the deal" Bill replied kissing her neck, which smelled of her perfume.

"So you won't be here tonight or tomorrow" Ruth asked.

"I will be back late tonight. Tomorrow, I will borrow a vehicle from Jimmy Ray and go visit the other murder site while you're spending my money," Bill said, chuckling into Ruth's ear.

❦ CHAPTER 10 ❦

ARRIVING EARLY, BILL DROVE THE rental car into the parking lot and continued around back. As he looked to his left, he saw Jimmy Ray sitting under a big beach umbrella with his wife Ellie Sue.

He honked and waved. Jimmy Ray raised his beer mug, acknowledging Bill's arrival. After parking the Taurus, Bill walked across the parking lot. Opening the small gate, he held out his arms for Ellie Sue and gave her a hug.

Time had not been kind to Ellie Sue. She had gained about a hundred pounds. Now her teeth were stained from all the coffee she had drunk and cigarettes she had smoked. Once beautiful, her face was now drawn and haggard. Her skin looked hard and calloused and her breasts, which had once been the envy of every girl in the city, had disappeared, hanging from her body like useless appendages. No doubt the excessive use of alcohol and tobacco had taken their toll on her body.

Bill noticed many changes in Jimmy Ray also. Some of his front teeth were missing. His once hard, masculine body was now flabby. The glasses he wore made his blue eyes the size of saucers. It was obvious Jimmy Ray had not cleaned his glasses, as they were covered in fingerprints. His body reeked of unwashed body odor and cigarettes.

Neither Jimmy Ray nor Ellie Sue was dressed appropriately for dining out. It was now obvious to him why the hostess had seated them outside. Disappointed upon seeing them, Bill wondered if this had been such a good idea after all.

As they sat down, the waitress asked him what he wanted to drink. He pointed to Jimmy Ray's glass and asked for the same. She smiled and walked back inside, leaving the three alone momentarily.

"Where is Billy Bob?" Bill asked, folding his arms across his chest to keep his body warm in the cool sun.

"He will be here tomorrow, just like we originally planned," Jimmy Ray said.

"That's just as well. I have work to do tomorrow and we can meet for dinner at your place," Bill said.

"How does fried chicken, home fries, green beans and apple pie sound to you?" Ellie said, smiling.

"Sounds wonderful to me," Bill said, reaching out for her hand and squeezing it.

"So what does a famous psychiatrist working for the FBI want of his two cousins? It ain't for the home cooking' and it sure ain't because we're close kin," Jimmy Ray bluntly said, looking at Bill from behind a beer mug, as he gulped down the last of his beer.

Bill waited for the waitress to set the three beer mugs down and take the empties away. She also left three menus and of course, the silverware wrapped in a paper napkin.

"Jimmy, are you and Bill still connected with the Klan or any other hate group?" Bill boldly asked.

"Why? You plan on arresting' me if I say yes?" Jimmy said.

"No, I need your help."

"Help for what!" Jimmy Ray said, sarcasm radiating in his voice.

"To kill shines—millions of them with one bold calculated plan of action. We will kill them from the west coast to Washington D.C. with one deliberate act to coincide with a flu epidemic or some other type of viral disease that will leave the medical community in a panic. Thus forcing the health authorities to burn the bodies and in so doing destroy all evidence of foul play."

Jimmy Ray and Ellie Sue sat dumbfounded. Speechless, they couldn't believe their ears. Then the booming laugh of a redneck and his wife broke the silence of the outdoor patio. A few people looked over at them. However, no one paid any particular attention. For all anyone knew, someone had just told a dirty joke.

"What's that French word for being someplace before?" Jimmy Ray asked.

"You mean déjà vu?" Bill replied.

"Yeah, that's the word," Jimmy Ray said as he slapped the table. "We were at a "Sons of White Men" meeting last night. Billy Bob proposed that same idea then. Now here you are, not twenty-four hours later saying the same damn thing."

"What's more important, I just bet you have the plan to do it," Ellie Sue said, sitting back and waiting for Bill to answer.

"Yes, Ellie, I have the plan and I have the knowhow. I can keep the authorities chasing their tails while we're contemplating and exercising our plan to commit genocide. Tomorrow night at dinner with Billy Bob and both of you, I will explain it all. Now let's eat and enjoy ourselves."

⁂

About ten that evening Bill stumbled into his room. He had to urgently pee and his head hurt. It had been almost twenty years since he had been so drunk. One thing he did remember was asking the waitress to call a cab to take him back to the hotel.

Suddenly, he felt light headed and his stomach began to roll. He felt a burning sensation in his stomach then almost without warning an explosion, as beer, whiskey; rum and vodka came up from the depths of his stomach. His head began to spin and he fell to the bathroom floor unable to stand, the cold tiles feeling good against his cheek as vomit dribbled from the corner of his mouth.

The next thing he knew, he awoke up around noon, lying in his hotel bed. How he got there he did not know. However, he was nude and Ruth was lying beside him, also nude. It bothered him that he could not remember anything except the cab ride home.

When he once again stood in front of the toilet to answer nature's call, he smelled and then saw what he had done last night. Again he experienced the same familiar rumbling of his stomach and the same burning sensation returned once again. Immediately he was reminded about the sins of drink as he puked into the shower stall.

Hearing him, Ruth turned on the shower, letting the water wash away any trace of his drunkenness down the drain. As they dried their bodies, Ruth asked. "Does this sort of thing happen often with you?"

"Last time was about twenty years ago when I was graduated from the University of Georgia and notified I had been accepted into medical school," Bill replied, looking at his face in the mirror.

"I'm afraid you will have to take a cab to see Doctor Furbish, Ruth, or you can walk. I was so drunk I took a cab home. Now I must take a cab back to the bar in order to get the rental car and then drive out to check the murder site. After that, I will go to Jimmy Ray's for dinner," Bill said, shaking his can of shaving cream and preparing to shave.

"Furbish's office is on Oak Street, up the street maybe two blocks on your right. Oh, by the way, Ruth, what happened to my clothes? I don't remember undressing."

"You did not undress yourself. I undressed you. You were covered in vomit," Ruth said, snapping her bra straps.

"Sorry about that!" Bill said, applying shaving cream to his beard that made his face feel like sandpaper.

Ruth did not say anything. She walked out of his room and into hers to finish dressing. He was pretty sure that in a few hours Ruth would be making love to Regina. Maybe a better way of saying it was that Regina would be devouring Ruth. Anyway, he was not going to worry about Ruth. He had other things to think about.

Victim number eleven had been another co-ed. She had been found not far from Valdosta State University, where Route 133 connects with I-75, just at the end of Baytree Street. There, on a cold, rainy, Sunday morning, a man walking his dog before church, found the body of a nude girl. Forensics had been able to determine she had been savagely assaulted many times over an extended period of time. She, had been sodomized after her death.

Unlike the others, this girl was not a prostitute. According to the police report, she was a part-time waitress at a local restaurant. She had been a full-time college student majoring in education.

Bill walked the area even though knowing he would not find anything of significance. Obviously victim eleven had been killed somewhere else, and discarded where found. The more Bill understood the son-of-a-bitch, the more he hated him. In the worst way, he wanted the killer caught and destroyed.

Upon further investigation and reading the reports, Bill now suspected the man might have a background in criminology or perhaps forensics. The guy was careful, thorough knowledgeable, and above all, lethal and he hated women.

Bill walked back to the rental car and his thoughts suddenly turned to the car: *I didn't need to take a cab to the restaurant in order to pick up the car because it had been in the hotel parking lot. How did it get back to the hotel? If I took a cab from the restaurant, how did the car get back to the hotel?*

Leaning against the fender, Bill reached into his jacket pocket to pull out a package of gum. Lost in thought, his mind concentrating on the crime scene, he did not hear the car drive up behind him.

"Who are you?" a deep male voice demanded.

The voice startled Bill.

"Sorry, mister, I didn't mean to scare you."

Bill turned. Standing behind him was a huge man. Next to him stood a woman carrying a white cross, wrapped in flowers. He rationalized they were the girl's parents.

"Mister, I asked you question. Who are you and what are you are doing here!" The man asked.

Standing up straight, Bill turned around, facing the couple. "My name, sir, is Bill Bradshaw. I'm with the FBI out of Washington D.C. I'm here investigating the murders of eleven young women."

"Our daughter, Robin, was found over by that stand of trees. She had been assaulted, then killed," the big man said, trying to hold back his tears.

"Well, sir, I will tell you what I have found out, but please keep this a secret, okay? I do not want any word leaking out that will scare off our murderer. I know this man is cold and calculating, charming and has money. I suspect he is a traveling mortician or a salesman selling mortuary supplies. I know he is a tall man who likes to wear multi-colored suspenders and drives a black Ford Taurus," Bill's words were like a tonic to the emotionally distraught couple.

"So you're getting close?" the big man asked, pulling his wife closer to his side, as if he expected her to faint or fall.

"I know without a doubt the man is from these parts. I'm sure of that, sir. I have the police in Atlanta and Valdosta searching, as we speak."

"May God bless you, sir," Robin's mother finally spoke, tears rolling down her cheeks. "Sir, you get the bastard. You get him before he can kill again."

"Yes, ma'am, I'm doing my best, Bill replied. "Now I must go and leave you to your private matter," Bill said, nodding at the cross.

Bill turned back to his car, opened the door and got inside. After starting the car, he pulled away slowly as he watched Robin's parents and feeling their pain and sharing their grief. It made him think of AJ. His eyes began to tear-up as he got back on the highway and headed east out of town to his boyhood home.

⊷⚘⊶

The drive took less than twenty minutes. He turned off the highway when he reached the county road that he had walked as a boy. In the distance, he could see his boyhood house where he had lived. It looked pretty much the same, except it needed a coat of paint. Then as he drew closer, he could see the changes. Several windowpanes were missing from the windows over the front porch. Where there had once been a big kitchen window, now there was a large piece of cardboard held in place with duct tape. As he turned into the drive, he noticed the down spouting was missing from the corner of the house, the eaves over the porch were gone and the three porch steps were rotten. It was evident that time, apathy and laziness had taken their toll on the once proud house. Two large dogs greeted him as he turned into the driveway.

He honked the horn announcing his arrival, but also for someone come and remove the dogs. As they did not appear to be friendly. Bill honked the horn two more times before Jimmy Ray came to the kitchen door, calling each dog by name: "Here, Martin! Here Luther!" He yelled. Both dogs backed slowly away from the car. Jimmy Ray yelled and both dogs took off to the barn.

Bill opened the car door, watching the dogs disappear into the barn.

"Hurry up will you, before they decide to come back and tear up your ass," Jimmy Ray said, motioning Bill to hurry.

Once inside the safety of the kitchen, Bill looked around. The smell of rotting garbage permeated the air. Bill walked into the dining room trying to escape the smell of rotting garbage only to be met by the smell of overflowing kitty litter boxes. By the time he reached the front parlor, Bill was about to throw-up. There he was greeted by the overpowering smell of two humans who had not bathed in weeks, if not months. Bill ignored the formalities of helloes and handshakes. Instead, he walked to the front door and pulled it open.

"What the fuck are you doing, cousin?" Jimmy Ray yelled.

Bill did not respond. Instead, he motioned his head to the side, indicating for Jimmy Ray to come outside with him. Once outside, Bill looked down the county road, being sure to keep his head turned downwind of Jimmy Ray. The smell of booze and cigarettes, plus Jimmy Ray's lack of body hygiene, forced Bill to walk to the end of the porch.

"Cousin, how would you like to help wipe out thousands, if not hundreds of thousands of shines from this planet?"

Jimmy Ray's whiskered jaw dropped as he expelled a disgusting blast of hot air from his lungs. "Oh, yeah, cousin!" Jimmy Ray exclaimed, smiling.

"Do you think Cousin Billy Bob will help us?" Bill asked, holding his breath so as not to share the same air, as his cousin.

"Billy Bob hates niggers, as much as he hates women." Jimmy Ray muttered his voice resounding as if it were a matter of fact.

"Billy Bob hates women?" Bill stammered remembering his cousin so many years ago as being the biggest cock hound in the county.

"You betcha he does, and in a big way," Jimmy Ray said, turning his head to look over his shoulder to see if anybody was listening.

"You see, cousin, Billy Bob killed his wife, Betty Lynn in a fit of jealous rage when he caught her in bed with the mailman. He found them together on the same day the news story broke that the GM plant was closing. I guess it was more than he could take because he walked back into his living room, took out the forty-four he kept next to his chair, walked back into the bed room and blew the two of them to kingdom come. Then he called the police, told them what he had done and waited for them on his front porch.

"When the police walked into the bedroom, the poor son-of-a-bitch's cock was still in Billy Bob's wife. They had a trial, and he was found not guilty. Of course, the jury was mostly old Klan friends and other extremists. I guess you could say it was a fair trial and all. The district attorney was voted out of office the next election and a Klan sympathizer was elected.

"Billy Bob applied for retraining. Under the union agreement, he also was eligible for his pension. So, he became a mortician. He is raking in the money now bought himself a big fancy house on the Witchlacoochee River. He keeps pretty much to himself these days. You know, cousin, after your daddy's death, Billy Bob quit the Klan and joined that Nazi skinhead group called the Aryan Nation. He even went to their boot camp somewhere in Utah to be indoctrinated. Now, five years later, he is a high-ranking officer with all kinds of connections and lots of influence in these parts."

Bill's imagination began to run wild. His first thought was: *Could it be? Is it just possible that my own cousin, Billy Bob Lee is the murderer? If so, this is too good to be true.*

All of a sudden, Bill felt two very powerful hands shaking him like a rag doll, bringing him back to the present. He had zoned out. That is what AJ called it when he was lost deep in thought. He blinked his eyes then smiled at Jimmy Ray. "Sorry, cousin, I got lost in my own world," Bill said, feeling his body turning in the direction Jimmy Ray was pointing. Bill squinted his eyes trying to see what Jimmy Ray was pointing at, as the bright Georgia sun was blinding him, causing a sudden pain to develop behind his eyes. He heard Jimmy Ray announce that Cousin Billy Bob was coming up the road.

Then he saw it; a long, black car. The closer it came the bigger it got until finally Bill recognized it. It was a Cadillac hearse—long, black and shiny, with tinted windows. Bill thought to himself: *No Georgia farmer would like taking his last ride in it, as it was much too fancy and showy for these simple folk. A Ford or Chevy Pickup with the tailgate down would be just fine for them.*

Bill and Jimmy Ray stepped off the porch and walked across the yard to meet their cousin. He watched as his cousin turned into the driveway, honking hello and causing Martin and Luther to charge out of the barn. Seeing them coming, Bill jumped into the front seat of the hearse while Jimmy Ray dealt with the dogs once again.

"Hello, cousin," Bill said softly, extending his hand.

"Hello yourself," Billy Bob replied, his eyes watching as Jimmy Ray chased the dogs into the barn. "So I hear from the family you're with the FBI and that you're some kind of fancy, high muckety-muck."

"Yes, I'm with the FBI and yes, I'm a Doctor of Psychiatry," Bill replied. He never took his eyes off his cousin because he was looking for telltale signs of a sociopath. Also, he was eyeing a pair of multi-colored suspenders.

"So, cousin, what brings an important doctor with the FBI down to southern Georgia?" Billy Bob asked. "I hear you want to kill all the niggers in the good old U S of A and you want your cousins Jimmy Ray and Billy Bob to help you."

"Once again, you are correct," Bill replied, watching Jimmy and Ellie Sue talking near the kitchen door.

"So you want to use the resources of the Aryan Nation, the Klan and the Sons of White Men to help you in this endeavor." Billy Bob's Georgian drawl had suddenly became very thick and distinct, as if putting on an act for an audience of Yankee do-gooders and trying to convince them he was just a big bubba, meaning no harm.

"Yes," Bill replied, looking back over his shoulder for the first time and noticing the body of a young woman with long black hair. Covered only in a white a sheet, her arm hung loosely down off the gurney showing a unicorn tattoo plainly visible on her upper arm. "We have company," he said, looking at the young woman's body.

"She was nothing much, just a simple whore," Billy Bob replied.

Bill began to laugh, trying to amuse his cousin. "How can a whore be simple?" he asked, trying to draw his cousin out of the self-induced protective shell where sociopaths run and hide.

Suddenly, Bill became aware he was sweating profusely. He could feel his sweat as it dripped down the side of his face, onto his neck and then down his chest and back. Looking over at the controls, he saw the air conditioner was running full blast. His eyes traveled back to the girl's body, lying wrapped only in a sheet. Then, for the first time, Doctor Bill Bradshaw realized he was afraid for his life.

∽ CHAPTER 11 ∽

WHEN THE ELEVATOR DOOR OPENED to the county morgue. Dr . Ruth Schwartz stepped out, her nostrils immediately assaulted by the smell of the harsh chemicals associated with the dead. She walked down the long, corridor holding a white piece of paper in her hand that contained the detailed directions to Doctor Furbish's office. Her high-heel shoes announced her arrival, their sound echoing off the pristine, white tile floor. She took giant strides, trying to escape the smells coming from the various rooms used for autopsies.

Reaching the end of the corridor, Ruth turned right and then made a hard left. There, in front of her, was an office door. The embossed gold lettering must have been six inches high. It spelled: "Doctor Regina Furbish, Medical Examiner."

Ruth put the directions into her purse and pulled out her FBI identification. She turned the oversized doorknob, and as she pushed, the door swung open with such ease it momentarily startled her, causing her to grab the door with her other hand and drop her ID.

Ruth turned and bent over to retrieve her identification card and then straightened up. Standing in her office doorway was Doctor Regina Furbish. During those few seconds when Ruth had been bent over, Regina had admired Ruth's body. When Ruth turned and smiled, Regina's heart skipped a beat—she wanted this woman!

"Hello, I'm Doctor Schwartz," Ruth said, looking at the tall, dark-haired beauty standing at the doorway. "I'm with the FBI and have an appointment with Doctor Regina Furbish."

"You found her," Regina said, holding out her hand.

"Hi," Ruth replied, walking over to shake Regina's hand.

Regina turned and led the way into her office. She pointed to a high-backed leather chair with overstuffed armrests. Regina took her seat behind her large desk, pulling her desk chair up close. She turned and rifled through her folders.

"Here we are, Doctor Schwartz," Regina said, looking up just in time to see the FBI agent running her tongue over her lips, making them moist and glossy. Regina ignored the universal signal that gay women use to subtly indicate sexual attraction, there would be time to play later. two folders that contained pictures of the dead women, Regina handed them to Ruth.

"Please note, Doctor Schwartz, the imprint of a circular mark just to the left of the throat on victim number eleven. That same circular mark appears at the side of victim number nine's throat as well. They appear to be impressions caused from a large heavy ring. Furthermore, note the red under both the girls' noses. Those are definitely chemical burns. I'm not sure, but I would suspect ether or chloroform. He sodomized both women after they were rendered unconscious or perhaps dead.

"I also found a piece of skin in victim number eleven's teeth. Evidently, she bit her attacker severely. The piece of skin has been sent to a lab for

DNA testing. Furthermore, I found an imprint of a bite just inside the labia. Whoever did these murders is a sick, sadistic bastard," Regina said, her once professional demeanor now giving way to hate, as she reviewed the autopsy results. The beautiful FBI agent, who was sitting in front of her with her long, slender legs crossed leaned forward, showing Regina her ample cleavage.

Ruth was lost in her own thoughts as she read the reports and viewed the photos. She saw at once the red burns on both girls' faces, and the circular indentation made by the ring of the murderer. None of the previous victims had such marks upon their bodies, leaving her to conclude that the ring was either recently purchased or awarded.

"Tell me, doctor, do you know of any mortician here in the city or in the surrounding area who wears such a ring?"

Regina sat back in her chair, her eyes staring off into space as she thought about the agent's question. She leaned forward, her eyes resting on Ruth's cleavage. Then she pushed herself away from her desk. Standing she proceeded to walk out of her office to the tall file cabinet located just outside her door.

As Regina opened up a drawer, Ruth watched her pull out a folder and walk back into her office. Regina placed it on the corner of her desk and pulled her chair around, pushing pictures and her phone to the side. Then she sat down and opened the folder.

"Here, Doctor Schwartz, are all the morticians in the county who are legally authorized to pick up bodies for disposal. They are required to fill out a personal data sheet and supply a colored picture of themselves and what mortuary or company they represent. I know of two new morticians who have just recently graduated and finished their internship. They may have bought a graduation ring. In fact, one of them killed his wife a few years ago and was acquitted. He is older and is what we here in the south would refer to as a 'good old boy' or 'bubba'," Regina said, handing Ruth the photos of the two new morticians.

Doctor Schwartz opened the file folder of victim number eleven. Looking once again at the ring imprint, she ascertained the ring was on the left hand of her murderer. When she closed the folder, Ruth turned and was aware Regina was staring at her. Maybe ogling would be a better word.

"Since I have helped you, have I earned a lunch" Regina asked looking into Ruth's big, blue eyes.

"Regina, you have earned a lunch and then some," Ruth responded.

∽ CHAPTER 12 ∽

BILL'S CRISP, CLEAN, WHITE shirt was now completely soaked with his own sweat. His mouth was dry as a desert; a slight but noticeable palsy suddenly appeared in both hands. As Doctor Bradshaw, had faced and treated many homicidal maniacs, but none of them could hold a candle to Billy Bob—he was evil incarnate.

Bill became fearful not only for his own life, but for all the prostitutes and white women in Georgia. He knew that if they caught his eye, smiled at him, even so, much, as nodded their heads or looked him in the eyes; they were as good as dead. That is how lethal his cousin Billy Bob was. Bill could feel his sweat as it slowly crept down his chest and over his stomach wetting his underwear and creating a very unpleasant odor to his nostrils.

Just when he was about to open the hearse's door, Billy smiled and announced, "Here comes cousin Jimmy Ray with the liquid refreshments." Bill opened the door and got out, enjoying the cool breeze on his skin. He breathed deep, savoring each breath; thankful that he would live another day.

As Jimmy Ray handed each cousin a cold beer he said, "The wife will bring us out some sandwiches. Let's go sit behind the house where no one will see us." In perfect step, the three men walked the short distance to the back of the house, out of sight of any nosy neighbors; not that there were any neighbors within two miles.

The real reason was to get out of the sun and sit down at the same picnic table Bill used on those lazy Sunday afternoons while growing up. Grandma Bradshaw and his mom would cook fried chicken, make potato salad, baked beans and perhaps a chocolate cake or an apple pie. Grandpa Bradshaw would tell Civil War stories he had heard from his daddy and describe life in the south when he was a boy. Now using the same picnic table, Bill was planning genocide. His mom would be appalled at his behavior. His dad and grandpa would be immensely proud.

"Okay, cousin, tell us your plan," Jimmy Ray said, taking a swig of beer.

Bill took a swig of beer, sat the long neck down in front of him, and then he looked at both men and began telling them what had happened to his AJ and why he wanted to kill all the shines.

"That's a very noble reason, cousin, truly it is, but tell us your plan and tell us what we can do to help you," Billy Bob said.

"Well, my plan is simple, direct and bold. It will take some very talented people who above all can keep their mouths shut. Shines must eat. The plan is this: We attack the food supply system. We do this by taking ripe tobacco leaves and boiling them in water. Then we filter the water and ship it to Arkansas in large barrels, where we take harvested, long stem rice and soak it in the contaminated water. We make gelatin and soak it in the same manner. We can develop body lotions and a hair wash using the contaminated water later. When the products are boiled or placed in water, the nicotine is released back into the product. Ingested, it will give off flu-like symptoms, or if applied to the skin, it will bring about death swiftly similar to a heart attack.

"We then use zip codes to disburse our free samples, using as many Middle Eastern people as we can and of course, black students, paying them with money and gifts. The gifts will be tainted with a very virulent pathogen, which can be homegrown in a Petri dish, virtually untraceable. They will overcome the body's natural defense mechanism, giving the appearance of the flu by causing high fever, diarrhea and death. This will cause the Center for Disease Control, (known as the CDC for short) in Atlanta to issue flu alerts and eventually an epidemic or better still a pandemic to occur nationwide.

"All the while, the shines will be dying by the thousands. They will die so fast the morgues won't be able to keep up with the autopsies, forcing the cities and counties to burn the carcasses or bury them in mass graves."

Jimmy Ray and Billy Bob sat silent. Both men were stunned by what they had just heard. Billy Bob was the first to speak, his glasses having fallen down the small, thin nose that seemed so out of place on his big round face. Looking over the rims of his glasses, Billy Bob started to laugh and smack his leg with his hand. He laughed so hard he began to cough, causing his face to turn purple. His laughter began to subside, and his color returned to his cheeks. With his laughter now behind him, Billy Bob spoke in a barely audible voice across the table to a very nervous cousin. "How do we know this isn't some kind of conspiracy by the FBI to entrap us and send us to jail?"

"This plan is way too complex for any one man to come up with." Jimmy Ray chimed.

"Cousins, it has taken me over seven months, endless hours at the library and many computer searches to find out the information I have just shared with you. As far as the FBI goes, what you are addressing, Billy Bob, is what is called a criminal investigation. I'm nothing more than a profiler who studies crime scenes and gives opinions as to the type of character and behavioral aspects of the criminal element that the FBI is searching for. I'm not a criminal investigator. As far as the plan being complex, Jimmy Ray, you are correct about that. That's why I wanted just few people involved. The people involved with this plan must hate the shines as much as we do…if not more so." Bill stopped talking and took a swig of beer and a bite of sandwich.

"So cousin, why are you in Valdosta? Are you profiling a criminal?" Billy Bob asked, his eyes burning holes into Bill.

"That is a correct assumption, Billy Bob. You see, there have been a series of ghastly murders up and down Interstate 75." Bill had anticipated this question and knew the question would come from Billy Bob. "I have asked the Valdosta Police Department to search the area for a mortuary supply salesman. We know he is left-handed and must be very charming, good-looking, and have money, because prostitutes are not cheap. He kills by charm, as he makes his victim very comfortable and then in an act of passion, he strangles them. He always disposes of the body in a public place and arranges the body in what I term, are religious positions, leading me to suspect the person is a religious zealot. However, I think this is just a ploy. In reality, the individual is a homicidal paranoid schizoid who actually hates women because he was betrayed by women or perhaps by his mother and then by his wife."

"Woo—wee, that is a powerful lot of guessing, cousin," Jimmy Ray said, turning his head and looking over his shoulder at Martin and Luther.

"When do you need an answer?" Billy Bob asked.

"I'd like a response by next week. I will leave tomorrow with Doctor Schwartz, and we will be driving back to Atlanta to catch a plane back to Washington D.C. in the morning. I want you to write me at my office. Address the letter to me and be sure mark it: Eyes Only. That way, my administrative assistant will not open the letter, log the letter in or make a file for the letter. Furthermore, this way we will have patient-doctor confidentiality, and the law cannot touch us. We will use the Internet sparingly and always in code. We will not phone each other except to plan fishing trips. Instead, we will use messengers or go-betweens that you have picked. They will become my patients, and we will do our correspondence that way. Moreover, I will fly down to visit, say every two or three months, depending on your progress."

"Hmm, so you stay nice and safe while we take all the risk." Jimmy Ray said, spitting out a large wad of yellow mucus, just barely missing Luther.

"You forget, Jimmy Ray. I will be giving false diagnoses and misinformation to the criminal investigators. If I sense danger, I will get word to you both."

"Where will the money come from to pay for your plan?"

Bill turned his attention back to Billy Bob, who was now sitting up straight. His arms folded across his chest, his two beady eyes glaring at him contemptuously. Billy Bob's simple and very direct question had caught him off-guard; causing him to feel crestfallen that Billy Bob asked this question. In reality, Bill had hoped his cousins would be able to arrange for the Klan to fund his plan. For all his research, planning and deviousness, Bill did not have the money to fund his own scheme.

Suddenly, it dawned on him that neither of his cousins were members of the Klan. Bill now realized he should have picked up on this the day before yesterday when Jimmy Ray had told him that Billy Bob was no longer in the Klan. He should have thought this through more carefully and checked out more details. Because without funds he realized his plan was going to fail.

"Well, cousin, to tell you the truth, I was hoping the Klan would help with the money. However, I just now realized neither of you are in the Klan, and I do not have any influence with the Klan since my daddy's death. I guess it was all just a pie-in-the-sky dream."

Bill stood up and extended his hand to both men and said good-by. Turning away from his cousins he walked back to the car. He waved and honked the horn twice, as he pulled out of the driveway and headed towards town. Tears began to slowly stream down his cheeks, as he thought of his beloved AJ and the fact he could not afford to avenge her death.

∞ CHAPTER 13 ∞

THE ATMOSPHERE IN THE CAR on the drive back to Atlanta was subdued. Both doctors were non-communicative lost in their own thoughts. Bill sat on the passenger side staring out at the countryside, but seeing nothing, concentrating mostly on how he could get the money to carry out his plan. Ruth was remembering Regina and how she had felt in her arms. They had lain together for almost five hours, each enjoying the other until they were physically exhausted. Upon leaving Regina's luxurious apartment, Ruth had given Regina her home phone number and asked her to give her a call. However, Ruth knew in the back of her mind that Regina was just a one-night stand.

They arrived at the airport early, having made the trip in record time, due in part to Ruth's heavy foot. After returning the rental car, they took the shuttle to the airport. Once inside, they stopped and checked their tickets against the schedule board, learning their flight to Washington D.C. was delayed due to inclement weather. So, instead of waiting at the airport, for who knew how long, they both decided to check into a nearby motel and take the later flight at 6:00 P.M.

Bill hailed a cab and twenty minutes later he, and Ruth were in a hotel room. The room was clean, and the king-sized bed looked especially inviting, as both were tired. While Ruth slipped into the bathroom, Bill turned on the television and searched until he found the weather channel. I became obvious why so many flights had been delayed. A large and powerful weather front was moving slowly towards Washington D.C. and the surrounding area, bringing with it strong winds with thunder, lighting and the chance of tornadoes. Ruth came up behind him and watched the screen also.

Bill turned and walked to the bathroom. As he stood over the toilet, he stopped wondering about the money and began wondering what she knew that he didn't. He walked back into the room, picked up his suitcase, opened it and took out his ditty bag removing his toothbrush and toothpaste. Instead of taking a shower he decided to wait until after he had made love to Ruth. Just the thought of her made him larger, as he walked back into the bathroom. This time Bill deliberately left the door open in order to hear what Ruth had to say.

As he walked out of the bathroom, he heard the statement, " …I have cracked the case. The murderer is Oh, no, not another one! Where was she found?"

We need to go back to Valdosta to seek out and investigate a man named William Robert Lee, a mortician. I saw his photograph in Regina's office. Bill, he was wearing multi-colored suspenders and matched the description that Emmy Lou gave us. He is our man, I am sure of it."

"Well, we are not going back right now. We have a couple of things we must do first…"

"Oh? And what must we do right now?" Ruth asked with a smile, sensing Bill's need.

"I want you to stand up and undress, but leave on your high heels," Bill said, standing back to allow Ruth to get up from the bed.

Smiling, Ruth turned off her cell phone and then extended her hand for Bill to help her off the bed. Once she was standing, Bill walked around the bed, climbed onto it and watched Ruth as she began to undress. When she was completely naked, she slipped back into her high heels and climbed back onto the bed.

Bill positioned her in the center of the bed. Slowly he leaned his body into hers all the while looking her into her eyes. As he pressed his lips to hers, he felt her passion as she plunged her tongue deep into his mouth. Their tongues entwined, encircled, searched and probed, all of it heightening their sexual hunger. Adjusting his body, Bill positioned himself on top of her slim body. Then he rose up onto his knees, lost in her smoldering blue eyes he lowered himself to her. Eagerly, Ruth reached for him, as he slowly slipped inside of her. Resting her hands on Bill's chest she looked directly into his eyes. Staring back, he leaned down, and kissed her gently. Bringing her hands up, she encircled his back while she raised her legs, locking them around Bill's back. Involuntarily, Ruth moaned as he lay on top of her, kissing her neck and biting her ear lobe. She was lost in her own ecstasy as Bill continued to create new sensations that were driving her wild with passion.

Excited almost beyond control, Bill intensified his rhythm thrusting harder and deeper. Each time he thrust into her, Ruth would cry out in ecstasy. As he kept up the steady pace, he found her mouth and kissed her, gently at first and then as his passion overwhelmed him he plunged his tongue deep into her mouth. With his hand he pinched her nipples, causing her to moan into his mouth. Bill could feel her heart beating against his chest, her breath coming in gasps. Throwing her head back, Ruth screamed for her release. Knowing she was almost ready, caused Bill's super-charged libido to pump harder and faster. He could feel his own orgasm beginning to travel up his loins until he could no longer hold back. They climaxed together, Ruth so hard that she fainted.

Exhausted, Bill lay on top of her, watching her as he tenderly kissed her neck, cheeks and lips. He savored it all because he knew this would be the last time for them—he was going to ask Billy Bob to kill her.

∞ CHAPTER 14 ∞

REGINA WAS ON THE PHONE; her long legs crossed and perched on top of her desk. She was oblivious to the two people who were standing silently in the doorway, watching her, admiring her shapely legs. When she turned and saw them She motioned for them to enter her office pointing at the two chairs in front of her desk.

She pulled her long legs down and deposited them under her desk, while holding up her finger, signaling that she was almost done. She took the initiative and handed Bill the folder of the young woman who had been brought in the day before.

Like all the others, she was strangled. Unlike the others, the killer left ligature marks; using a piece of rope instead of his hands. The woman must have fought valiantly for her life, only to be bested by a man twice her size and probably three times her strength.

The ME's file was complete and accurate in every detail. Bill handed the folder to Ruth, while he opened the enclosed envelope and removed five photos. As he looked at them, he saw the body of a beautiful young

Georgian co-ed, who had made a serious mistake. She had said "yes" to a serial killer, and he had obliged her by ending her life. There were three things she had in common with the other eleven young women, who had occupied cold metal slabs in the city morgues of Atlanta and Valdosta: They would never feel the warm, Georgian sun on their cheeks again, nor smell the salty breeze as it blew in from the gulf coast. Worst of all; they all had known his cousin Billy Bob Lee, intimately.

The third and fourth photographs had Bill's attention for sure. They were photos of two tattoos, one located just above the girl's pubic bone. It was a blue and purple butterfly. *Very beautiful,* Bill thought. Then he picked up the other picture. He hoped the two ladies did not hear the small sound he made, as his breath caught. He had seen this tattoo before. It was on the arm of a young woman lying on a gurney. Her body draped in a white sheet for the purpose of modesty, her arm dangling motionless at her side. The small, gold and white unicorn had been clearly visible on her delicate forearm. When he had been in the hearse driven by his cousin.

"Doctor Bradshaw, here is the picture of the man I told you about," Ruth said, pulling Bill from his reverie, as she handed him the photo along with the completed form that gave all the pertinent information about his cousin, Billy Bob. Automatically, Bill took the photo from Ruth's hand and looked at it, his eyes focusing immediately on the multi-colored suspenders and then the face. His suspicions were now confirmed: Cousin Billy was the murderer. Picking up the folder, he looked in it, trying to decide what he must do give up his cousin or protect him to further his own plans?

"Please tell me, Regina, why is this form and a picture required?" Bill asked.

Regina laughed and told them about the two very industrious medical students who went around the state and claimed bodies that had listed, 'no next of kin, as their long lost relatives. Then they sold the bodies to medical schools around the country. They had made a lot of money doing this until the day a family acquaintance reached a son who lived out of state and told him of his mother's death in Georgia. When he had driven down from Ohio to claim her body, the morgue attendant insisted her son had already claimed the body. The real son politely informed us he was the woman's only living relative and he had *not* claimed the body. His story had checked out. Ever since then, our office has been required to gather the information you have in your hand."

"Were the students ever caught?" Ruth asked.

"Yes, they were caught. Nothing very serious happened to them. They used the money to pay for medical school. And except for the one woman having a son, none of the others had any relatives to make a complaint."

Bill handed both folders back to Regina. She placed them on her desk and then turned and asked, "Did I earn another lunch?"

As Bill smiled at the raven-haired beauty, one part of his brain comprehended what was being said, while another part was busy calculating the cold, hard facts. His choice was clear: Either remain silent and exact his vengeance on an unsuspecting populace, or he must do his duty to God and country and turn in his cousin. The answer to his next question would be the determining factor.

"Regina, have you ever met the man in the photograph?" Bill asked.

"No I haven't," she replied.

"Let's go to lunch," he said, grabbing both women by an arm, his decision made.

Bill knew that Doctor Ruth Schwartz, a noted psychiatrist and profiler working for the FBI, must die. His problem was Regina. He didn't know if Ruth had told her of her suspicions or, if in fact, she even knew his cousin.

On the drive to the restaurant, Bill sat in the backseat, his conscience trying to come to terms with what he must do. Ruth was beautiful and rich, her family both powerful and influential. If she was permitted to pursue cousin Billy Bob and if the FBI or even the local police apprehended him, Billy Bob might confess Bill's plan to the authorities, besmirching his impeccable reputation with the FBI—something he could ill afford. Another point of concern was whether Ruth had told Regina who she thought it was. It figured it was most unlikely, as the Bureau's policy was not to discuss an on-going investigation with individuals outside law enforcement.

When the car came to an abrupt stop in the restaurant's parking lot, it interrupted his thoughts. When he blinked his eyes, he saw they were at the End Zone, the very place where he had gotten drunk only two days before and where he had met with his cousin. *How ironic*, he thought as he got out of the back seat and followed both women into the restaurant.

The conversation was light and lively, until both women began male-bashing and telling off-colored jokes. Bill sat amused, smiling and watching the tender touching going on between the women. He recognized it for what it was—foreplay.

With each passing drink, the jokes got raunchier. Pretty soon, Bill put a quick stop to it. All he needed was one of these "good old boys" chiming in and then the fight would be on. Some of these old boys took their manhood seriously, and were not above punching two loud-mouthed, man-hating females in their faces.

Not knowing or caring who they were, no jury would convict southern men defending their honor in these parts, that's for damn sure, he thought. Bill paid the check, left a nice tip and took the car keys from Ruth then asked, "Regina, where to now?"

"I want to go home," she replied.

"You want to go home and not back to work. Is that right, Regina?" Bill said, opening the back door of the car so Regina could slide inside.

"Bill, I have had too much to drink and I need a nap."

From personal experience, Bill knew that two glasses of wine mixed with rum and coke, chased down by two beers, with only a shrimp salad in your stomach, made for a good drunk.

"Home it is. Oh, by the way, how do I get there?" Bill asked, opening the passenger door for Ruth, who was surprisingly quiet for some reason.

Twenty minutes after leaving the restaurant, Ruth was lying on the bathroom floor in their hotel room. He smiled down at her and left her to her misery. He had things to do.

***

The drive to cousin Billy Bob's took over an hour, as Cousin Jimmy Ray's directions had been sketchy at best. Actually, it was just pure luck when he spotted a hearse sitting in the driveway of a large home that was beautifully landscaped.

He pulled into the drive and parked behind the hearse. Bill noticed that the hearse's motor was running, and by the pool of water that was collecting on the drive, the air conditioner was cooling the occupant in the back.

He walked up the long winding sidewalk, taking deep breaths, trying to clear away the smell of the putrefied flesh he had just seen. He rang the doorbell, listening as the entire house reverberated from the vibrations of the Westminster chimes. As he waited for his cousin to respond to the doorbell, he turned his back to the door, so he could marvel at the scenic beauty surrounding him. On three sides, he was surrounded by forest with the Witchlacoochee River gently flowing south on its way to Florida. The silence was broken by an eagle screeching as it flew low over the river looking for a fish to eat. He was about to ring the bell again when the door opened.

Billy Bob was eating a sandwich, as he opened the door. He did not smile or say anything, merely walked back into the kitchen Bill not far behind him. Billy Bob poured two cups of freshly brewed coffee.

"So what brings the FBI to my house? Have you come up with the money?" He said handing a cup of coffee to Bill.

"Well, I came to warn you that the FBI will be coming soon to arrest you, as the serial killer of twelve women."

"Oh, is that all?" Cousin Billy said taking a sip of coffee.

"Is that all? You mean there are more?" Bill asked, watching his cousin's eyes and facial gestures.

"Oh, my heavens yes at least thirty over all."

The thought of so many missing women shocked Bill into a sense of rage; however, he dared not display it.

"Cousin, have you ever been diagnosed by a psychiatrist." Bill asked.

"Yes I have Bill."

"May I ask what diagnosis the doctor gave you?" Bill asked taking a sip of his coffee.

"I'm a paranoid schizophrenic with severe homicidal tendencies."

"In other words, Billy Bob, you're functionally insane," Bill said, taking another sip of the coffee, as he watched his cousin for any warning signs of aggressive behavior directed at him.

The kitchen exploded in laughter that echoed off the walls, as Billy Bob's face turned red and the deep hacking cough started, reminiscent of the days when Billy Bob smoked three packs of Pall Malls a day.

"Functionally insane, now that's one diagnosis I've never heard before," Billy Bob said. Sitting down at the kitchen table that was located in front of a huge picture window that over-looked the back yard and the valley below.

"Are you here to arrest me, cousin?" Billy Bob asked, taking the last bite of his sandwich.

"I have no authority to arrest you. I only have influence and the power of persuasion." Bill replied, taking another sip of his coffee.

"So what happens when the FBI comes to arrest me?" Cousin Billy asked, in the softest gentlest voice Bill ever heard his cousin use. It was almost child-like.

"Well, I can only guess, but I would think they would put you in a hospital and treat your illness with drugs. They would keep you safe and warm for the rest of your life. And maybe the warden would let you grow flowers. That's what I would guess." Bill said pushing his empty cup towards Billy.

"Would I be allowed to have sex with the nurses or other female inmates?" Billy asked.

"I doubt it Billy. You will be heavily sedated and your libido will be severely depressed." Bill replied watching for any violent reaction.

"Well, if you're not going to arrest me, then why are you here?" Billy asked throwing his massive frame against the kitchen chair.

Bill sat silently knowing what he was about to propose was the betrayal of a colleague. He was about to order the death of a woman who stood between him and his planned vengeance. He was quite fond of Ruth and he even admired her. However, he did not love her. As Ruth loved only Ruth and other women. Men were just a means to an end that helped keep her homosexuality a secret.

Furthermore, Bill thought how Billy Bob would find the money to fund his project out of gratitude to him for not going to the police.

He finally spoke: "Last week, when we met at Jimmy Ray's, I sensed your reluctance helping me. You and Jimmy Ray felt it was a trap or a conspiracy. Hell, Jimmy Ray said no one man could think like that. Well, I wanted to prove myself to you both. I felt that if I told you what was going down concerning you, then you could disappear and prove your guilt, or you could stay and help remedy the problem and have some sexual excitement as well."

"I'm listening," Billy replied, as he made himself another ham sandwich.

Warming his coffee Bill began detailing his plan for a murder. Emotionless, he laid out the cold brutal murder of his colleague in such gruesome detail that cousin Billy stopped eating his sandwich and just listened.

∽ CHAPTER 15 ∽

BILL WALKED INTO THE VALDOSTA Police Department Metro Division around 4:00 p.m. that same afternoon. Upon seeing Bill's FBI Identification card, the desk sergeant immediately dispatched a young, female officer to escort the doctor to a vacant interrogation room. The young woman informed him he should make himself comfortable and she would tell Detectives Buford and Davis that he had arrived.

Immediately, Bill's eyes traversed the room, looking for the hidden microphone and camera. He found the camera easy enough, but the microphone eluded him although he knew it was close by. The seats were hard, the metal desk was caked in grime and coffee stains ringed the table from one end to the other, each ring representing an interrogation. Bill stood and walked from the room, looking for a washroom. He wanted to wash his hands as they smelled after he had touched the dirty table. On his return, he saw Detective Buford walking towards him, holding a cup of coffee.

"You want a cup, doc?" The small, rotund detective inquired, as he walked into the room that Bill found so disgusting.

Smiling, Bill shook his head. "No, thank you, Detective, I'll pass," Bill replied, waiting for the detective to sit down before taking a chair for himself. "Will Detective Davis be joining us?"

"He'll be he shortly. He had to make a couple of phone calls first," Buford replied, sipping his coffee as he eyed the doctor over the rim of his cup.

"Very well, Detective Buford, I have been to the medical examiner's and have read the report on the young girl murdered the day before yesterday. I do not think our serial killer murdered this victim. I say this because our serial killer has always killed his victims with his two hands. That girl was strangled with a piece of rope, as indicated by the ligature marks on the girl's throat."

"So what you're telling me, sir, is that this crime was a crime of passion, revenge or a crime of opportunity?" the detective asked. He held his coffee cup loosely in his hand, causing the coffee to spill on the table.

Bill watched in disgust as the detective used the side of his hand as a squeegee, forcing the spilt coffee to fall to the floor. However, what really turned his stomach was when the detective licked his hand, sucking the coffee into his mouth.

"What I'm suggesting, Detective Buford, is that our serial killer did not commit this murder unless he has changed his modus, which I find very doubtful after twelve murders."

"Hmmm, you may have something, doctor. Detective Evans feels we have two good suspects: The girl's ex-boyfriend and her ex-husband. Neither have what you would call ironclad alibis. However, the ex-husband did say he went to the house, picked up their daughter and took her to the mall to buy her shoes and school supplies. Afterwards, they had dinner. Though we cannot seem to find him on the mall's surveillance tapes, he did have a receipt from both the shoe store and the restaurant, but nobody remembers seeing him or the daughter.

"Evidently the ex-boyfriend is a real winner; a druggie with a big cocaine and crystal methadone habit. The ex-husband volunteered that when she found out her boyfriend was a user and a pusher, she dropped him like a like bad habit. Also, he supposedly threatened to kill her and her daughter. So I will tell Detective Evans and we will pursue your theory. It makes sense."

Bill smiled and shook the detective's hand. "Good," he said. "This will give Doctor Schwartz and I more time to investigate her lead. In fact, she is chasing down her theory as we speak.

"You know, doctor, she shouldn't be running around chasing a serial killer without backup. This man is lethal. I don't believe he would hesitate to kill her." Detective Buford's concern was genuine and heartfelt, obvious by the tone in his voice.

"I agree," Bill replied. "I can only assume that she has backup, as she is on the phone with her boss every day."

⚜

As Bill was talking with Detective Buford, Ruth was driving the rental car into the parking lot of the Silent Home Mortuary. The mortuary was situated about five miles north of town on State Route 31, adjacent to the Silent Hill Cemetery.

This will be quick and easy she thought. I'll just go in and ask the attendant if he a Mr. William Robert Lee works here and is he working now. If he working then I'll call for backup, have him arrested simple as that and that will be that. How utterly simple and straight forward Ruth thought as she parked the rental car. *How Bill found this place or even knew of it is anybody's guess. But if he is correct, one more sick-o will be locked away for the rest of his life.*

⁂

As Bill had let Ruth use the rental car, he had walked from the hotel to the police station. He needed the exercise and the station was only a mile from the hotel. Since AJ's death he had not been working out and he also needed the time to think. As Bill stood at the traffic light waiting to cross the street he glanced at his watch and thought: *I did my job by persuading the police to look elsewhere. Ruth should be at the mortuary by now. What a surprise Ruth will have when she meets cousin Billy Bob face to face. Today will be the last day of Ruth Schwartz' distinguished, but oh-so-short life,* he thought as he crossed the street. Then he started whistling "Dixie," something he did only when he was happy

∞ CHAPTER 16 ∞

RUTH GRABBED HER PURSE AND checked to make sure she had her FBI identification badge before opening the car door and easing her body out and standing. She adjusted her clothing and then began walking up the well-kept sidewalk towards the front door of the Silent Home Mortuary. She was quick to notice the manicured lawn and all the various plants. The sidewalk made a very gentle, sweeping dogleg to the right, where visitors were greeted by the overpowering smell of roses. Before continuing, Ruth stopped to admire all their colors, enjoying their beauty. Slowly she bent down and breathed in their smell, noting that the fragrance of each rose was similar to the one before it. Puzzled, she decided to ask her mom why that was so. Reaching the mortuary door, she opened it and walked in, noticing how clean and elegant the lobby looked. She unzipped her purse and reached in for her ID.

"Hello, is anybody here? " she inquired in a loud voice. There was no response. Looking across the lobby, she saw a sign with a small, dainty looking arrow that said "Office" underneath it. *The place lives up to its name.*

She thought as she walked down the corridor. "Hello, is anyone here?" she yelled, putting more emphasis into her question. Once again, she was greeted by silence.

As she was about to turn and leave the silent mortuary, she heard what sounded like a door opening and slamming shut. *Ah at last, life among the dead,* she thought as she walked further down the corridor. She was greeted by two antiseptic looking, steel hospital doors that were labeled: "Embalming Room."

Slowly, she pushed the heavy doors inward, feeling the rush of cool air hitting her in the face and causing her nipples to react under the thin, white material of her blouse.

"Hello, is anybody here?" she asked in her normal tone of voice.

"In here," a masculine voice replied.

Ruth walked towards the voice, passing through another set of double doors that read "Crematorium." She noticed a gurney against the wall, and wondered if the latest occupant of the gurney had been cremated. She did not have long to wonder; as she felt the steel grip of a man's hand on her neck and something white being clamped tight over her mouth. Ruth was quick to recognize the smell of ether, as it deadened her brain.

Once the woman was safely secured to the gurney, he grabbed a pair of surgical scissors and began cutting her clothes away. He started with her tight fitting, black leather skirt and cut up the middle, revealing her long slender legs. Then he grabbed the waistband of her panty hose and began cutting downwards towards her feet. Billy was careful, being sure to place each item in a garbage bag for disposal. He cut and snipped her clothes until she was completely naked before him. Her breasts stood firm, as her nipples reacted to the coolness of the room.

"I hear through my sources that you have been looking for me. I also know that you're not a real FBI agent, but a wannabe agent. I also hear that you like to have sex. Well, girlie, that is just what you're going to have."

Through droopy eyelids and a brain still craving sleep, Ruth watched in muted horror as Billy Bob undressed before her. Even in her drug-induced state of mind, Ruth now knew why there was never any DNA evidence. This pervert was castrated. Where a man's penis normally should be was an artificial phallus about nine inches long. What made it, particularly gruesome was that it was not flesh colored, but black.

Penis envy, she thought, as she watched him apply the KY jelly to his pretend thing. Another strange thing was that he applied surgical gloves. *Why,* she wondered, as he approached her. She felt his hands as they forced her thighs apart, then the sudden entrance of the foreign object, his brutality causing her to cry out in pain. She could feel his hot breath on her stomach as his lips kissed her soft flesh. Then out of the corner of her tear-stained eye she saw something red begin to move down a tube in her arm. She saw her blood being drained from her body. She began to scream, as her life poured out of her into a plastic, two-dollar bucket.

Bill was shaving when the phone rang. He put his razor down and walked into the other room where he picked up the phone, mentally noting the time was eight thirty. "Hello?"

"Hello, Doctor Bradshaw, this is Ryan O' Neal of the FBI."

"Yes, Mr. O' Neal. How may I help you?" Bill asked in a very polite tone of voice.

"Sir, Doctor Schwartz wouldn't be there by any chance, would she?"

"No, sir, I haven't seen Doctor Schwartz since yesterday at lunch. She left me to follow-up on something while I went to talk with Detectives Buford and Evans of the Valdosta Metro Police Department. We were to go to dinner last night but she stood me up. Why are you asking me about Doctor Schwartz anyway?" Bill asked, feeling the shaving cream begin to harden on his face.

"Well, we had a deal. She was to call and report in twice a day. She has not reported in and I know she was on to something because she told me she would check out her lead and then call me. I know she is not a trained investigator, but I figured with you and the local police there, she would be safe. Now I'm not so sure that she is safe."

"Agent O' Neal, I will ask around and see what I can find out. Give me your number," Bill said, writing the number down before he disconnected. He stood up, smiled, and returned to his shaving. He placed his razor under the hot water to warm his blade, and began to whistle "Dixie."

As he dressed, he looked at his watch. Twenty minutes had elapsed since Agent O'Neal's phone call. He looked about the room and grabbed his suit jacket; his mind flashing back to the day he and AJ had gone clothes shopping for him.

He smiled, remembering that day so vividly. It had been a beautiful fall day when AJ had walked into his office that Saturday morning and told him to get his jacket on as he was taking her to lunch. They had only been dating for a couple of months, but even back then he had been crazy about her. He had laughed and said, "Okay." Since he found it hard to refuse her anything, he had always said, "Okay," to her. After lunch, they had walked by a men's clothing store and she had literally pulled him into the store and started picking out suits and sports jackets. When she was done, he was in debt over a thousand dollars.

Bill pushed the "down" elevator button and waited, all the while thinking about how one act of kindness directed towards his cousin Billy Bob had now come full circle. Bill stepped off the elevator and walked up to the front desk. He waited for the desk clerk to finish with the person in front of him. When she was finished, the blue eyed, raven-haired beauty with the perfect smile, whose name was Kitty, asked if she could help him.

The doctor felt a stirring deep within his loins but suppressed it. "Yes, Kitty, I was wondering if you have seen my colleague this morning, or perhaps yesterday afternoon, say after four?"

"Your colleague being whom?" she asked.

"Doctor Ruth Schwartz. We're with the FBI," Bill said throwing that tidbit of information in to impress the young woman.

Kitty's eyes got big and her voice dropped an octave, as she whispered softly, "No, sir. I just came on duty at 6:00 this morning and I have been busy with checkouts and reservations."

Bill thanked Kitty and walked from the hotel lobby and into the parking lot where he looked up and down the parking lot as if he were looking for somebody. Spotting the rental car they had been using, he noted it was parked in a different parking space. Upon checking it out, he noticed the keys were in the ignition and all the doors were locked.

He pulled out the slip of paper with Agent O'Neal's telephone number and dialed it. A soft and sexy feminine voice answered. Bill quickly asked for Mr. O' Neal.

"Hello, this is Agent O' Neal. How may I help you?"

"Sir, this is Doctor Bradshaw. I have checked with the hotel staff and no one has seen Doctor Schwartz. What I find peculiar is that the rental car she was driving is here in the parking lot and the keys are in the ignition."

"Thank you, doctor, I will take it from here."

"Agent O'Neal, I will be flying back to Washington this afternoon, unless you want me to stay and help."

"Delay your flight until tomorrow."

"Okay, I will." After hanging up, Bill turned, walked back inside the hotel and headed for the restaurant. He was suddenly hungry.

∞ CHAPTER 17 ∞

AS BILL SIPPED HIS COFFEE. He thought about what now had to be done. With his money problems resolved, the next major problem was finding the talent to execute the plan. He knew that his plan was feasible and doable, depending upon the people and their ability to keep quiet He had to find large, ripe, tobacco leaves and then find large cauldrons, or perhaps barrels in which to boil the leaves. After that, the hazardous material had to be transported to another state. There, people he did not know would soak various types of rice in the contaminated water until the water was absorbed into the rice.. The idea being that when the rice product was cooked in water, the poison would be released. .

Next the product would be boxed, identified and shipped, to various parts throughout the country where they would be disbursed. All this must occur before a major flu epidemic.

Just as he was about to leave the restaurant and go back to his room to make some calls, his phone rang. Quickly, he flipped open his cell phone, noting the number was long distance. The area code was Washington D.C. Without a moment's hesitation he answered. It was Agent O' Neal. The call was short and direct. O'Neal informed him that he, along with two other FBI agents—one from D.C. and one from the Atlanta office—would be in Valdosta tomorrow. Bill was to make suitable arrangements for them.

Bill knew the drill. He had been through this before. He walked to the front desk where Kitty was leaning upon her elbows reading something that looked like a college textbook. He watched her a few moments fantasizing about her. Then reality set in when she asked, "Yes, doctor, what may I do for you?" He reserved four non-smoking rooms in the name of the FBI and returned to his room to do some thinking.

Bill lay on the bed. His fingers interlocked behind his head. His eyes wandered across the ceiling until they found the remains of a housefly that obviously had pissed someone off.

Slowly, he began his deep breathing exercises, taking as much air in through his nostrils as his lungs could hold, then exhaling through his mouth. He found that this relaxed and helped him concentrate on whatever issue was before him.

Soon, he realized he had to break the plan down into segments because it was so critical and complex. Each segment would need to be straightforward and simple in nature, but would become quite complicated when combined with all the other plan segments. To keep things simple, Bill decided to assign an operational codename to each segment. The military and FBI were good at naming their plans, so why not him?

The first segment would be called Nightshade. He reasoned that since tobacco is related to the deadly nightshade plant, the code name was appropriate. Bill thought his cousin Jimmy Ray and a few of his associates from the Sons of White Men could oversee Operation Nightshade. All they would have to do was boil the tobacco leaves, pour the water into some barrels and then transport the barrels to Arkansas, since that was where the next segment would be taking place.

The next segment of his operation would be named Razorback. He reasoned that since Arkansas produces so much of the nation's rice, he would buy a few tons of it at auction and then transport the rice, via truck, to an isolated, predetermined destination. There the rice would be husked and soaked in the poisoned water. Once the water was completely absorbed, the rice would be dried, packaged under a fictitious name, and stored until needed.

The operations dealing with female cosmetics, body lotions and shampoos, would be difficult, as the FDA closely monitored the cosmetics industry. However, cosmetics manufactured in Mexico could be shipped across the borders of California, Arizona and Texas without any suspicion at all. Bill reasoned that most, if not all, lotions, shampoos and cosmetics had a common ingredient. Perhaps he could contaminate that ingredient, if he could find out what it was, sell the contaminated ingredient to a Mexican cosmetic company and have them manufacture it under a name who caters to people of color. He would call that segment Black Beauty.

Next he would buy the merchandise and distribute it in bags that could be hung on doorknobs. Each bag would have a box of rice, cosmetics, shampoo, body lotion and whatever else he felt could work. That segment would be called Black Knight.

First thing when he got back to Washington D.C., he would do the necessary research. The overall operation would be called Bitter Vetch. As he lay there, his eyes began to get heavy. Sleep was not far away. He let his mind think pleasant thoughts of Kitty, imagining her nestled in his arms, her warm body lying next to his as he kissed her neck, tasting her skin.

Somewhere in the deepest recesses of his sleep-clogged brain, Bill heard the ringing of the telephone that was perched so precariously next to the bed. Slowly Bill extended his arm, his hand grasping the receiver. He turned on his back and placed the mouthpiece under his chin. Just as he was about to speak the phone fell to the floor, pulling the receiver with it. An immediate series of curse words followed. Slowly, he picked up both the phone and receiver. Placing the phone in his lap, he finally said in a gruff voice, " Hello."

"Doctor Bradshaw, this is Special Agent Tyrone Anderson. I am with the FBI out of the Atlanta office. Agent O'Neal told me to call you so you can brief me about Doctor Schwartz."

"Oh, he did, did he?" Bill responded, buying time for his sleep-drugged brain to start working.

"Yes, sir, he did," Agent Anderson said in a matter-of-fact voice.

"Where are you?" Bill asked, as his mind started to engage once again in both thought and reason.

"I'm out of the Atlanta Office. However, I'm currently in the lobby of your hotel."

"Okay, tell you what. Let me splash some water on my face and get dressed. You go into the restaurant and order me a club sandwich with fries and a Coke. I'll be down in ten minutes or less." Bill hung up the phone, slipped into his shoes and did the necessaries.

The restaurant wasn't crowded, and Agent Anderson stood out in the crowd. He was the biggest, blackest man Bill had ever seen. Agent Anderson had to be six foot six and weigh at least three hundred pounds and he was not fat!

As Bill approached the table, Agent Anderson stood. "Doctor Bradshaw" It was both an acknowledgement and a question.

"Yes, I am Doctor Bradshaw," Bill said, extending his hand.

The two shook hands and sat down at the table Agent Anderson had selected.

"So, did you order for us?" Bill asked.

"Yes, doctor, I ordered two club sandwiches and two sodas."

Bill knew at once that Agent Anderson was a southerner, as the drawl was a dead giveaway. Secondly, only Yankees called soft drinks pop instead of soda.

"So where did you play ball, Agent Anderson?" Bill asked, folding his hands in front of him.

"Sir, I played my college ball right here in Georgia. I played my professional ball for Houston and Tampa."

"So, you got your law degree from the University Of Georgia," Bill said, his voice trailing off as he waited for the agent to answer.

"Texas," the agent replied, unfolding his paper napkin.

"Hmm, very interesting," Bill said as he unfolded his napkin and placed it on his lap.

"Why is that interesting, doctor?"

"Well, sir, your whole life has been sports. I would have guessed you would have gone into coaching or sports journalism—anything but the law and especially the FBI. Hell, with a law degree you could be a sports agent, making millions of dollars."

Both men began to laugh as the waitress placed their food in front of them.

"Tell me, doctor, when was the last time you saw Doctor Schwartz?"

"Let's see… we had gone to see the medical examiner and reviewed her findings about victim number twelve. After looking at the medical report and photographs, I concluded that the girl had died at the hands of someone other than our serial killer. Then the three of us went to lunch. Afterwards, I went to see Detectives Evans and Buford. I walked back to the hotel and waited for Ruth to call me as we had made plans for dinner. However, she never called me. So I ate here at the hotel by myself and went up to my room and watched television and then went to bed. That's about all there is."

"So you have no idea where Doctor Schwartz went?"

"That's correct," Bill replied, taking a bite from his sandwich.

"You say she had the rental car, and you walked from the police station to the hotel."

Bill could feel his anger beginning to rise. How dare this shine question his veracity?

"Yes, I walked. It was a nice walk, about three, maybe four blocks from here."

"What time was that" Agent Anderson asked, taking a sip of Coke.

"A little after four, I would say."

"Well, doctor, the time-line is very short."

"Time line what is a time line?" Bill asked.

"It is a window of opportunity for someone to kidnap Doctor Schwartz. Kill her, then drive her car back to the hotel, park the car, lock it with the keys in it and walk away."

"You think Ruth is dead?" Bill questioned.

"Yes, I do!" Anderson replied.

Bill became silent, his eyes staring straight ahead. His skin became pale and beads of sweat began forming on his upper lip.

"Agent Anderson, if you are correct—and I sincerely hope you're not—that makes two women whom I have known intimately and both are dead. My girlfriend, AJ, was murdered by two male youths looking for drug money. Now Ruth may be lying dead somewhere as well."

"AJ? Do you mean Doctor Alexandra Jackson" Anderson asked?

"Yes, I do," Bill replied.

"Why did you ask me that question in that tone of voice, Agent Anderson?" Bill asked.

"Because, doctor, we all thought AJ was a lesbian and Doctor Schwartz was her lover. Well, that's what the rumor mill was saying."

"Hmm, really" Bill mumbled as he took a sip of soda to wash down his anger. He could feel his anger, deep down, inside welling up, ready to explode. He wanted to exact his vengeance on this uppity agent for blaspheming his memory of the woman he loved. However, he remembered that Agent Anderson lived in Atlanta, and Atlanta was one of the cities targeted to receive his free gifts. So, Agent Anderson would not be among the living much longer.

Bill remained silent, his mind reflecting back to the countless conversations he, and AJ had about moving in together and about getting married. Each time, AJ had said, "No."

Many times he had wondered if there was somebody else. He remembered asking her one evening as they sat in her kitchen drinking wine, if there was another man. She had replied, "No, silly, there is no other man!" Bill hadn't thought to ask if there was another woman. No, the thought had never entered his mind.

"Well, no matter what happens, Agent Anderson, tomorrow I will leave for Washington D.C. of course I will make myself be available to the FBI. I have told you everything I know, except the Medical Examiner's name, which is Doctor Regina Furbish."

"Well, have a good trip and thank you for your help and support. It is appreciated, doctor," Agent Anderson said standing to shake Bill's hand.

Bill handed the waitress a twenty and told her to keep the change.

∽ CHAPTER 18 ∽

THE NEXT MORNING, AGENT ANDERSON briefed the investigative team, explaining in detail what Doctor Bradshaw had told him and what he had been told by the police. Doctor Bradshaw had indeed been with Detective Buford and that Doctors Bradshaw, Schwartz and Furbish, had lunched at a restaurant called the End Zone. The waitress and hostess remembered them as Doctor's. Furbish and Schwartz got inebriated and mouthy about men. Doctor Bradshaw stopped them before they had gone too far and possibly gotten hurt.

"So...we could be looking for a good ole' boy who is sensitive about his manhood," Agent O' Neal said, sipping his morning coffee.

"Yes, sir, I was thinking along those lines. However, I suspect more than one individual—perhaps as many as three. One man to kidnap her, another to drive the car back here to the hotel and possibly another to drive our murderers away," Agent Anderson replied, taking a bite of his cream-filled doughnut.

"So you think our doctor is dead. Is that what I'm hearing?" Agent O' Neal asked, looking at agent Anderson square in his eyes.

"Yes, sir, I do. I think Doctor Schwartz was playing John Wayne and in the process got herself kidnapped. Her body probably has been disposed of in some remote area around here and the chances of finding her body is remote at best."

"So, in other words, we're just wasting our time here? "Agent Demetrius Gallopli asked in a rather agitated voice. "Shit! I get pulled off a real case just to come here to south Georgia to look for a queer doctor who thought she was a trained investigator and is probably dead. That's just fucking great!"

"Agent Gallopli you're here to look for a FBI profiler who was on to something. I know this because she told me. I did not know she was going to pull a John Wayne and go after the serial killer by herself," O'Neal said, looking Gallopli and the other agents in their eyes.

"Further more, she is not a queer, is that understood? She is an employee of the Federal Bureau of Investigation who is missing and presumed dead. And on that premise, we shall investigate. The only strong clues we have are the medical examiner and Doctor Bradshaw. According to Detectives Buford and Evans, Doctor Bradshaw is convinced the serial killer did *not* kill the last young woman murdered here in Valdosta."

"Excuse me, Agent O'Neal, I have a question." All eyes turned to Agent Anderson as he stood and asked, "Why is the FBI investigating murders that should belong to the local police departments and perhaps the state police? I can see offering them help with forensics, but to actually commit man-hours that can be better utilized elsewhere just seems like a waste of time to me."

The other agents were quick to agree with the Anderson.

O'Neal waited patiently for the bitching to subside. As he stared at each man, he spotted agent James West, a very experienced agent with more than twenty years with the bureau and another fifteen as a police detective. It was probably true he should have been retired years ago, but he knew all the right people and he did know the law. He would tell the government lawyers where to look and often times how to proceed with a case. This he could do in such a way that nobody ever took offense with him.

"Agent West, would you care to tell these fine, young dumb-asses why we're investigating a serial killer and helping out the local police?" O'Neal said, taking a swig of coffee.

"You're correct as usual, Agent O'Neal, they are a bunch of dumb-asses." The room began to explode in laughter, boos and hisses. Agent West held up his hand and the room went silent. All eyes were now on Agent West.

"These murders have been committed on or near an interstate highway, as far as we can ascertain. Said highways are funded by the Department of Defense, and are federal property and as such, come under our domain. This dates back to the days of President Eisenhower when he initiated the National System of Interstate and the Defense Highway System. As you know, Ike was the Allied Commander in World War Two and he was impressed with the Autobahn Highway that Hitler had built. It allowed for rapid mobilization of his armies and helped develop the German economy. Thus Ike implemented the same type of program to develop local economies and build up the infrastructure of the United States, which was primarily rural back then. That is why we're investigating the killings of these young women and why we are now looking for one of our own.

"Agent Anderson has verified Doctor Bradshaw's account and his alibi. Today, in force, we start looking for the individual that Doctor Schwartz typed and labeled. Now due to her inexperience she is undoubtedly dead."

The room remained silent, all eyes waiting for O'Neal to give them their orders. They did not have long to wait.

O'Neal remembered a conversation sometime earlier, where Doctor Schwartz had informed him she and Doctor Bradshaw were looking at a mortician or a person who sold mortuary supplies as their prime target. On that basis, he dispatched Agents West and Anderson to follow up on that part of the investigation. He planned to talk with the medical examiner himself. Gallopli was to work with forensics, examine the rental car, get the mileage at the time of the rental and develop a definable timeline. Using the hotel as home base, he was to try and figure the average daily mileage, thus any abnormal spike in the mileage would tell them how far out and back the killer or killers had driven. It was a shot in the dark and the agents all knew it, but many a killer had been caught with less.

Agents Roy Dow and Timothy Richards were sent to the End Zone Restaurant to interview the hostess and waitress and perhaps if they were lucky, some of the good old' boys who were there at the same time Doctor Schwartz was there.

⁂

O'Neal looked at his watch. It was exactly 10:00 a.m. when he walked into Doctor Regina Furbishes office. He stood in the doorway, looking at the tall, dark-haired beauty with the long, shapely legs resting on top of her desk. When their eyes met, she flashed her smile showing off her beautiful white teeth; he felt an immediate reaction. For a split second, he forgot why he was there. Regina motioned for him to come into her office then pointed to the chair directly in front of her desk.

When Agent O'Neal sat down he couldn't help but stare at Regina's legs. It had been almost a year since he had been with a woman and he could feel his manhood stir, as he looked up her skirt.

Regina did not sit up nor did she pull her legs down and place them under her desk. Instead, she was toying with this tall, good-looking stranger. Teasing him would be a more accurate description. As she talked to someone about budget concerns and possible cuts, she dangled her shoe on her big toe; fully aware the stranger could see up her skirt. Her conversation ended with a terse good-bye.

"Hello," Regina said, remaining seated.

"Hello," Agent O' Neal said, his eyes staring directly into hers.

"How may I help you?" she asked, looking at the handsome stranger with a whimsical smile and curiosity in her voice.

"My name is O'Neal and I'm with the FBI. I was hoping you could tell me the name of the man Doctor Schwartz was investigating."

Regina pulled her legs down and placed them under her desk. Her demeanor changed from the flirt to the consummate professional. "I don't remember the name. In fact, I'm not sure I ever heard her or Doctor Bradshaw mention it. However, I know where the information is kept." Pushing back her chair, Regina stood and walked out of her office.

Agent O' Neal was in lust as he watched her walk out of the room. He began to fantasize about making love to her. Imagining her naked, lying in his arms while he kissed her. As his thoughts grew so did his manhood. The dark haired beauty walked back into the office.

"I found the folder Doctor Schwartz was so interested in. However, the picture and the biographical page are missing," she said, handing the folder to him.

"Who had the folder last—Doctor Schwartz or Doctor Bradshaw?" O' Neal asked.

"Hmmm, if I remember correctly it was Doctor Bradshaw who handed it to Doctor Schwartz," Regina replied her eyes locking onto the large bulge in O'Neal's crotch.

"Are you sure?" O' Neal asked.

"I'm positive," she replied.

"She probably took it then. What I don't understand is why she just did not ask you to make a copy of the bio sheet," O' Neal said, staring up at Regina and admiring her beauty. "Want to go to lunch?" O' Neal asked without preamble.

"I thought you'd never ask," Regina replied, picking up her purse. "Let's go before someone calls."

⚜

Using the infamous Slim Jim, the police officer opened the door of the rental car. The first thing that struck Agent Gallopli was the smell inside the car. It smelled of perfume. Quickly he opened the glove compartment and found the rental agreement. He backed away from the car and let the forensic team do their job.

He found a seldom-used break room and poured himself a cup of coffee. Then, taking a seat near a window, the agent pulled out his note pad and pen and started to add and subtract. The car had been rented at the Atlanta Airport, which was 230 miles from Valdosta. So, adding that figure to the odometer reading on the rental agreement, he got his starting figure. Per Agent Anderson, he knew that both doctors had used the hotel as home base. Therefore, in two days they had driven sixty miles. Immediately his mind quickly rejected the numbers. No way could they have driven sixty miles in two days! Maybe at best five miles, as everything they did was within ten blocks of the hotel. The only deviation would have been the restaurant, which was about three miles from the city morgue. That would mean a twenty-five mile trip out and back. His curiosity peaked, Agent Gallopli walked back into the forensic garage and asked for a county map.

He was quickly, but ever so politely, told that the forensic department did not have maps. He was told he should go upstairs and see the sergeant at the front desk. The agent smiled, thanked the forensic tech and did, as he was instructed.

The sergeant was a very tall, hawk-nose man with two, deep scars on his face, obviously from wounds received in the line of duty. Gallopli explained what he was doing and why he was doing it. Smiling, the sergeant nodded his head. He took the agent into the emergency response room and showed the agent two maps. One was a city map, the other a county map.

Using his ink pen, the sergeant pointed to the hotel. Then carefully explained that Valdosta was only thirty square miles and using twenty-five miles as a hypothetical figure and starting from the hotel parking lot, Doctor Schwartz could have gone anywhere within the county. However, the sergeant knew that Gallopli was looking for a mortician or a person who sold mortuary supplies.

"Using that premise I would discount everything north of this point," the sergeant said pointing to State Route 84, "and concentrate your search from Quitman here in the west, down to Claysville in the south and on over to Naylor here in the east."

Gallopli was impressed with the sergeant. "Why these areas and not to the north?" Gallopli asked.

"Because there are no mortuaries until you get to Adel and that is farther than twenty five miles from the hotel. Quitman has a mortuary and so does Claysville. If my memory is correct, there is one in Naylor," the sergeant said, sticking his pen pack into his shirt pocket.

"Very good. I'll run this by my boss," Gallopli said, shaking the sergeant's hand.

⚜

They sat in a booth way in the back of the restaurant. Since they were early for lunch, the place was deserted. O'Neal watched her. In fact, he could not take his eyes off the woman. He loved her smile and her smell. When she reached across the table, she took his hands and held them in hers, he knew he wanted this woman—wanted her for his lover. It was his lust he wanted her to satisfy. Hell, he wanted her to be the mother of his children!

Lunch was a glass of white wine and a salad. Finished, O'Neal paid the bill. Back at the car he opened the door for her and he walked around and climbed in behind the wheel.

"What time is it?" Regina asked.

"About 11:45 a.m.," he replied, starting the car and adjusting the air conditioner vent away from her face.

"Good, we have time then," Regina said, looking at him and smiling.

"Time for what?" he replied.

"Some afternoon delight!" she said with a laugh leaning over and kissing him on the mouth.

CHAPTER 19

D R. BRADSHAW WAS PLAYING THE age-old game of catch-up. He used to play the game well but now he could care less. He had other things on his mind. Mary was helping him immensely and he appreciated her help. Slowly, things were coming together. As they worked, he filled Mary in on what he had learned in Georgia. Of course, he told her of Doctor Schwartz's disappearance and his fears that she might be dead He told her of the couple he had met alongside a country road, carrying a cross to mark the spot where their daughter had been found murdered.

It had been two weeks since he had returned from Georgia. Sitting at his desk, Bill wondered about his cousins: *Had they been able to get the money? Would the Aryan Nation and the Sons of White Men help him with his plan?*

The court trial for AJ's killers was coming up in a couple of weeks. According to his source, Gonzo, the usual wheeling and dealing was going on in the judge's chamber. Their defense attorney wanted them tried in juvenile court where they would get a slap on the wrist and sent to counseling until they were rehabilitated in six months. However, the government's prosecuting attorney wanted life, as Doctor Jackson was an FBI employee and fell under the same accord as killing a police officer, or any other member of the law enforcement team.

Where it would end, nobody knew except for twelve jurors all black. *Hope they do the right thing;* Bill thought taking another sip of coffee and wondered fleetingly how he could kill all the blacks that were already in prison. The simple ringing of the phone brought him back to the everyday life of a successful doctor. "Hello," he said.

"Doctor, are you ready for your nine o' clock appointment, or do you need a few more minutes." Mary asked chuckling into the receiver and causing him to smile.

"Send him in, Mary."

Mary entered the office carrying the familiar purple folder. He knew by the color of the folder that this person was a new patient. Handing him the folder, Mary stepped aside and introduced a Mr. Jonas Tubbs. Quickly, Mary grabbed the mail that was in his outbox and walked to the door and shutting it.

"Please, Mr. Tubbs, take a seat," he said, pointing at the chair in front of him.

"Don't rightly reckon I'll be long enough to warm your chair, doctor." Mr. Tubbs said with a slow deliberate drawl. His green eyes were cast downward, his hands holding a hunter's cap in front of his groin. His demeanor was of a man who was out of place in a big city, let alone sitting in front of a psychiatrist.

"How may I help you, Mr. Tubbs?"

"Your cousin, Billy Bob, sent me. He asked me to tell you he got the money and that your cousin Jimmy Ray is going forward with his part of the plan."

"And just what is Jimmy Ray's part of the plan?" Bill asked.

Jonas looked up at him for the first time. "Don't rightly know for sure except it involves killing a lot of filthy niggers."

"Is there anything else Mr. Tubbs. I appreciate the message. So I will say thank you and please tell my cousins thank you. Will you do that for me?" Bill asked standing up and extended his hand. "I will do that, doctor." Jonas replied shaking the doctors hand, turning towards the door.

"Mr. Tubbs, do you have money to make it back home?" Bill asked.

"Yes, sir, I do." Mr. Tubbs replied placing his hand on the door knob.

"Very well then," Bill said, patting Jonas on the back.

After Jonas had left, Doctor Bradshaw took the information page in the purple folder and tore it up, removing any evidence that Mr. Tubbs was ever here. He put the empty folder on the corner of his desk for Mary to reuse.

Bill looked at his watch. Only ten minutes had elapsed since Jonas had given him the message; almost an hour before his next patient. He felt good. Getting up from his chair, he went into his private bathroom. . Examining his feelings, Bill realized that he was excited, like a little boy on Christmas Eve. *With luck*, he thought; two *parts of his plan would be completed in less than six months.*

He sat down at the computer and began searching for this wonder bean that his Grandma Bradshaw told his mother about from Africa. Though he could not remember the name of it, he decided to read the list of ingredients on a tube of AJ's bath lotion. Perhaps that would jog his memory.

Agent Gallopli left the Valdosta Metro Police Station and proceeded to walk back to the hotel. He checked his watch, as he wanted to know how long it would have taken Doctor Bradshaw to walk the same distance. However, his real reason was that he needed time to think. Knowing

O' Neal wanted to cover his own ass. He had all the men starting at the beginning and working backwards. That is what they were doing.

He looked at his watch as he walked in the front door of the hotel. Eleven minutes elapsed. Doctor Bradshaw had said maybe fifteen minutes to walk from the police station to the hotel, at least that part of his story checked out.

Walking by the restaurant, Gallopli looked in to see if anybody was in there. Surprisingly, the restaurant was empty. Then he walked by the front desk and headed towards the elevators where he pushed the "up" button and waited. While waiting, he pulled out his room key and loosened his tie. Having been so self-absorbed in thought, he hadn't realized until that moment he had to take a leak and fast.

Once his bodily function was satisfied. Gallopli rested on the bed and read the phonebook. He was looking up the addresses of mortuaries. Out of luck, he called Agent O'Neal's room; still no response. To hell with it he thought; I will *go, investigate the three mortuaries and then call it a day*

He decided to shower, shave and put on clean clothes before he left for Naylor. One never knew whom you might run into, and he wanted to look good.

An hour later, Gallopli was standing in front of P.D. Bertram's Funeral Home that offered a wide range of services. So the hand painted, black-

and-white sign said. Gallopli opened the door and walked inside. Hearing a radio, in the distance, playing a Beatles tune, he headed towards the music. When he got to what looked like an embalming room that doubled as an office, He called out, "FBI!" Suddenly, the room fell silent. Somebody turned off the radio. A voice yelled back, "Just a second I'll be right there."

Gallopli stood at the ready not knowing what to expect. Then a small man appeared. He was stooped-shouldered, his hands crippled from arthritis, and he was wearing a sweat-stained white shirt and black tie with brown shoes and black pants. From behind the heavy wooden door that said, "Keep out—authorized personnel only!" he emerged.

"Did you say FBI" the old man asked.

Agent Gallopli relaxed; this old boy was harmless. "Yes, sir. My name is Gallopli, and I'm with the FBI."

"Gallopli? What kind of name is that?"

"It is Greek"

"You mean to tell me that they have goddamn Greeks in the FBI now?"

"Yes, sir, we also have Italians and Jews and even Niggers."

"Shit, boy, no wonder this country is so fucked up! It's when the likes of you and those other communist sons-of-bitches can infiltrate the FBI that you spread your filthy doctrine to our youth."

"Yes, sir, that is exactly what we do, alright. We corrupt young boys and girls, encouraging them to kill, rob and steal, so we can keep our jobs." Gallopli responded indignation ever present in his tone of voice.

"What do you want? I'm busy." The old man asked.

"Are you P.K. Bertram?"

"Yes, boy, I'm P.K Bertram. Now that we got that straight what in the hell do you want?"

"What does the P.K stand for?" Gallopli asked.

" It stands for Percy Kelvin."

"Really, I thought it stood for pecker knocker," Gallopli said, his disgust and contempt for this old racist son-of-a-bitch being hard to hide. "Percy, that's a good name for a queer. Percy the faggot" with that statement, Gallopli turned and left, the old faggot to his pain and sorrow.

Gallopli was familiar with racism. He faced it as a child and in school growing up. However, never before had he seen the hatred behind the racism. Now he had and it bothered him. Shit, it did more than bother him; it downright scared him. Thankfully, people like Bertram were dying out. He guessed that was a good thing. It must have been pure hell back in the old days when black men had to step aside for the lowliest white trash that passed them by. Perhaps that is why the blacks were so patient. They just sit and wait and let time pass by, because they know it cannot stay this way forever.

Gallopli decided to head to Claysville. He figured an hour tops until he would be back at the hotel, in time for the evening meeting and supper.

The drive there took approximately thirty minutes. Looking at his watch, he saw he was doing better than he had expected, time-wise. As he drove through downtown Claysville, he just happened to spot a sign that said "cemetery." Not knowing why, he followed the sign. He had gone about a mile further down the road when he saw the sign that said, "Silent Home Mortuary." Slowing down, being sure to put on his blinker, he pulled into the driveway, and followed it up until he reached the parking lot.

Parking the car, he got out and looked around. Nothing moved. There were no sounds. *Geez, it is as quiet as a tomb,* he thought. He walked down the sidewalk, making a slight turn to the right. Noticing the rose bushes in bloom, he thought them pretty. Gallopli opened the door and walked into a very large, immaculately clean lobby. Still, there were no sounds at all. Seeing an arrow that pointed towards the office, he headed that way. "FBI" he called.

He heard a door slam, then what sounded like something metallic hitting something. Not taking any chances, he slowly walked down the hallway with his hand on his gun. *Fuck protocol!* He thought just before he again yelled, "FBI!" He continued walking down the hallway heading towards two stainless steel doors.

Slowly, Agent Gallopli pushed one door open, his eyes doing a complete sweep of the hallway. Finally, he heard what sounded like a television news broadcast. He could hear someone in the room to his right. "FBI" he yelled again. *They had to have heard me this time, or else they are deaf.* He thought to himself.

"Come on down G-man, we won't shoot." A male voice yelled back. Gallopli heard the voice chuckling. He relaxed and walked into the room that said, "Embalming." Suddenly, he felt a vice-like grip around his throat then something white was placed over his nose and mouth and then silence.

Agent Gallopli would not have to worry t any more about bullshit cases. Nor would he ever have to worry about looking good, in case he met somebody important. For Agent Gallopli, did meet somebody influential and that somebody was Death!

∽ CHAPTER 20 ∾

THE PHONE RANG AND Doctor Bradshaw picked it up on the second ring. "Hello! Yes, this is Doctor Bradshaw. How may I help you?" Doctor Bradshaw listened intently, as Agent O' Neal, explained that another agent had gone missing. It appeared this Agent Gallopli had been working on a theory. Problem was, he did not tell O'Neal, or anybody else. Now this Agent Gallopli was missing, and presumed dead, just like Doctor Schwartz. O'Neal asked him if there was anything, he could remember that might help catch this killer.

Bill asked, "Did you or one of your agents talk with the medical examiner."

There was a pause and then a slight chuckle, followed by a clearing of the throat. Agent O' Neal responded, "I talked with the medical examiner."

Immediately, Bill knew by O' Neal's actions and voice, that Regina, the mantrap, had seduced him. She always got her man.

Taking a sip of wine, Bill placed the glass back on his desk. He right-clicked on his mouse and began to browse, reading all he could about an ingredient that is commonly used in lotions and shampoos, even as a decongestant. The ingredient was called Shea butter. The butter was made from a bean grown in Africa. As he read about its mystical properties, he found the article was quick to point out that the Shea bean was distilled, using petroleum-based products and that the butter extracted in this manner still contained harmful chemical residue. As such, its mystical properties were seriously diminished. His mind immediately processed this information. He knew he needed to find a large quantity of Shea butter, inject it using the Bitter Vetch and then sell it to a company who specialized in bath and body products that catered to blacks. If it was ever discovered what killed these people, it could be blamed on the processing of the Shea bean back in Africa.

He stopped reading the article that glared back at him on the video screen. Suddenly images of Cousin, Billy Bob began flashing in his brain. The visions were so vivid that he actually saw the agent walking up the sidewalk and enter the lobby of the Silent Home Mortuary. He saw the agent flashing his badge and his right hand was on his weapon, yelling for anybody. He watched the agent walking down the same hallway that only two weeks ago Ruth had walked.

The agent pushed his way through the heavy steel doors, and yelled, "FBI!" Then proceeded to walk down the hall to the first door on the right. There, Cousin Billy would be waiting and there, the young energetic and most capable agent would die. He would not die a violent death, he would not be tortured, nor would he lie in a darkened room, lingering in pain. No, his death would be quiet and peaceful.

Agent Gallopli would be put on a stainless steel gurney and wheeled to the oven gate. Still unconscious from the heavy dose of ether or chloroform. His body would be placed on to the oven table. Probably next to another soul whose family was paying for the cremation. After that, Billy Bob would turn on the gas, wait for the pressure gauge to reach its desired range and then simply hit the igniter switch. A slight noise would break the silence and Billy Bob would know that the furnace was doing its job. He would turn and clean up the room, removing any sign that the agent was ever there. He would polish the stainless steel doors and of course, the front door.

Once done, he would then drive the agent's car to some place in town. Call his cousin Jimmy Ray to come pick him up and take him home. It was that simple no fuss, no muss. One agent disposed of nice and neat, and he could get on with his business.

Of course, this was all conjecture, how did he know if Cousin Billy Bob was actually involved or not?

∽ CHAPTER 21 ∽

IT HAD BEEN ALMOST a year since AJ's murder. The newspapers were silent about the up-coming trial, preferring to concentrate on some other type of debauchery or senseless act of violence. However, in Washington D.C., violence was an everyday occurrence. Bill could still remember his grandfather saying, "Niggers lack social skills, and they are too tribal to live in peace with each other. They needed the white man's influence and judgment in order to live peacefully in white society. When the blacks congregate in close proximity with each other, violence is the result."

Bill thought it must be difficult for the newspapers and television news crews to pick a story that would excite the locals that, over the years, had become immune to violence.

Sometimes, Bill wondered what the public reaction would be if a newspaper printed a story about a boy scout helping a little old lady across a busy street; or a young man finding a handbag full of money and returning it to the owner in Washington D.C. That would be big news. However, he knew that would never happen in D.C.

Bill took another sip of wine, refreshed his browser, and looked up flights to Valdosta. He felt like going fishing with his cousins just to get away for the upcoming weekend. With the trial for AJ's murderers, only ten days off Bill needed to check in with his cousins and to monitor their progress.

✦✦✦✦

He looked at his watch. The flight had taken less than four hours, and that included a stop in Atlanta. After picking up his rental car, it was five hours from the time he had left Reagan International Airport, and he was sitting with Cousin Jimmy Ray, drinking coffee at the same picnic table where five weeks before he had outlined his plan to his cousins.

Jimmy Ray informed him that he had picked up both moral support and a sizeable cash donation from the Klan. He was going to use the cash donation to purchase two hundred additional barrels, bringing the total barrels to five hundred thousand gallons of the poisonous alkaloid ready to be transported to Arkansas. Then when the barrels were emptied they would be returned and refilled. Billy Bob had estimated it would take another hundred thousand gallons to implement Bitter Vetch.

"Very good, Jimmy," Bill said, taking the last sip of his coffee. "So your part of the plan is in full operation."

"What do you want us to do when we finish?" Jimmy Ray asked.

"After you have fulfilled Billy Bob's estimates, I want you to remove all traces of where you brewed the tobacco. Furthermore, pay off your help and then wait until you're needed. I'm thinking that we're looking at sometime this fall."

Bill turned, waiting for Jimmy Ray to come up alongside him and walk with him to his car. Martin and Luther followed at a respectable distance.

"What can you tell me about the FBI agent that is missing?" Bill asked.

"Nothing, really the newspapers, and television news showed pictures of the two FBI people. One a woman, the other a man. Both missing and presumed dead." Jimmy said tossing his cigarette into the grass.

"Hmm, that's too bad," Bill replied. "I knew the woman. The man I never met."

The two men shook hands and said their good-byes.

As Bill backed out of the drive, he looked at the dashboard clock. It read 2:30. He did not want to drive to Billy Bob's house, as he knew he would not be home. Instead, he decided to check into a hotel and call from there. Perhaps they could have a nice dinner before he caught the plane back to Washington on Sunday.

Dinner with Billy Bob was a joyful, almost festive occasion. Bill knew his cousin had probably not taken his medicine for a few days as he was looking at the manic-depressive side of his cousin, as evidenced by the extreme euphoric high that he was exhibiting. This was dangerous. Bill knew, as Billy Bob could start bragging about the plan or the killing of Ruth for that matter.

"Tell me, cousin, how is Operation Razorback progressing?"

"Well, the Aryan Nation purchased about twenty-five metric tons of both white rice and brown rice. It did this on purpose, so if the government comes investigating, the Nation will show them the records and the storage facility. We will tell them that this rice is to feed our people when the war comes between us and the blacks or the government. In reality, we purchased one hundred tons of contaminated rice that was involved in some chemical spill a while back. This contaminated rice is being shipped to a location known only to me and two other high-ranking officials of the Nation.

"We have constructed large holding tanks where the poisonous water will be mixed with the rice at a ratio of about four to one, letting the rice absorb the water. Then the water will be drained, and the rice allowed to sun dry. The rice will be picked up and poured into large vats. Then it will be packaged under the name of Uncle Adolph's Wild Rice.

"The remaining water will be poured into large kettles, then along with bones of cows and horses. The water will be boiled to make gelatin. We are going to flavor the gelatin orange and cherry, as kids seem to like those two flavors the most. Thus, we will give the little ones what they want. We are naming the gelatin "Darla's Delight."

For some reason, Bill had never thought of the children.

"We have a very capable chemical engineer who happens to work for the state of Arkansas. He is the one who came up with the ratio. It will save money and allow us to contaminate more rice and gelatin. He did happen to mention that when ingested, nicotine gave off so many different clinical symptoms that medical personnel would not be able to effectively or accurately diagnose anyone. Depending on the age of the person and their prior medical history, the symptomology could range from burning of the mouth, throat and stomach, to nausea. Followed by projectile vomiting, rapid heartbeat, dizziness and convulsions. Death could occur as quickly as five minutes or less and usually from respiratory failure. Much like the flu, don't you think, cousin?"

Bill said nothing. He was pleased with what he had been told. He was glad to see that Cousin Billy Bob's whole demeanor changed. Now he had become quiet, almost subdued, when he began discussing what he and his friends had done.

"So when will Operation Razorback be completely finished?" Bill asked, sipping his iced tea.

"Everything will be completed in six weeks."

"That soon" Bill replied, sitting quietly his head bowed as if in prayer. He was thinking about Shea Butter and how to purchase it and get it to the right manufacturer for processing. Most of all, he was wondering if the manufacturing process would change the nicotine's lethal properties.

"Tell me something, Billy Bob, does the wholesaler you used to buy the rice know of a way to purchase large quantities of Shea butter?"

Cousin Billy Bob looked up from his plate. Setting his fork to the side, he quietly asked, "What the fuck is Shea butter?"

Bill began to laugh, his cousin's response taking him by surprise. When his laughter subsided, he explained in detail what Shea butter was and how it was going to be used. He went on to explain that he had to find a manufacturer in either Mexico or South America that could make and ship the end items to a predetermined location for packaging and eventually distribution and delivery along with the rice and gelatin.

Billy Bob sat perfectly still. His arms folded tightly around his torso. His head bowed, listening to every word that his cousin the doctor was saying.

When Bill had finished, Billy Bob looked up at him and asked, "Is that all?"

"Yes, that's all for now" Bill replied.

"I'll see what I can do," Billy Bob promised.

"I also have one more item to discuss with you, cousin."

"Yes, I know," Billy replied, looking over the rim of his glasses at him.

"You know what I'm about to ask you?" Bill asked.

"You are going to ask me about the FBI agent who has gone missing," Billy said, his face peaceful and serene as if he were in church.

"Well, yes I was."

"Ask your question, cousin."

"Do you know what happened to the second agent?"

"Yes, I do. I made him disappear just like the first one. No fuss and no muss, nice and neat," Billy responded, clapping his hands back and forth as if was cleaning dirt off them.

Each man sat in silence, neither looking at the other, and both wondering what the other was thinking; each man playing the "what if" game.

⚜

On Monday, The trial for AJ's killers began. It had been almost an entire year since her death and still Bill grieved for her. At night, when lying in bed, he would often reach out to check if she was there. Sometimes he could still smell her perfume coming from her bathroom.

Now he sat in a court of law, directly behind the prosecutor. Detective Gonzales sat next to him along with the medical examiner, the two police officers that had caught the two boys riding in AJ's car and the detective who had interrogated Kareem.

Bill looked at the jury. All were black seven women and five men. The youngest juror perhaps was in her forties while the oldest maybe seventy. They sat silent, their eyes staring directly at the two young men who sat across the room from them. Both were being tried as adults for killing a federal agent. The death penalty was evoked as required by the law when a federal agent is murdered.

Just before noon, the prosecutor rested her case. All the witnesses had been sworn in and had testified. Each one pointed to the two boys stating, "Yes" these are the two men who were driving the stolen car. Yes, these are the two men whose fingerprints were all over the murder scene and that yes, the DNA evidence from the semen found in AJ matched one of the boys." The defense attorney sat still, doing nothing and saying nothing. The trial was a slam-dunk.

It was over except for the penalty phase. AJ's killers would be punished harshly. *However,* Bill thought to himself, *this city of violence, this city of liars and cheats, this city with its own society and sub-culture that had produced such vermin, would know the depth of AJ's lover's wrath. This city and others like it would be made to pay and pay dearly. These people, who only ten generations ago had come to this country with bones in their noses and war paint on their faces, would suffer and suffer greatly. Their dead would pollute the air, as fires would burn night and day removing the last vestiges of their race in America.*

Bill walked out of the courtroom, the need for revenge seething from every pore in his body.

∽ CHAPTER 22 ∽

D R. BRADSHAW SAT AT HIS desk, his fingers interlocked behind his head, staring at a large painting, lost in thought. It had been over a month since he had visited his cousins. He knew Jimmy Ray had completed his part of the plan. Billy Bob had told him Operation Razorback would be completed in six weeks. That meant one more week remained—two at the most—before that part of the plan would be completed.

Still, he wanted to know about the Shea butter. *Had Billy secured someone to help him procure enough Shea butter to interest a cosmetic manufacture in Mexico or South America? Could he sufficiently contaminate the Shea butter with the Bitter Vetch?*

Mary walked into his office with her correspondence file, thus bringing him abruptly back to the present. She informed him there was an agent O' Neal on line three. He pulled out his ink pen and picked up the receiver just as Mary pushed the button connecting him.

"Hello, Doctor Bradshaw here, how may I help you?"

"Hello, sir, this is Agent O'Neal. I just wanted to take a moment to thank you for your help and support during the investigation of Doctor Schwartz's disappearance. As I lost another agent during that investigation, I have been fired as a special agent. Now I'm just plain, Agent O' Neal and have been reassigned to our office in Minot, North Dakota. That means, I'm being forced to quit or live in limbo for the rest of my career. Since that was really no choice at all, I have decided to take a job with the Atlanta Police Department, working in Internal Affairs. Doctor Furbish is going to take a job in Atlanta as well and we are going to live together. At least that is the plan."

"So, you or the other agents have no idea what happened to either Doctor Schwartz or the other agent? Is that correct?" Bill Bradshaw asked, a puzzled tone in his voice.

"Sir, no one knows anything or have they seen anything. There is no DNA evidence, no fingerprints and no witnesses. It is as if the earth opened up and swallowed them."

"Hmm that is very strange indeed. How about the picture and bio-sheet that was in Doctor Furbish's office?"

"Gone. Obviously Doctor Schwarz took it with her," Agent O' Neal said with disgust.

"What about the Valdosta Police Department? Are they still going with the premise we're looking for a mortician or a sales person who sells mortuary supplies?"

"As far as I know they are, sir."

"So, with you gone who is your replacement?"

"Agent James West has been promoted to special agent. He is a very capable man and in my opinion, should have been promoted a long time ago."

"That's good!" the doctor responded, trying to sound positive. "Well, Agent O' Neal, good luck with your new job and I wish you and Regina much happiness."

"Thank you, doctor."

Bill handed the correspondence file back to Mary. While talking with the agent, he had been signing letters, not bothering to read them as Mary had already done that.

"So the FBI is stumped," Mary said, picking up the folder and walking back to her desk.

"Perhaps befuddled would be a better word," Bill said, shaking his head. "Who's next?"

"Doctor, it is time to go home. We are done for the day. Hell, we're done for the week! Did you forget it is Friday?" Mary said.

"My God, this week went fast!" Bill said, "I had no idea it was Friday."

✦

That night Bill made reservations for an early morning round-trip flight to Valdosta. He also made a room reservation at the same hotel where Ruth and he had previously stayed. Once that was done, he reserved a car.

The flight down was anything but exciting. However, Bill did manage to get some long overdue journal articles read. Upon landing, he rented a car then drove the short distance from the Valdosta Regional Airport to his hotel. After he registered, Bill proceeded to his room. He had purposely chosen a non-smoking room on the second floor that was close to the stairway exit. It was his intention to use the stairway instead of the slowest elevator in the whole state.

When he had settled into his room, he first called his Cousin Billy Bob and set up a meeting for later in the day. Next, he decided to pay a visit to the Valdosta Police Department and check in with them. What he really wanted to know was what they did or did not know.

Bill knew it was a long shot at best as it was a weekend. Also, more than likely, no one at the station would be able to give him the information he sought. It was his fervent hope that the mere fact he had came down and was paying out of his own pocket would count for something.

He was in luck. The same, very attractive police officer that helped him the last time he visited was on duty. She smiled, recognizing him at once.

"Hello," Bill said, smiling at the young officer.

"Howdy," she replied.

"I was hoping to talk with Detective Buford or Evans is that possible? I do not have an appointment."

"Let me see who's back there," she said, picking up the phone and punching an extension number.

Looking more closely, Bill noticed she was wearing gym shorts, tennis shoes and a tee shirt stained with her sweat. "Oh, by the way, my name is Doctor Bradshaw and I'm with the FBI," Bill said, trying to impress the young beauty that was smiling up at him. As he looked down her shirt, he could view more than an ample cleavage. Immediately he became aroused.

"Yes, Detective Evans, a Doctor Bradshaw is her and wishes to talk with you." Hanging up the phone, she then stood up, walked around the desk and said, "Please, follow me."

Bill was glad to follow as it gave him a chance to eye the young officer from behind. She was a cutie—nice, firm and compact, with a nice smile.

"Officer, may I ask your name?"

"My name is Jennifer Culpepper. Most people just call me Pepper."

Bill smiled and extended his hand. "Nice to meet you, Pepper."

"Nice to meet you, doctor."

Pepper stopped short. As Bill was paying more attention to her behind than where they were going, he bumped into her. She didn't say a word, just extended her hand and pointed to Detective Evans who stood as Bill walked into his office.

The first thing Bill noticed was that Detective Evans was also wearing gym shorts, tennis shoes and sweating like a pig. Next, as the detective walked towards him with his hand extended, the doctor observed he walked bent over, his back obviously giving him some trouble. He was pale and his breathing was fast and erratic.

Taking the outstretched hand, Doctor Bill quietly urged, "Detective, please sit down." Then he called in an authoritative tone, "Pepper, come here!" Looking more closely at the detective, Pepper immediately recognized the problem—Detective Evans was having a heart attack. Bill placed his finger on Evan's carotid artery, checking the detective's pulse. It was too fast. "Call 911, Pepper!"

Two hours later, with Detective Evans safely situated in the cardiac care unit, Bill and Pepper walked back into town. Fortunately it was a short walk from Pineview Hospital to the police station, or "The Tombs" as the police officers referred to it. That was because the station was located on Toombs Street.

They could have called for a patrol car to bring them back to the police station, but it was a nice day, so why not walk? Besides, it gave Bill time to ask Pepper out to lunch. Pepper accepted, but said she first needed to shower and change into street clothes.

"Tell me, Pepper, is Fazoli's Restaurant still open?" Bill asked.

"Oh, my, yes, that is my favorite restaurant," she said. "The restaurant is only closed on Sundays and Mondays as are most family restaurants here in town."

Bill looked at his watch. He thought to himself, *It is almost 3:00 p.m. I arrived at the regional airport around 11:00 a.m. and before noon I had checked into my hotel and helped save a man's life. Now I'm taking this beautiful police officer to lunch and perhaps to bed.* Although he still wanted Kitty, Pepper certainly excited him.

Dinner with Billy Bob was tentatively set for 7:00 p.m. at some shake and bake chicken place out near the freeway. So, he had four, maybe four and a half hours to feed and then seduce Pepper. That is if he could and if she would let him. It was at times like this when he missed Ruth the most. Of course, if Pepper did not want to have sex with him there was always Regina. So what if O'Neal thought Regina would be true to him? Regina was a creature of habit and comfort. Plain and simple, she liked sex. If you were not there to enjoy her, then she would find somebody who would.

Lunch was superb. The wine was excellent and it helped set the mood. It made Pepper frisky and she made it clear she wanted to play. Bill was quick to capitalize on the moment. Looking around the dining room, he quickly noticed the dining room was empty except for them—one of the benefits of coming in late. He grabbed her hand and held it under the tablecloth, holding it close to his crotch so she could feel what she was doing to him.

She took another sip of wine and leaned forward. As he looked down at her, she smiled and said, "Tell you what. You take care of the check and I will go to the ladies' room. Then we will go to your hotel room."

Sitting in his rental car, Bill again looked at his watch. It was 7:15 p.m. and Cousin Billy was not there. He let his mind drift back to the afternoon and Pepper. She had been like velvet in his arms—so soft and smooth. Molding her body to his, she anticipated his every move. Bill could not get enough of her body. He was in lust and he knew it. Before separating, she had given him her phone number and directions to her place. Also, she told him she was off duty the next day and if he wanted, he could stop by.

Though he was waiting for his cousin, he really wanted to go to her; to hold her body against him once again and feel her lips on his. No doubt about it, he wanted to feel her breath on his neck and fuck her. He was becoming thoroughly aroused when the sudden honk of a horn forced him to jerk back to the present. He looked to his left where his Cousin Billy Bob had pulled up next to him and sitting next to Billy Bob was Jonas Tubbs. *How odd,* Bill thought. *Something must be wrong.*

∞ CHAPTER 23 ∞

THE THREE MEN SAT AT a table drinking a southern drink called, "Sweet Tea." Bill was listening to both men describe, in detail, how they convinced the elders of the Aryan Nation to help procure 625 barrels of Shea butter.

Next, they had been able to sell the Shea butter to a cosmetics company in Mexico, using a dummy company with an overseas address that could be traced back to Rhodesia. The name was Black Beauty's Secrets. A greedy and unscrupulous Mexican broker was its sales representative. Actually, this company manufactured products under various names. In turn, these products were sold to distributors, who then sold the beauty products to discount stores.

The beauty of it all was that the products changed hands many times crossing just about every state line in the United States. In this way, it would make it difficult, if not impossible, to determine where and when the product had been tampered with, should the contaminated products be detected. There were virtually no paper trails, only e- mails and false custom's documents.

From a Mexican customs agent Jonas had bribed, he had learned the manufacturing company in question was also a front for the illegal distribution of narcotics. Jonas went into detail about how he, and Billy Bob injected each barrel with the bitter vetch, using two sizeable syringes and a huge hypodermic needle.

Cousin Billy told Bill that Operation Razorback was completed. There were over two million boxes of contaminated rice and about six million packages of gelatin sitting in two warehouses, awaiting distribution to selected cities.

"According to the cosmetic company's customer service representative, the products manufactured under the trade name Black Beauty's Secret could be delivered to any city or cities that we select. So which cities are we going to target and when." Jonas asked.

"I will have to let you know when and where. This next phase of the plan will require exact timing, so I have to do some serious thinking." Bill replied

The meeting took less than thirty minutes. As he drove away, Bill reached into his pocket and pulled out Pepper's number. He had to see her again and soon.

⁂

The flight back to Washington D.C. was very turbulent. Bill was bemused as he watched his fellow travel companions grasping their armrests, their knuckles white. As the plane pitched and yawed in the cold gray sky, the passengers were bounced up and down as the flight attendants passed out vomit bags. Soon, the smell of vomit permeated the cabin. One woman across the aisle began saying her rosary while another began reciting the Lord's Prayer. Bill's stomach was a little queasy, but otherwise, he was fine.

What he was waiting for was a flu epidemic or better still, a pandemic outbreak of influenza to cover the implementation of Bitter Vetch. W this event occurred, AJ's death would be avenged. Only then could he take satisfaction in knowing that he was responsible for the deaths of hundreds of thousands of shines and other scum.

The plane managed to land safely and ahead of schedule. As Bill stood up and stretched his legs, he saw many men and women were pale, their eyes glazed over with vomit residue on their shirts and blouses. As he reached for his carryon luggage, the stench of vomit still permeated the cabin, making him anxious to get out into the fresh air. Glancing toward the back, he saw a young flight attendant tucked behind a curtain, crying, obviously overcome by emotion. Just then the hatch door opened and blessed, fresh, cold, clean air rushed through the cabin. People began breathing normally, as the stench of vomit began to dissipate.

⚜

Bill was home less than an hour later. As he changed his clothes, he listened to his phone messages. The third call was from Pepper. She had called to find out if he had made it home safely and to say she missed him.

Flopping down on the bed, he dialed Pepper's number. On the third ring, a deep voice answered. "Hello, this is Technical Sergeant Harlan

Culpepper. We are not at home right now. Please leave a message and telephone number. We will get back to you as soon as possible."

Bill was stunned perhaps devastated would be a better word. His mind had trouble grasping what he had heard. Laying there, his mind raced: *Pepper is married? She wore no ring. Her apartment had no pictures to indicate she was married. Perhaps she is divorced, and that was an old recorded message she had not gotten around to changing... Tomorrow I'll call the station and ask.* Placing the phone on the bed, he closed his eyes.

⚭ CHAPTER 24 ⚭

ONCE AGAIN BILL WAS AWAKENED by the sound of his own scream, his body wet with sweat and, his arms wrapped tightly around AJ's pillow His dreams had become increasingly vivid. In them he saw the headlines of The Post described, in detail, the deaths of African-Americans by the thousands Medical evidence revealed some type of undefined genotype disease related to the Asian flu. The he watched, as the country become paralyzed and cities like Oakland, Detroit, Columbus, Cleveland, Newark, Trenton, Philadelphia and Atlanta were in anarchy Law and order was breaking down, giving way to fear and panic.

He could smell the sultry, humid air, heavy with the stench from the dead. City governments, already stretched to the breaking point, were digging mass graves using every power shovel and bulldozer they could beg or borrow. Bulldozers and front loaders pushed the bodies into large pits as men wearing facemasks poured lye on the corpses to speed up decomposition…

Quickly, Bill blinked his eyes and sat up on the side of the bed. He bowed his head and rested it on his hands. Though he was thirsty, his thirst could wait. What he needed most was a shower.

Sitting at the kitchen table was something Bill rarely did. He preferred instead to carry his food into the den and watch TV. Now, he waited for the microwave to finish, while his mind began to diagnose his mental and physical health: *My physical health is deplorable, although still athletic-looking my muscles are flabby and my stamina is basically non-existent. I have to begin working out he muttered to the microwave as it chimed, notifying him his pancakes were ready. In college, I used to lift weights and jog. He thought. Tomorrow morning, I will begin jogging.*

If I have to diagnose my mental health, I would say I have some form of schizophrenia. I'm thinking acute rather than chronic, only because I'm developing the typical clinical abnormalities associated with acute schizophrenia. The reason in my case being the sudden loss of a loved one who was killed violently, which has created an emotional upset in me.

In other words, the sudden death of AJ had created a hole in his soul, and now he was he in full-blown depression. That was not unusual, really. Personality disorders like his often resulted in a retaliatory mentality. Why should he be any different just because he was a psychiatrist?

⚜

The alarm clock announced that it was Monday morning, and time to go jogging. The night before, Bill had laid out his gym stuff. AJ had taught him to do this as it helped speed up the process of dressing. He did not work out since the morning of AJ's murder. The cool morning air hit him square in his face as he opened the front door. He began to stretch his legs, and torso as he began to shiver. Bill knew that if he ran some and walked some, he might just be able to do a mile. That is all he wanted to do, a mile. He would take it nice and slow, trying not to overdo it as he had done so often in the past.

Bill walked into his office right on time. His lungs hurt, as did his legs, but it was a good hurt. Mary had brewed the coffee and was busy posting the out-going correspondence.

"Good morning, doctor," Mary said, smiling up at him. "I will be right in with your coffee and the paper."

Bill had never said anything, but he hated it when she brought him his coffee. However, she did not seem to mind as it gave her early morning one-on-one time with him. This way, she could plan her day around their discussion.

He waited until they had finished discussing office business and of course, her life. A day would not be complete without discussing her life. Though he really did like Mary, she was neurotic, of that there was little doubt. However, she was the best administrative assistant in the city, and her salary reflected her worth.

"Mary, please call this number in Valdosta and ask for Officer Culpeper. I want to speak to her."

"Yes, doctor. Remember, your first appointment is in twenty-five minutes. It will be Sally Pritchard."

Bill reviewed Sally's folder as he waited for Mary to put his call through to Pepper. He had just taken a sip of coffee when Mary buzzed him, announcing that Officer Culpepper was on line three.

"Hello, Pepper. I tried returning your call yesterday but got a male voice on the message machine."

"Oh, Bill I'm so sorry to tell you this, but I'm married. My husband is in the air force, and he is always gone. I get so lonely and horney, I just have to have sex. And since you're a stranger here in town and a doctor and all, I chose you, knowing you were a safe bet."

"I see," Bill said, tapping his pen on Sally Pritchard's folder. "Okay, then. Thank you for explaining the situation to me and thank you for the favor."

Bill did not say good-bye. He took another sip of coffee and continued to read his notes on Sally. Next time he would try for Kitty.

∽ CHAPTER 25 ∾

THE COLD, NOVEMBER RAIN UNRELENTINGLY pounded against the bay window of Bill's condo. He was reading the morning paper and enjoying his coffee, while listening to the TV news. It was Saturday, and he had no real plans except to go grocery shopping and return a new shirt that had a flaw. In addition, he wanted to go into the library and check out a couple of movies. Otherwise, that was going to be his day.

Funny how a simple glance at a TV screen could change not only a life, but the lives of a whole country, even the world. Fate had walked into Bill's life, and the country would never be the same.

It was twenty-seven months since AJ's attack and death. Now, at last, her death would be avenged. The little red banner that flashed across the bottom of the TV screen announced that according to the CDC in Atlanta, the flu season was fast approaching, and it was expected to be severe with the possibility of becoming an epidemic in various parts of the country.

This was just the news Bill had been waiting and hoping for! He turned off the TV, walked over to his computer, clicked the mouse and the screen came to life. Quickly, he found the e-mail addresses for which he was looking. He only wrote four words. His message to the Aryan Nation and the Sons of White Men read "COMMENCE OPERATION BITTER VETCH." Within forty-eight hours, the deadly gifts would be trucked to predetermined destinations. Forty-eight hours after that, the gifts would be hanging on door knobs, lying on apartment house floors and handed to unsuspecting people, as they departed from their grocery stores.

Bill decided implement his plan in the mid west. Starting slowly, he directed the deadly cargo to Chicago, and Milwaukee. Before sending more, he wanted to see if the hospitals could handle the sudden and overwhelming influx of sick and dying people. Also, he wanted to see if these cities had an effective emergency response plan to handle the dead.

His next assault target would be Kansas City, followed by Saint Louis, Oakland and Los Angeles. These cities were chosen because they were points of entry into the United States from Asia. The next target would be Houston, then Atlanta and Miami. Houston and Miami were also ports of entry for large cargo ships coming in from Asia. Atlanta was where the CDC was located.

Bill figured the rest of the country would be waiting for news on how to combat this flu epidemic if it hit them. He was also hoping the CDC would be overwhelmed and make an incorrect evaluation of the flu strain. If that was the case, doctors across the country would misdiagnose the real cause of all the deaths.

Although not widely known, Bill was aware that the World Health Organization had predicted there would be a very mild flu season this year, thus causing pharmaceutical companies around the world to reduce production of their influenza vaccines. Right then, the country was a sitting duck, and he was going to blow the country out of the water!

∞ CHAPTER 26 ∞

D
R. AARON HILL WALKED FROM the physician's parking lot towards Saint Elizabeth's ER, where he would soon be going on duty. As the cold north wind cut right through him, he walked quickly. He was not a big man, nor a man with a lot of fat to insulate his body from the cold. As he drew closer, he noticed large numbers of African-Americans standing near the side entrance of the ER door. He looked back over his shoulder and saw more African-Americans arriving. Some were crying. Others were bleeding from their noses, and a few were so weak they just simply had to give up and sit down on the cold, wet ground.

As soon as Doctor Hill entered the ER, he knew the night was not going to be an easy one. The first thing he did was hang up his overcoat and then put on a white lab coat. Next, he grabbed his stethoscope, made sure his penlight worked and stuffed his pockets with latex gloves.

Taking a good look around, he saw immediately what was happening. Only ten days before, he had been in Thailand as part of the Doctors

Without Borders Program. There, he witnessed first-hand the ravages and devastation of the flu. While there, he and his colleagues had prayed this would not happen in the states. Their prayers were not answered.

Quickly, he called for the charge nurse, the nursing supervisor and housekeeping. Susan Leininger was the charge nurse on duty that night. She was a tall, dark, raven-haired beauty who had been an NICU nurse and a critical care nurse before coming to the ER. All the nurses on duty that night were qualified in multi-specialties and very experienced. Two of the nurses were even combat nurses, having seen duty in Afghanistan and Iraq. Aaron knew he had the right crew with him, and that made him feel confident.

Nurse Leininger stood before him, her dark eyes looking through him, as she also knew what they were facing. The other six nurses, the two lab technicians, the radiologist and Anne Todd, the nursing supervisor for the entire hospital, stood silently waiting for the doctor's orders. He looked into their eyes and saw apprehension and even fear. However, still they stood tall waiting for his command.

"What we have here is the beginning of a flu epidemic. I saw this not more than ten days ago in Thailand, and I prayed we would not be ravaged by it. Well, ladies, it is now here. This is only the first round. It will get worse, that I can assure you. So we will all wear masks and latex gloves. I want housekeeping to spray down the walls in the hall and exam rooms. Also have house keeping wipe down the gurneys with bleach. Every hour, I also want the floors mopped. This strain of flu is extremely virulent. Before this is over, thousands, if not millions of people will die. If you do what I tell you, then you will survive I promise.

"First, I want to set up a special triage. This is what the common complaints will be: Body aches, muscle and joint pain, headache, sore throat and unproductive coughing. You will also hear harsh breathing. The person may have a fever between 100 and 104 degrees. I want you to look for redness or hemorrhaging of the mucous membranes and note if the person is experiencing dizziness and sneezing. Furthermore, they may be experiencing diarrhea and vomiting. Those are the primary symptoms which you must look for first. You must remember, that the real danger of influenza infection is that it has the tendency to progress into the often fatal, secondary bacterial infection of pneumonia."

Each nurse stood silent, grabbing a handful of latex gloves from the box that was being passed around. Nurse Todd picked up the hospital intercom handset and paged housekeeping for some more help. She then turned to the nurses and told them she would round up more staff and open up the cafeteria in order to allow the people who were outside to come in and sit while they waited to be seen. Next, she told Mrs. Anderson and Mr. Davis, who were the intake specialists, not to charge these people. Instead, she asked them to help her set up a triage station in the cafeteria.

"Nurse Todd, if we don't charge these people, how will we get paid?" Mrs. Anderson asked as she shut down her computer.

"The CDC and the state will pay us. This is a national health emergency. I know it hasn't been declared yet, but it will be by morning. Not more than ten minutes ago I got two calls from Bethany Hospital and one from Saint Ann's. They are also under siege. So let's get ready, shall we?"

"Yes, ma'am," Mrs. Anderson said, throwing back her shoulders and raising her head high. She knew she was about to become very important.

By then, Mr. Davis was already in the cafeteria telling the patrons to leave, as he was confiscating the room for a medical emergency.

Mr. Davis was a medic in Vietnam. He already retired both from the Army and the United States Postal Service. The reason he had taken this job was at the request of his wife who had told him he was a bad retiree. He couldn't just sit around; he had to be involved in something. working part-time, he became an intake specialist, working nights.

"Doctor Hill, I have requested the pharmacy tech to call her supervisor for more help. She agreed when I explained what we would be facing," Nurse Todd stated.

"Thank you," Doctor Hill said, walking towards the cafeteria.

He knew that the hospital's pharmacy did not have sufficient broad-spectrum antibiotics to satisfy the immediate need. In fact, if he was right, the entire city of Chicago did not have enough meds. This was going to be bad. He could feel it. Putting on his facemask and gloves, he began his shift.

❦ CHAPTER 27 ❦

CLIFF PFEIFFER, PhD, was the senior microbiologist and director of all labs at the CDC. Standing without moving, his eyes were glued to his 5300-inverted contrast microscope eyepieces. On the slide he was watching the microbial villain that was causing the illness of so many people across the country. He had isolated the *Bacillus Influenza*, which he had accepted as the true virus and identified it as a mutant strain of the H2N2A.

He loved working at the CDC. It was a facility that was multi-faceted and always-in motion. Personally, he felt he had made a difference in the country and in the world, as did most, if not all, of the staff. He was proud to be one of its directors.

Looking back at the culprits on the slide, he noticed this strain had two rather nasty peculiarities to it. First, it was resistant to the anti-viral agents generally used to treat respiratory tract infections usually associated with influenza. Second, for some inexplicable reason, it was attacking mainly African-Americans and Hispanics. He did not know why that was.

Perhaps it was some sort of genotype virus, but he figured this virus was a mutant. No matter what, it was going to be a bad flu season.

He was about to call the director of the CDC and his boss, Doctor Nancy Moore, when Kathy Tyler, his lab chief and his personal assistant, showed him her results. By rights, they should have been the same as his but they weren't. Then Raymond Rucker, another microbiologist, asked him to look at his slide, as he was viewing something, he did not understand. What was really strange and scary was that the virus being evaluated was from three different regions of the country and each was different?

Doctor Pfeiffer knew he was in trouble. He also knew that if he was in trouble, the country was in trouble. Not knowing what he was dealing, he instructed his staff and all lab personnel to wear face masks in addition to face shields. Though they would hate it, he was not going to take any chances with his staff.

He made the call to Doctor Moore and reported what he knew for sure. "...Furthermore, and this is the strange part. This microbe is similar to those found in tuberculosis patients and in children with whooping cough, measles, chronic bronchitis and scarlet fever," he told her. Then Cliff laid the big one on her when he suggested that this virus could be a new mutant.

"Nancy, I'm afraid we are in for a very rough time of it. I think people will die by the thousands, if not by the hundreds of thousands. Conservatively, the United States could lose twenty to thirty percent of its population in a matter of weeks if this cannot be stopped and fast."

Nancy's knuckles went white as she gripped the receiver tightly. She had always known it was possible this day might come. Although she and Cliff often butted heads over budget and staffing needs, she knew his reputation was above reproach. She learned to take his word and his work to the bank. "Thank you, Cliff," she said, putting the receiver back into its cradle. She buzzed her administrative assistant.

"Yes, doctor" came a small voice over the intercom.

"Carol, please get me the Surgeon General," Nancy said trying not to let her voice betray her fear.

Ever since she was in high school back in the big city of Ada, Minnesota. Nancy Moore had known she was going to be a doctor. However, she never dreamt that one day she would be called upon to be the Director of the CDC. Nor did she ever imagine she would be a Professor of Medicine at Emory University. But she was and with the other dedicated medical professionals at her side, she was truly committed to protecting the health and welfare of Americans.

⚜

While Doctor Nancy Moore waited on that cold and rainy Monday morning to speak with the Surgeon General, six hundred miles to the north, Doctor Bradshaw was sitting in his office talking on the phone with an Agent James West of the FBI. He was investigating the disappearance of two FBI agents and the murders of fifteen young women. What he wanted was insight and any information Doctor Bradshaw might give him that could help him find this murderer.

Bill listened intently as Agent West described in detail the murders of the young women. He knew from Agent O' Neal's reports and Agent Anderson's interview that he had developed a workable profile of the killer.

"Excuse me, Agent West, did I hear you say fifteen women?" Bill asked.

"Yes, sir, the total is now fifteen," West replied in a matter-of-fact tone of voice, betraying no emotion.

"Were the women prostitutes?" Bill asked.

"Yes, they were," West replied.

"Were they put in various positions reminiscent of religious postures?"

"Yes, sir, you could say that!"

"Were the bodies found in and around Valdosta or were they found up and down Interstate 75?"

"One body was found in Albany down by the riverfront. She was found sitting up. Her hands folded in prayer. The other two women were found in Tifton. Their bodies were perhaps a hundred yards apart. One of them had been sodomized according to the medical report."

"Agent West, who was the medical examiner that did the autopsy?"

"Don't remember his name. Is that important" West asked, warming up to Bill's charm and professional demeanor.

"I guess not. What does it matter? The girls are dead and we both know it's the same man. What I might suggest is that you meet with Detectives Evans and Buford of the Valdosta Metro Police Department and advise them to issue a warning to all women in the area."

"Sir, Detective Evans has died. Detective Buford has retired and moved to Florida to be closer to his daughters."

"So, who has taken over the case?" Bill asked.

"As far as I know, nobody, yet!" West replied, anger starting to creep through his professional veneer.

Bill smiled to himself. He knew Billy Bob was still safe.

"Agent West, were there chemical burn marks around their noses and mouth, like they had been knocked out with ether or chloroform, or were they strangled?"

176

"Two had been strangled. The other was rendered unconscious." West replied.

"I suppose there is no DNA evidence." Bill asked.

"None at all," West remarked coldly.

"Well, Agent West, it is still the same man. I would think the girl killed in Albany may be a copy-cat killer. I would have to come down to Valdosta and investigate for myself. However, with this outbreak of flu spreading across the country, quite frankly, I'm afraid to fly, as we both know airplane cabins are breeding grounds for germs," Bill said, taking a sip of coffee.

"Well, Doctor Bradshaw, thank you so much for your time and insight. I do appreciate it and hopefully we will meet again," Agent West said, his voice trailing off, knowing that the conversation was about over.

"Good-bye, West and thank you for the update and remember, my friend I'm only a phone call away." Bill said hanging up the phone.

Bill hung up the phone and buzzed Mary. There was no reply. *That's strange,* he thought. He looked at his watch to see that it was only 10:00 a.m. Getting out of his chair. He walked out to see what was happening. Mary's back was to him. He could see she was engrossed in the news channel on the TV. Obviously, something big was happening.

"What is it Mary? What's going on?" Bill asked, concern in his voice.

Mary looked up at him, her eyes red from crying. She was clutching some Kleenex in her hand. "Doctor, according to the news report, there is a pandemic of influenza. Right now, it is in Chicago, Milwaukee, Saint Louis and Oakland. The flu is killing black people by the hundreds. According to the CDC, this strain of flu is from Thailand and there is no cure. It is resistant to any medication. The CDC says it will spread south and then turn north. They are telling people not to panic and to wear face masks and latex gloves. They're are asking people not to kiss, or even shake hands. Why would the flu only attack black people, doctor?" Mary asked.

"I'm not really sure, Mary, other than to say it might be related to demographics, in that they live in such close proximity to one another. That's the only thing I can think of right off," Bill said, turning to go back into his office.

Once in his office, Bill turned on the TV and switched the channel to CNN.

He listened intently as the news reporter pointed at a map of the United States. The map was showing the natural progression of the flu as it traveled across the country. Each state had a different color that ranged from yellow for normal, orange for moderate and red for severe. Bill noticed the states of New Jersey, and Pennsylvania, were not in red.

Quickly, he turned to his computer and called up the e-mail addresses that would see to it that those two states would be in red before the week was out.

Doctor Paul Erlich sat in his office at the Health and Human Services Building in Washington D.C. He was listening to Doctor Nancy Moore of the CDC as she explained the influenza virus and what the CDC and ultimately, the entire country was facing. Her voice showed no emotion, but the inflection and tone of her voice revealed fear.

Paul was a tall, lanky man with a soft, gentle smile that matched his demeanor. He was a product of the 1960s, a high-school dropout who enlisted in the Army in hopes of finding himself. While in the Army, he received his General Equivalency Diploma. After extensive training, he was chosen for the Army's Special Forces where he became a medic, thus beginning his career in medicine. Now more than thirty years later he was the Surgeon General of the United States with the rank of Admiral. Not bad for someone who had been a high school dropout from the hills of Pine Grove, West Virginia.

Now, three days after Doctor Moore's call, he, along with his staff and the Under Secretary of Health and Human Services, were at the CDC headquarters in Atlanta, waiting for Mrs. Amanda Brown to give a quick overview of what they were facing. For the most part, Amanda was the spokesperson for the CDC. However, in actuality, Amanda was a statistician and research specialist. Nancy looked at each person's face as the members of the group took their seats. She noted the dark circles under their eyes. *How refreshing,* she thought with a bit of cynicism. They *are as stressed as me* how *uplifting is that!*

Nancy paid particular attention to where her boss and Paul's boss sat. His name was Leon Gonzales, and he was the Under Secretary of Health and Human Services. Leon—that's what everyone called him behind his back—reported to the Secretary of Health and Human Services, Mr. Gregory Simon. From previous meetings and discussions, Nancy had learned that if Leon sat close to Paul, she could be assured the Secretary of Health, and Human Services was very concerned. If he sat apart from the others, he was here on a fishing expedition, trying to gather information that he could downplay to the media to lessen the fears of America. *What a horse's patoot,* she thought.

Amanda walked to the podium and opened her binder. The binder was blue with a police badge embossed on it. The caption read: To Protect and Serve. Paul thought it was so appropriate. One of the guys who just happened to be sitting next to the light switch turned off the lights plunging the room into darkness except for the light of the teleprompter. Amanda cleared her throat and began her briefing:

"Ladies and Gentlemen, this flu season, which started in the Midwest, has taken off and is growing exponentially across the country. Presently, it has infected 28% of the United States' population. So far, this strain of flu has been most deadly for people between the ages of twenty-eight and forty. This pattern of morbidity is unusual as flu is usually the deadliest for the elderly and the very young. At its present rate, the flu will kill approximately 675,000 Americans, mostly poor blacks or underinsured whites living within close proximity to large black populations.

"We are presently at a loss to explain why the states of Montana, Wyoming and North and South Dakota are experiencing very little signs of the flu epidemic. I know of one case where a third grade-school teacher has instructed her students to wipe down their desks using bleach, and the other teachers have followed suit. The children have taken this measure to heart and are disinfecting their homes as well. This may be one of the viable reasons. However, I choose to think it's because of the lack of population density, and the fact that people in those states do not travel in the fall and winter.

"This influenza virus has such a profound virulence that the mortality rate may reach 2.5% or higher. The death rate for the fifteen to thirty-four-year-old men and women may exceed 20%. It is thought this will reduce the overall U.S. population because this is the largest age group in the country. Furthermore, it must be stated that the effect of this influenza pandemic may be so severe the normal life span of the peoples in the US may be depressed by ten years.

"Of particular interest, is that this strain of influenza is also starting to appear in Mexico, Brazil, Africa, the South Pacific and Asia. Presently, we named this strain of flu after the country of origin, which is Thailand. Thailand has reported to the World Health Organization a morbidity rate of 5%, or fifty deaths per thousand. At that rate, it is expected that Thailand will lose nearly eight million people. China has closed its borders and has suspended all air travel in and out of the country. They have not reported anything to the WHO, but our sources at the embassy and consulates say the dead line the streets and funeral fires burn brightly throughout the night.

"For those of you who are wondering why this virus is attacking primarily African-Americans, the only thing I can say is poverty, coupled with poor diet, is prevalent among this group. No immunity, fear or apathy toward immunization shots are allowing this virus to propagate and spread. Doctor Pfeiffer has reported this microbe is immune to any of the antiviral antibiotics currently being used to treat influenza. John Hopkins and Sloan Kettering have verified this fact. Plus, for years we have over prescribed and over medicated the population until viruses are immune to the medications prescribed.

"According to our sources, this virus strain masks its true symptoms until it is a full-blown viral infection. Then it strikes with such a vengeance that it overcomes the body's natural defense mechanism, and subsequently, the patient dies. If a person suffers with breathing difficulties, it may be a heart attack or perhaps some sort of allergic reaction to a med given as another reason. For example, a doctor in Chicago diagnosed a woman with a heart attack. All the symptoms were there, even the EKG showed she was having a heart attack. What she died from was the flu. She was taking a shower, simply washing her hair when she called out for help.

Thirty minutes later she was dead. With the variety of other symptoms associated with other illnesses, diagnosing this virus will be difficult, if not impossible."

Amanda was finished. Her briefing took less than five minutes, and it encapsulated the entire situation. The Surgeon General of the United States stood and bowed his head to Amanda, silently thanking her.

"Does anybody have something they wish to add?" he asked.

No one spoke; the room remained silent.

"Well, then, I do. I have a gut feeling, we are going to lose nurses and doctors in this fight. Even though they are trained professionals, this virus is an equal-opportunity killer and does not care what the color of your skin is or your profession. I foresee an economic collapse as well as a social collapse that may bring this country to its knees, if not its complete demise. As I stand before you, CNN and MSNBC are showing rioting, looting and shootings in almost every major U.S. city presently inflicted with this virus. The smaller towns are holding up very well so far. Mr. Gonzales and I will brief Secretary Simon this afternoon. So I say good-bye to each of you and good luck."

Nancy sat transfixed as Paul spoke. Never before had she noticed how tall he was or how handsome he was in his uniform. She thought to herself: *Funny, here we are in the middle of an all-out microbial war that we're losing and people dying right and left, and I'm thinking how good-looking the Surgeon General is. I need a vacation.*

❧ CHAPTER 28 ❧

AGENT JAMES WEST WAS SITTING in front of the Medical Examiner of Lowndes County, Georgia. The first thing he noticed about her was the smile. It made you feel warm and important. Immediately, she put you at ease. Then you happened to notice she was beautiful.

He began by saying, "Doctor, I know you're busy and I will make this short and painless. I know in reviewing the notes of Agent O'Neal and in talking with Doctor Bradshaw that Doctor Schwartz was sure you showed both Doctor Bradshaw and her the picture of the person we are looking for. Now that picture has disappeared. I was wondering if you knew who took the picture? I was also wondering if perhaps the state of Georgia requires all licensed morticians to be fingerprinted and photographed?"

Regina sat straight in her chair, her arms resting straight out in front of her, hands clasped, holding a pencil. She cocked her head slightly to the right, thinking, then turned back, her eyes looking over the head of the love-struck agent. "Agent West, I believe the State of Georgia does require its morticians to be fingerprinted and photographed. I also seem to remember that we require a *colored* photograph. This requirement has only been in effect for the past couple of years."

Regina reached across her desk and pulled a folder out of her combination correspondence and anti-clutter basket. Opening the folder, she showed Agent West the remaining photograph. It was in color and the back of the photo was stamped with the name, T.W. Evans Studio.

"Doctor, can I trouble you for a phonebook?" Agent West asked.

Regina handed the phone book to the agent. Immediately he turned to the yellow pages and looked for T.W. Evans Studio.

"Hmm, seems old T.W. Evans is no longer in business," Agent West said, flipping the phone book closed and handing it back to the doctor.

" Well, I don't know if this is important, but his son is the police chief here. Perhaps if you asked him, he might able to help you," Regina said.

"Good idea! I think I will call and make an appointment with the chief. You see, doctor, my colleagues mistakenly feel they are so big and important and that being a Federal Agent gives them special rudeness privileges. It doesn't. I find that by calling and asking for the person's time I get better service."

"Nothing wrong with that, Agent West. By giving respect to others you earn respect, especially from those you desire to help you," Regina said, standing up and extending her hand.

"Thank you, doctor," Agent West said, taking her hand.

Bill had asked Mary to cancel the last two appointments of the day as he feigned illness. Actually he wanted to get home and watch CNN.

Once home, Bill sat in front of his TV, watching the red banner strip at the bottom of the screen that gave the details of each state's misery. In his hands was a road atlas he had bought when he and AJ had driven to Nova Scotia the summer before her death. On a whim, he had decided to keep score. By taking the population that was printed in the fact box on each state map and then dividing the population into the number of deaths flashing across his TV screen, he was able to get the percentage of deaths.

He even went one step further by using the data of the U.S. Census Bureau he had previously downloaded, in order to get the official count of blacks in each city that he had targeted. With no more thought than he used when making up his grocery list, he recorded his results. As the camera panned to the roadside leading to the morgue, he found himself yelling and cheering. All that could be seen were row after row of the dead, lying under white sheets. As far as the eye could see, bodies of men, women and children lay rotting in the sun, their corpses fouling the air with the stench of death.

Soon, his cheers turned to uncontrollable cursing. Then he was silent as his lower lip began to quiver. Jumping to his feet, he shouted at the TV "FEEL MY PAIN!" Then with a hysterical laugh, tears began running down his cheeks. Bill became inconsolable. Pushing his face into the sofa cushion, he hit the cushion with his fist as hard as he could and screamed for AJ.

The Surgeon General stood before the Secretary of Health and Human Services of the United States with Leon to his right. They had just given Secretary Simon the news. Dejectedly, he leaned back in his chair, his face pale, with perspiration quite noticeable on his forehead and upper lip. He was obviously physically and emotionally exhausted. Though the Secretary of Health sat silent for only a minute, to Paul it seemed like an hour.

Then the secretary sighed and said, "So, there is nothing that can be done but watch our people die by the hundreds of thousands? Is that what you're saying? I'm to brief the President of the United States, who must then go on national television and tell millions of Americans they are going to die because they're poor and black? He is to tell America that this virus is so insidious and so virulent that it will decrease the average life span of all Americans by ten years? I get to tell him that we are not alone, as other nations are experiencing the same effects as we are?"

Still standing straight and tall, Paul turned to look at Leon. Leon was gone and Paul realized he was alone. Leon had left him alone with an irate Secretary of Health and Human Services and he was looking for a scapegoat.

"No, Mr. Secretary, you tell the president that this disease is a mutant; a throwback to the early days of whooping cough, measles, tuberculosis and scarlet fever. You tell him that when we were treated as children or young adults, we were over-medicated, thus allowing this microbial virus to become immune to the antibiotics that have been prescribed around the world for decades. Now the world is facing a killer that it cannot see, smell, or touch and if unchecked will cause the virtual extinction of the human race. It's all right to be afraid, Mr. Secretary. I would be more worried if you were not afraid, sir. This is not a time for arrogance or bravado. We must be prudent and accept the virtual outcome. Death will walk the streets, invade our homes and ride our highways. It will pass quietly through our airports, arriving in foreign destinations and introducing itself to the populace as nothing more than a common cold. Then when those countries least expect it, the disease will strike with such a vengeance that fear will give way to panic, which will lead to economic chaos and the eventual collapse of governments around the world."

Secretary Simon looked at Paul, his eyes focused, his face stern, his lips pulled back tight in a sneer. Paul had just committed political suicide and he did not care. First and foremost he was a doctor of medicine before he was the Surgeon General and he was not going to be a scapegoat for this man or anybody else.

Paul bowed his head in respect to Secretary Simon and then walked out of the office. He picked up his cap, noted the time and realized he had been on the go for forty hours and he was tired. He headed home, knowing there was nothing that could be done until morning.

∽ CHAPTER 29 ∾

D R. PFEIFFER WAS SITTING AT his desk, holding a cup of hot, black coffee with his left hand. In his right hand he held a magnifying glass. He was looking at photographs of the influenza microbe taken at different stages in its development. One thing he could not understand was why the microbe appeared so different in blacks than it did in whites. His thinking was that perhaps genetic makeup might have something to do with it. That was when he decided to have one of the geneticist look at the slides to get their input.

Nancy walked into his office holding a coffee cup that read: Hire the left-handed. It's fun to watch them write. She walked over to Cliff's personal coffee pot, poured a cup of coffee and then sat down across the desk from him. Her eyes were bloodshot; the dark circles under her eyes made her look older than her years. Like the rest of the staff, she was physically and emotionally exhausted.

Crossing her legs, she leaned forward and said, "Paul called me a little while ago. He has briefed the Secretary of Health. He seems to think he will be made the scapegoat along with the CDC. That we will be blamed for allowing this pandemic to occur." Nancy paused to sip her coffee then proceeded, "If Paul is correct, I suspect we will be vilified and crucified both by the press and congress."

"Nancy, I just might have something for us. I have been examining my slides and these photos, trying to understand why this virus is attacking primarily healthy blacks and Hispanics. I'm of the opinion that what we are looking at is not a mutant, as I first thought, but something else. Perhaps some sort of alkaline derivative or perhaps a long-term environmental issue associated with poverty. However, with this virus and its peculiar traits, I cannot be sure. I'm going to ask Doctor Cecilia Stokes at John Hopkins to look at these slides and photos and give me her thoughts."

Nancy waited, making sure Cliff was finished before she asked, "Who is Doctor Stokes?"

"She is head of the Genetics Department at John Hopkins," Cliff replied.

"Do it and do it fast," Nancy said.

❦

Bill sat his calculator down on the coffee table. He had reasoned correctly that the death toll was climbing. In Oakland, Saint Louis and Kansas City, the death toll was at fifty deaths per thousand, or 5%; an increase of 2.5 % in just twenty-four hours. In Tulsa and Detroit the death rate was in excess of one hundred deaths per thousand or 10% and climbing by the hour.

Taking a bite of his ham and cheese sandwich, Bill then turned back to his computer and brought up the cities of Atlanta, Richmond, Boston and Washington D.C. They were the next to be selected for the distribution of his "gifts." He reasoned that it would take four days to get all the required products to their assigned destinations and then another three days to distribute the packages door to door. By Thursday he figured there would be a sudden and dramatic increase in influenza cases leading to the deaths of thousands. He could hardly wait until CNN started reporting those deaths so he could keep score.

⁂

Her assistant handed Doctor Stokes the FedEx package. She knew what was in it as her friend, Cliff, had called to ask for her help. Although she was buried in her own research work, how could she refuse when so many were dying? Besides, she owed her friend Cliff just a few too many favors. Opening the envelope, she read the handwritten note:

> Armageddon is knocking at mankind's door. Humanity is under attack by an enemy called pestilence. Outcome in serious doubt. Mankind on the verge of extinction as death waits for no one. May God keep you and bless you. Cliff

Cecilia set the note aside. The note was both a warning and a plea. *This must be more serious than is being reported if Cliff would write something like this,* she thought as she picked up the slides and headed for her lab.

⁂

Agent West arrived a few minutes early for his appointment with Chief Evans of the Valdosta Police Department. He was greeted by a very attractive police officer. Her nametag said her name was, Culpepper. She smiled as he approached and asked him his name and business. He pulled out his identification and introduced himself. Then he stated he had an appointment with Chief Evans at 3:00 p.m.

"Yes, sir, please follow me."

She led Agent West down one corridor, up another, then up a flight of stairs and down another corridor. Officer Culpepper knocked on the door then slowly opened it, announcing the somewhat bemused agent.

The chief stood and extended his hand. "Chief Josiah Evans, sir."

The agent took Josiah's hand, measuring his grip. It was very powerful, almost painful. Instinctively, West knew this man was a leader and somebody who could be trusted. His work experience had taught him how to judge a man. The strength of their handshake was the first indicator. The second thing was how they tied their tie. Was the tie tied in a full Windsor knot or a half Windsor knot? A full Windsor knot indicated a man who paid attention to detail. A half Windsor indicated a person who was more a nuts and bolts kind of guy who had to be in on the action and did not care much for details.

The third and most bizarre indicator, at least he had always found it so, was to watch the man eat. If the person seasoned their food before they tasted it. It showed lack of forethought and a lack of trust; that they were not to be relied on with anything important. He knew there were no actual scientific facts to back up his theories but they worked for him and that was good enough.

Simultaneously the two men sat down. Chief Evans, the quintessential politician and very knowledgeable police chief, opened the conversation with the most typical question, but he asked it with such politeness it took Agent West by surprise. "Sir, how may the Valdosta Police Department be of service to the Federal Bureau of Investigation?"

"Chief Evans, I understand that your father used to be a professional photographer here and I was wondering if perhaps he still had negatives of individuals who were required by state and federal law to be finger printed and photographed. This person would have been photographed perhaps two, maybe three years ago. A mortician to be exact." Agent West stopped talking as abruptly as he had started.

" Well, sir, I don't know. Let me call my dad and ask him."

Josiah picked up the phone and pushed a button. The chief looked up, noticing that the agent was sitting very patiently, his eyes looking about the office at pictures of various dignitaries who had once visited the city. There were: Jimmy Carter, George Wallace, Bill Clinton and Al Gore. Then there were a few entertainers: Ray Charles and the group called Alabama.

"Hello, dad, I have an Agent James West of the FBI sitting here in my office. He was wondering if perhaps you still had the negatives of the people who were required by the state and federal government to be photographed."

Josiah covered the mouthpiece and looked up from his chair and said, "Dad says he may have a few. He is checking."

Agent West looked up and smiled. "Ask your dad how far back his records go if you can."

"I can hear my dad. He is cursing a blue streak. I think he banged his head on the cupboard door. He forgets to close the damn thing and it gets him every time. Now, mom is telling him to quit blaspheming," Chief Evans said as he began to chuckle. "Mom has just ordered Dad to sit down and be still."

"How long have your mom and dad been married?" West asked politely.

"Wow, I'd have to think on that one. I know more than fifty years, as the church had a party for their fiftieth wedding anniversary. I'd say close to fifty-five years. How about your folks? How long have they been married?"

"Well, I never knew my dad, chief. My dad was killed in Vietnam before I was born and mom never re-married. Instead, we lived with my grandparents and mom went back to school and became a nurse…"

Agent West's voice trailed off as Josiah began speaking into the phone, "You do! That's wonderful, dad. We will be right over. Yes, mom, soup and sandwiches will be fine with us."

Agent West began to grin as both men stood up. "Your dad found the disk?"

"No! Mom found the negatives because she remembered a man called Robert William Lee came into the studio and asked for his picture to be taken. The reason mom remembers him is because he killed his wife and then because he was in the Klan, he was acquitted and got off scot- free and that just irked my mother no end."

∽ CHAPTER 30 ∾

P AUL SAT IN HIS OFFICE watching CNN. He had sent his wife, Andrea—known to her friends as Andy—to visit and care for her parents in Seattle. The twins, David and Timmy, were at sea. The boys were naval aviators assigned to the Indian and Pacific Oceans. They were not due to rotate stateside until late summer. It had been his decision to stay and man the helm. As he was fond of saying, "Sailors only run from hurricanes." Truth be known, he was scared. Amanda Brown's words kept echoing in his brain: "… 20 % of America's population will be dead in weeks." According to the news, the figure was already at 12% and climbing.

Irate politicians were calling Paul but he didn't return their calls. His thought was, *Why waste time discussing something I have no control over, when I can provide the leadership and management oversight needed to protect the health of the nation?*

He called a staff meeting for 9:00 a.m. to discuss educating the public and advocating disease prevention. Before he did that, he wanted to be briefed on what was happening with the influenza vaccine from Great Britain. Also, he needed to know what the holdup was on the anti-viral facemasks and the latex gloves. Plus, he wanted to know what home remedies, if any, could be used to alleviate the symptoms of this virus, although he already knew that his ploy was nothing more than a panacea for a scared populace. According to the news reports, Baltimore, Washington D.C. and Richmond were starting to experience a dramatic increase in influenza cases.

The staff was assembling in the outer office. He could hear them as they lined up. They always lined themselves up from the shortest to the tallest before walking into his office. Lieutenant Adams would call them to attention and they would salute in unison. Paul would return their salute, and then tell them to stand at ease. They were his honor staff, the best of the best: Dedicated medical professionals who had chosen public health as a calling.

He began by first asking, "Ok, which one of you is working on the vaccine from Great Britain?"

"That would be me, sir."

"Ok, Lieutenant Adams. Give me the status," Paul stated.

"Well, sir, the news is not good. There is a flu vaccine shortage both in this country and in Great Britain. You see, sir, according to the president and CEO of World Wide Pharmaceuticals in Liverpool, the Brits opted to reduce the production of the flu vaccine because of the projections from the World Health Organization. Then in March, they were asked to increase production from eighteen million doses to thirty million. There was no way the company could produce that much vaccine in the time-frame they were given. In April, coinciding with the increase in reported flu cases, they were asked to produce eighty million doses for the United

States alone, not including the demands from other countries also experiencing catastrophic casualties related to this flu virus.

"On Saturday, a routine quality control check revealed that the doses contained 25 mcg of mercury per dose. The EPA's safe limit is 0.1mcg, which means that anyone given the contaminated dose would receive an overdose of mercury, resulting in death or very serious brain damage.

"The company had to destroy fifty million doses destined for the United States. The bottom line, sir, is we just do not have enough vaccine to protect our people."

Paul was devastated. He leaned back in his chair, afraid to speak. Knowing if he spoke his voice would betray his fear. "Thank you, lieutenant. That will be all for now."

"Yes, sir!" Lieutenant Adams stood at attention, saluted and then walked out of the office..

Adams headed back to her office with her thoughts. *That is the way the Surgeon General is. He wants us working, getting involved and making a difference. I feel as if I let him and the country down. I just can't change reality. The fact remains, we do not have enough vaccine to make a difference.*

Paul looked at the very tall, gangly looking Lieutenant Black, who reminded him of himself so many years ago. "Lieutenant Black, I hope your news is better than what Lieutenant Adams reported?"

"Sir, my news is just as dismal as Lieutenant Adams." Sir, China has closed all its ports and has suspended all shipments to the world. The antiviral facemasks that were ordered by the health department last fall have been confiscated by the Chinese Government and are being distributed to the people of China. According to the Bureau Chief of CNN, the stench of death is everywhere in China. The government has stop counting the dead and are burning the corpses or burying them in mass graves a mile long and a half a mile wide. Sir, I'm afraid we will not receive any help anytime soon from Asia. As I was told last night, the death toll is in the millions and still climbing."

"Thank you Lieutenant, that will be all."

Like Adams before him, Black rendered a salute and walked out.

Paul began tapping his pen on the desk, something he did only when he was angry—and he was very angry!

"Ok," he said, "I will listen to two more reports and if they are no better than the first two, I will send all of you out into the field where you can do the most good."

Captain Milton Jackson was the next to report. He stood only five foot six and was built like a fireplug with a huge neck and a barrel chest. His biceps were over-developed from countless hours in the gym. He reminded Paul of a bulldog.

"Ok, Captain Jackson, report," the admiral said, his voice betraying his anger.

"Sir, I have looked at this situation in a different way."

"How so, Captain Jackson?" Paul said cynically.

"Sir, I have analyzed the progression pattern of this virus. If you look at this map you will see that I have circled all the infected cities."

"Yes, captain, so what?"

"Sir, all the cities, except for Chicago and Milwaukee, are in a straight line. Only the neighborhoods with the densest black populations have reported a disproportionate amount of deaths. Yet, cities like New Orleans, Jackson, Mississippi, Baton Rouge, Dallas and cities in the Carolinas have not been touched. Please note that not even Rhode Island, which is an easy commute from Boston, has reported no deaths from influenza.

"Sir, we are dealing with two very distinct and very deadly concerns. Sir, I want your permission to do more research and track down what the second problem is."

"It sounds to me, captain, that you already have an idea of what we may be facing," Paul said.

"Sir, I think our food supply has been compromised by a terrorist organization."

"Captain, have you told anybody else your theory?"

"No, sir, just you!"

"Ok, now listen up, all of you. You are all hereby ordered to a vow of silence. Not one word of this will leave this office. Captain, you have my permission to investigate your theory. I want you to contact Doctor Pfeiffer at the CDC in Atlanta. You met him last week. Start there. That's all," Paul said, dismissing his staff.

After they had left and closed the door to his office, Paul leaned back in his chair and interlocked his fingers behind his head as his eyes found the familiar picture hanging on the opposite wall. The picture depicted a colonial marine doctor administering to the needs of the sick and injured seamen in 1798. It was supposed to have been the U.S. Marine Hospital Service, the forerunner of today's U.S. Public Health Service. Just above the picture he had placed a small, round, flesh- colored band-aid. When he needed to concentrate, he would focus on it.

Captain Jackson's terrorist theory had scared him, but the longer he concentrated on the band-aid, the more convinced he became that this pandemic was not the result of a terrorist plot. However, the captain could be correct about the food being contaminated. His logic about the disease taking a straight line also had merit.

"Sir, the Under Secretary is waiting for you." Marty had walked into his office and had to shake him to get his attention. Paul had been concentrating so hard he had failed to hear the buzz.

Paul looked up and smiled. "You were saying, Marty?"

"Sir, the Under Secretary is waiting for you on line one."

"Thank you, Marty."Paul said.

∽ CHAPTER 31 ∽

AGENT WEST WATCHED AS MR. Evans developed the photograph of a man named William Robert Lee. For the first time, both the FBI and the police had a picture of a man who might be the killer of fifteen women, and maybe two federal agents.

Mr. Evans handed the photo to Josiah. Mrs. Evans walked up to her son and looked over his shoulder at the picture and stated: "Josiah, that man is evil. Evil I tell you."

Josiah handed the photo to Agent West. Looking at the photo, Agent West said as he handed the photo back to the police chief, "He's not exactly what you would call a good-looking fellow, is he?"

"Dad, print me two more copies," Josiah said.

"Other than my mother's claim that this man is evil, we have nothing. We cannot even get a search warrant. All we can do is pursue him as a 'person of interest', " Josiah said, walking over to the coffee pot and pouring a cup.

"Where does he live?" Agent West asked.

"I have no idea," the chief responded.

"He works at the Silent Home Mortuary in Claysville. That's what he told me anyway."

"Are you sure, mom?"

"Yes, Josiah, I'm sure."

"Agent West, do you feel like a drive?"

"Yes, chief, I do."

With the cruiser lights on, the trip to Claysville took less than fifteen minutes.

Both men got out of the patrol car, reached for their guns and automatically checked them. With guns in hand, they walked slowly up the walkway, their eyes surveying the rooftop, each man protecting the other as only years of police work and instinct could teach. They reached the front door only to be greeted by a note taped to the front door. The note was short and to the point. It read:

Sorry, we are temporarily closed. Please call P.K. Bertram Funeral Home at 235-8762.

" Now, isn't that a kick in the butt," the chief remarked, holstering his revolver.

Agent West did not respond to Chief Evans' comment. He was busy writing down the telephone number.

"Tell me, Chief Evans, where is Bertram's Funeral Home?" Agent West asked, putting the pad and pencil back into his pocket.

"That's over in Naylor, the opposite direction from here. I'd say about twenty miles…maybe a little more. Why do you ask?"

"Agent Gallopli was on to something. I'm not sure, but I think he was looking for a mortician. In the car he was driving the day of his disappearance, I found a state map of Georgia. Each town that had a funeral home or a mortuary was circled with an X beside it—all except for this one. Just maybe, chief, he never got to put an X next to this city because this is where he was killed. I'm thinking that if he went to Naylor, then perhaps we could establish a timeline."

"Then, let's go to Naylor!" said the chief.

As they entered the city limits of Naylor, Chief Evans turned off his lights, slowed down and reported to the county sheriff. Agent West said nothing, but he was curious as to why the Chief reported to the county sheriff.

Looking over at him, Chief Evans remarked, "The two police officers in Naylor are assholes. As Naylor does not have a police chief, the officers report directly to the sheriff. By reporting to the sheriff, I can circumvent the two village idiots. Plus, if anything happens, the sheriff would have a starting point to launch his investigation."

Agent West chuckled. He liked this young man.

"Here's the funeral home on the right. Hasn't changed in twenty years. That's when we buried granddad. He was shot."

"You mean he was murdered?" Agent West asked.

"No, not exactly. Granddad had a way with the ladies. Rumor has it he was shot behind the feed store in a duel of honor. He died from pneumonia while recovering from his chest wound."

"How old a man was he?" Agent West asked, grinning from ear to ear.

"I'm not sure. Let's see, he married grandma at fifteen. They were married sixty years when grandma died. I guess that would make him eighty-five or maybe a little older."

"How old was the lady in question?"

"Hmm…Darla would have been about fifty-five back then. Granddad loved younger women."

Both men were laughing as they got out of the patrol car. They walked into the funeral home, still chuckling when Percy Bertram greeted them.

"Hello, Mr. Bertram, I'm Chief Evans of the Valdosta Police Department. This is Agent James West of the FBI. We would like to ask you a few questions."

∽ CHAPTER 32 ∾

D R. CECILIA STOKES HAD JUST finished her analysis of the CDC slides and photos in her office at John Hopkins' Genetics Department. She found it frustrating and next to impossible to know exactly with what the CDC was dealing with. Cliff had reasoned correctly that this virus was not a mutant. Two of the slides indicated the virus was the same, although taken at different times and at different locations. But then things began to get confusing. Three slides taken from patients in Chicago, Oakland and Milwaukee did not match the other two. Everything was convoluted. However, of one thing Cecilia was sure, it was not a mutant virus nor was it a geno-type disease. She strongly suspected that whatever, it was, it was man-made.

Cecilia twisted the cap off her bottled water and took a healthy swig. Her eyes turned to her screen saver that showed various colored fish swimming to and fro, with no particular place to go. Her practiced mind was already formulating a letter to Cliff when her phone rang—

"Hello, Doctor Stokes," she said, turning her back to the computer.

"Hello, doctor, this is Doctor Milton Jackson of the Surgeon General's Office. I'm sorry to bother you but Doctor Pfeiffer of the CDC in Atlanta told me to call you."

"Yes, Doctor Jackson, how may I help you?" Cecelia asked, picking up her ink pen, ready to take notes.

"Well, doctor, this is rather difficult to explain. I have a theory. After talking first with Admiral Erlich and then Doctor Pfeiffer, it was suggested I run it by you. So here it goes: I think this influenza epidemic is not a mutant virus but the result of a terrorist attack against our food supply system."

Doctor Stokes held her composure, as she had just come to a similar conclusion not ten minutes earlier, although she did not think it was a terrorist attack. Actually, she suspected some sort of derivative with an alkaline base. It had been her plan to request a pathological review of tissue samples, or if available, a liver biopsy. Now some man with a very deep voice, whom she did not know, had called and confirmed her suspicions.

"Hello, Doctor Stokes, are you still there?" asked the voice on the other end of the phone.

"I'm sorry. Yes, Doctor Jackson, I'm still here. What makes you think that this virus is man-made?"

"I don't think the virus is man-made. I think this virus is a cover-up for a terrorist attack on our nation's food supply. Have you ever read or seen an epidemic travel in a straight line? Or for that matter, have you ever seen an epidemic that targets pretty much just one race? I think the outbreaks in Houston and Miami are a deliberate attempt to screen what's really happening. They are nothing more than a contrived deviation."

"Well, except for the part about a terrorist attack, I think you may be on to something big," Doctor Stokes agreed.

"Why not a terrorist's attack?" Doctor Jackson asked.

"Well, doctor, why would terrorists only attack one race? Why not the entire nation? I'd be more agreeable with your theory if you said a hate group."

"Hmm, that thought never occurred to me," Doctor Jackson said, still pondering Cecilia's remarks. "Doctor Stokes, I will discuss this with the Surgeon General. I hope I can rely on your discretion as to this conversation. We wouldn't want to panic the nation anymore than it already is."

"I agree, and yes, I will keep this concern quiet, Doctor Jackson. Good-bye," Cecilia said, as she turned back to her computer.

The message she sent to the CDC was short and to the point:

> **Virus NOT a mutant, NOT a geno-type. <u>This disease is man-made!</u>**
> **Stokes.**

She bowed her head and whispered, "Please God, help us.

∞ CHAPTER 33 ∞

C LIFF WAS SITTING AT HIS desk when his computer announced he had mail. Turning, he read the note and for one moment, his breathing stopped. Doctor Cecilia Stokes short message from John Hopkins sent shivers up his spine. A metallic taste began to develop in his mouth. Not even coffee could kill the taste of fear.

He bowed his head, but not in prayer. His mind was trying to fathom the basic questions of who could have done this and why. Standing up, he turned off his computer, walked to the door and turned out the lights. Though he felt sick, his main emotion was anger! Walking down the hall he pressed the elevator "down" button. Once outside, he walked across the complex to the headquarters building. There he showed his badge to Harry, the security guard.

Harry smiled and nodded his head. "Hello, Doc."

"Hello, Harry." They had been having this same conversation for more than twenty years.

"Is she in?"

"Yes, she is," Harry replied.

Cliff proceeded down the hall to Doctor Nancy Moore's office. Carol was long gone, so he entered the office, knocked on Nancy's door and walked in. "We need to talk. It's important," Cliff said without preamble as he sat down without being invited.

The director of the CDC watched as Cliff leaned forward. His shoulders were hunched and he grabbed his hands as if he was in church. Experience had taught her that when Cliff was silent and subdued, she'd better get ready, as the news was going to be bad.

"Yes, Cliff, what is it?" she asked.

At first Cliff could not speak. Slipping his hand into his jacket pocket, he pulled out a copy of Cecelia's message and handed it to her.

Doctor Moore looked at the message. "So we are tracking a very virulent influenza virus that is immune to antiviral antibiotics and some sort of mass murderer or murderers and we cannot distinguish between the two. Is that what you're saying?"

Cliff sat silent, stroking his chin as he pondered a response. Finally he said, "Well, Nancy, why does it matter? On Saturday, World Wide Pharmaceuticals destroyed fifty million doses of influenza vaccine because of contamination. China has closed its borders to all foreign traffic, so we cannot get the anti-viral facemasks we need. We already know that this strain of influenza is immune to any of the antibiotics anyway. We are losing this fight and we are losing badly. If we go public with this, we will surely cause widespread panic and more people will die because of it. If we remain silent, we will be accused of duplicity and racist behavior. I think the correct course of action is to pass this on to Leon, and let him tell Secretary Simon. I would also alert the Surgeon General, as it was one of his people who alerted Doctor Stokes to the fact we might be the victims of a terrorist attack.

Nancy grimaced. "Yes, Cliff, I agree. Let's e-mail Leon and let him tell Secretary Simon. I will also e-mail the Surgeon General and tell him what we're facing."

Cliff gave a half smile. He was so damned tired. "Goodnight, boss," Cliff said.

The director sat quietly, her mind starting to compose an e-mail message to Leon. She had decided to write in lieu of calling. Years ago she had learned, when dealing with the Washington bureaucrats, that the faintest of ink was better than the best of memory. Translation: Cover your ass at all times. This way there would be a record of the CDC's attempt to notify higher authorities, making it impossible for Leon to deny he had not been notified. Nancy also sent a copy to the Surgeon General, informing him of what the CDC had discovered, allowing him to take whatever action necessary to protect the country. That is if he could.

꙳

The Surgeon General was sitting at his desk reading e-mail when he saw one that said:

Urgent! Read me First!

The e-mail was from Nancy and it was sent at 5: 58 p.m.. He opened the file and read the message. He was about to break into a very un-gentlemanly barrage of curse words, when the object of his anger knocked on his office door. *The poor dumb son-of-a-bitch is about to feel the wrath of an admiral and may God help him*, he thought to himself.

"Come in, captain," Paul said, holding a pen between his hands, trying not to display his anger. Paul waited for the usual military customs and courtesies to finish then he asked, "What is it, captain?"

"Sir, I did as you suggested and talked with Doctor Pfeiffer of the CDC. He in turn requested I talk to a Doctor Cecilia Stokes, a geneticist located at Johns Hopkins. Fortunately, she had finished her evaluation of the slides and photos that Doctor Pfeiffer had sent her. It is her opinion it is not terrorists we're facing, but a hate group. She agrees there are two different situations: One is man-made while the other, sir, is the influenza virus. Although deadly, it is just a mere diversion for the murdering of innocent people."

Captain Jackson knew he was stretching the truth but continued: "When you look at the influenza epidemic in its totality, you see the deaths that are occurring in other parts of the country fall within the normal statistical range, mainly the very young and the very old. Then when you look at the immunization rates for influenza and pneumococcus among the blacks and Hispanics, it becomes painfully obvious that they are not protected and thus are susceptible to the flu and of course pneumonia.

"However, sir, not withstanding, I have never seen an epidemic that targets mainly blacks. The cities of Oakland, LA, Saint Louis, Kansas City, Chicago, Milwaukee, Atlanta Houston, Tulsa, Richmond, Columbus and Cleveland are all reporting death tolls now at about 20%. Washington D.C., Richmond, Philadelphia, Boston and Detroit are currently at 15%. The estimated death toll as of this morning is over a million."

Paul sat back in his chair; his anger subsiding as he realized what Doctor Nancy Moore, director of the CDC had meant by her E-mail statement:

Independent verification confirms virus is a mutant but also a mask for murderers. We are losing on all fronts. Have informed Leon of details. Good Luck! Nancy.

⚜

Leon Gonzales, the Under Secretary of Health and Human Resources, was furious! *How dare that bitch put me in this position?* He was powerless. Doctor Nancy Moore, Director of the CDC, had nailed him good. His political career was now over and he knew it. She had trapped him and had wrapped him up nice and tight. Whether on purpose or by accident, she had forced him to make a decision. Now he had to tell his boss, Secretary of Health and Human Resources Simon that the CDC had been wrong. The virus was not a mutant nor was it a geno-type disease, but in fact, a very virulent strain of influenza. In addition, someone was tainting something with a man-made substance that was killing thousands of American citizens. Also, he had to tell Secretary Simon that the Surgeon General's emotional outburst was accurate. But the biggest and most humiliating thing was that he had embarrassed both the President of the United States and the Secretary, making them look foolish and incompetent in a time of crisis. No doubt about it; he knew he would be fired.

In this case he had no maneuvering room or place to go. There was only one way out if he was to try and save his ass. Leon turned his chair towards his computer screen. He reread Doctor Moore's message and took one phrase out of context. He lied. Noting the time, he saw it was

5:58 a.m. *I bet within the hour the Secretary would be telling the President that this epidemic is the result of a terrorist attack,* he said to himself.

The President would give the problem to the National Security Advisor who in turn would pass it to Homeland Security, who would pass it on to the FBI and then just maybe, the pressure would go away from Leon.

∽ CHAPTER 34 ∽

D R. BRADSHAW SAT IN HIS office listening to CNN. The news was all bad. He heard the reporter relating that there were not enough body bags or coffins to bury the dead. Governors from the states of Pennsylvania, Ohio, Illinois and Michigan authorized the burning of the rotting corpses and the digging of mass graves.

The President had closed the New York Stock Exchange and suspended all foreign and domestic air traffic, except for military flights and a few humanitarian flights. Furthermore, he ordered the closing of both the Mexican and Canadian borders to all traffic and trade in the interest of public health and safety. The United States was now isolated from the world.

Feeling the adverse effects of the epidemic, many companies had suspended operations and told their employees to stay home. Banks closed, leaving only the ATMs to dispense money. When the ATMs ran out of money, that was it. To make matters worse, those states that had been the hardest hit by the epidemic, either suspended or curtailed the operations of many non-essential agencies. Furthermore, the governors of Michigan and Illinois informed the residents that a pandemic was not a legitimate reason to draw unemployment.

According to the news reporter, the closing of the Mexican border created yet another catastrophic situation. As the camera panned to the fields, the young Hispanic reporter announced, "There are no migrant workers in these field's gathering crops to help feed a hungry nation." Then by accident or design, he announced that crops were wilting or rotting on the vines in the Rio Grand Valley in Texas, thus adding to the food shortage.

The cost of bread soared to ten dollars a loaf, milk to twenty dollars a gallon and apples were six dollars each. American housewives went into a wholesale panic. Decent, law-abiding God-fearing people began to steal and even kill as they were unable to pay the exorbitant food prices. Within twenty-four hours, most of the food shelves in stores across the United States were empty.

Smaller towns across the nation formed what could only be described as Ladies' Auxiliary clubs; organizing local food drives within the safety and security of their churches and community centers. Here they shared fruits and vegetables that had been canned that season or the year before. They skimmed the cream from fresh cow's milk and froze it so babies and small children would have nourishment should anything happen to the livestock. Local police began screening cars that came into the towns, turning back anybody that did not live or work within their community. There was fear that big-city folks would come and steal food from them, then sell it at inflated prices.

Rioting and blind panic became commonplace. As the police took ill or left to care for their own families, law and order had disappeared. Mob violence became the rule. To make matters worse, hospitals were filled to the breaking point. Exhausted staff members walked off their jobs by the thousands for fear of their lives and the lives of their families. Many hospitals were just left open; the people were simply left unattended. Without medicine to treat them, people died by the thousands, and their bodies lay everywhere. There were no corpse hounds to carry them away.

Bill decided to cancel all his appointments, using the flu as the reason. He was going to take some time off…or so he thought. Just then, Mary walked into his office. She was pale, her eyes red from crying. Silently, she handed him the last of the correspondence to be signed, plus several checks. Then she said, "Doctor, the Deputy Director of The FBI is on line one waiting to talk with you. He says it's urgent."

"Thank you, Mary," Bill said, trying not to laugh at Mary's nonchalant manner.

"Hello, this is Doctor Bradshaw. How may I be of service?"

"Hello, Doctor Bradshaw, this is Harlan Fisher. I'm the Deputy Director of the FBI, and I'm calling on behalf of our country. It needs you. In fact, doctor, it needs you badly."

"How may I help?" Bill asked, wondering how a psychiatrist could help the country.

"Doctor, I'm sure you are aware of the present health crisis."

"Who isn't aware of it, would be the better statement, sir."

"Well, doctor, we have uncovered a diabolical murder plot, perpetrated by a hate group. We want you to help us develop a profile."

"Hmm," Bill muttered, "that is a very difficult assignment, Mr. Fisher. How do you know it's a hate group and not a mutant strain as the CDC has told us?"

"Tell you what, Doctor Bradshaw. I want you to go to Atlanta and meet with the Director of the CDC. I also want you to talk with a

Doctor Pfeiffer. If you are not convinced after your meeting, then I will ask someone else for help."

"Ok, I will do that. I was closing down my office because of the flu anyway. This weekend I will drive to Atlanta and meet with Doctor Pfeiffer and the Director on the thirtieth. I intended on driving to Valdosta, anyway, to meet with Agent West. I want to know what progress he has made in trying to catch a serial killer that Doctor Schwartz, and I had profiled."

"Ok, I will set up the meeting for Monday morning at 9:00 a.m. Will that be alright?"

"That will be fine, sir," Bill said, hanging up the phone.

The absurdity of it all, Bill thought. *Well, there certainly are enough hate groups to go around. I'll just pick one or perhaps invent a new one.*

He did one last thing before closing up the office and heading south. Getting onto the web, he typed one line:

Launch Operation Sweet Tea Newark, Trenton, Patterson.

Operation Sweet Tea was a code. It told everyone to finish dispersing the free samples in New Jersey, then destroy everything not used and go home. Long ago, at the Greasy Spoon Restaurant in Valdosta, Billy Bob had come up with this plan in order to destroy all vestiges of the remaining supplies when the time was right. Little did anyone realize that Billy Bob's plan would be needed and implemented.

∽ CHAPTER 35 ∾

AS CHIEF EVANS DROVE THE cruiser, Agent West sat in the front passenger seat with his arms folded across his chest, his head bowed and his eyes closed. Passing motorists would have thought he was sound asleep. However, the motorist would have been wrong. Actually, his mind was concentrating on what that old racist, P.K. Bertram had said. West had seen many really bad men and even a few evil men in his tenure with the bureau. However, he had never run into anyone so full of hate as P.K. Bertram. That man was plain scary! Hell, he was a maniacal bigot! He could be described as a throwback to another time and place in history providing, of course, that someone wanted to describe the dried up old fart. However, Bertram did admit that the "communist-loving, Greek commie bastard posing as a FBI agent" had been there. Now West knew two things he had not previously known.

Chief Evans was concentrating on the road. He was embarrassed he even knew anyone like P.K. Bertram. Fortunately, P.K was old and hopefully wouldn't be around much longer. As far as Evans was concerned, hell could have him.

He and West had learned that Agent Gallopli *had* been there prior to his disappearance. They confirmed that the ink markings on the road map found in Gallopli's rental car, did indeed correspond to Agent Gallopli's investigation. The Silent Mortuary was his last stop, of that both men were sure. What's more, they found out that a mortician named William Robert Lee had been scheduled to work the day Gallopli disappeared. Since he had not reported off, nor had he reported a pickup at any of the hospitals or nursing homes, in the area. West deduced Mr. Lee must have been at work.

When asked about Mr. Lee, Mr. Bertram had said, "Mr. Lee said he was going to take some time off for personal reasons."

Chief Evans had then asked the next logical question, "How long ago did he leave?"

A quick deduction showed that since Mr. Lee had been gone, no young women had been killed. Coincidence yes, but worth a second look!

<hr>

Billy Bob and Jonas left Newark, New Jersey around 2:00 p.m., Saturday. They had distributed the last of the boxes to the local Junior Achievement Club in Newark that morning. Just like they had done in every other city across the country. Who would ever suspect that a bunch of kids would deliver death to their friends, neighbors and even their own family's doorsteps? They paid for the delivery of the products in cash and left.

Outside Richmond, Virginia, they pulled into a roadside diner to eat. It had taken four hours, and that had included one stop for gas in order to make Richmond. Billy was going to drop Jonas off at his house then drive to Valdosta on Sunday.

They sat at a booth that overlooked the parking lot. In the distance, they could see the freeway that would take them into Richmond. They ordered sweet tea and asked for a menu. While the waitress was busy with the order, Billy Bob pulled out his homemade checklist.

Jonas listened intently as his friend started asking and answering his own questions. After every positive response, Billy Bob would take his pen and check the question. He stopped only long enough to look over the menu and order chicken gumbo. Jonas requested the same.

Jonas looked up at the waitress as she served their order. He smiled politely and said, "Thank you."

When the waitress had moved on, Jonas began buttering his bread. Then he spoke softly, after first looking around the diner to make sure he could not be heard: "Maybe next time we can kill lots of wetbacks and those fucking Cubans. We've pretty much destroyed those fucking shines. And if we haven't destroyed them, we sure did put a dent in them big time."

"Well one thing for sure, there will be a lot of job openings and our people can get back to work and make a decent living," Billy Bob said taking a bite of supper.

⚜

"If and when Mr. Lee returns home, we will be waiting for him," Chief Evans remarked, pulling his cruiser into his assigned parking spot.

Agent West smiled and nodded his head. "I feel good about this. My gut tells me he's our man. I sure do!" West said, closing the car door and walking towards his rental car that was parked across the street.

"You're not coming in?" the chief asked, pointing towards the back door that led to his office.

"No, sir, I'm going to call my boss and tell him what we found out. I want to fax this picture to Washington so the bureau can make wanted posters."

"You mean the FBI will print up wanted posters even though we have nothing but a pocketful of speculation and a dozen maybes?" Chief Evans asked.

"No, probably not. But it's fun to ask!" Agent West said, grinning.

Billy stood on the porch of his motel room, watching the rain falling straight down. It was a cold, winter rain that chilled to the bone. To make things worse, an ocean fog had come rolling into the area. Looking at the weather, he debated with himself whether to wait until it got light or leave now and get a jumpstart, and try to outrun the rain. After some deliberation, he decided to get an early start and hopefully stay ahead of the rain.

First, he showered, shaved and dressed. Then he threw his belongings into the back seat of his Cadillac and headed south. Before getting on I-85, he pulled over for gas, coffee and two cream-filled pastries. He hadn't eaten much of his supper the night before, complaining to Jonas it had tasted rather funny. With his car, radio turned on. He searched the radio stations until he found a news channel that told him what was going on in the country. *All those poor souls dying like that. What a shame!* Billy said to himself, as he broke out in laughter.

Jonas fell asleep in his over-stuffed lounge chair watching the evening news. Awakened by his churning stomach, he knew he was going to be sick. Nausea quickly enveloped him and to make things worse, he felt his colon tightening up, as it tried to hold in yesterday's lunch and dinner. Plus the countless number of peanuts inside his swollen rectum. His head felt funny and a deep, metallic taste began to develop in his mouth. Sweat began to appear on his forehead and upper lip. He was going to puke.

The miserable, lying, two-faced, son-of-a bitch broker Raoul evidently sold the rice to the restaurant. To add to his misery, his colon began opened, letting a brown chalky liquid escape that coated his shorts and then his pants.

As his breathing became labored, he began gasping for life. In that moment, Jonas knew his pathetic, hate-filled life was now over. "Damn those shines anyway…"were the last words Jonas uttered.

It was over. Jonas Tubbs lay dead in his own vomit; a victim of his hate.

The rain was now a torrential downpour. Fog crept slowly up from the valleys, crossing the highway and making driving difficult. Though Billy

Bob had the windshield wipers working at full speed, they were almost useless against the rain. A prudent man would have slowed down, but Billy Bob was not feeling very prudent at the moment. Instead, he was looking for a rest area or a gas station because he suddenly needed to take a dump and badly. When he began to sweat, he turned on the Cadillac's air conditioner hoping that would help. That was a mistake because it made the front windshield fog-up. Quickly, he hit defrost. The on rush of hot air cleared the window all right, but then caused him to sweat even more. Next, he rolled down his window, only to be pelted by the hard, driving rain. All the while, the urgency deep within his bowels was telling him to find a toilet…or else.

Out of the corner of his eye, Billy saw a road sign announcing an upcoming rest area. It did not say how far, but he now knew relief was ahead. He turned the Caddy into the right lane and slowed down, trying to see between the raindrops and the wiper blades. As hard as he tried, his colon could hold out no longer. The warm brown liquid began to leak out. Quickly, he sped back up, finally seeing the green rest area sign. As he began his exit, Billy Bob did not see the hard-right turn sign, nor did he heed the posted reduced speed limit sign. Realizing his error too late, he jammed on his brakes, causing the Cadillac to spin. It bounced over a small divider and slammed into a parked semi.

The eighteen-wheeler was en-route to deliver ten thousand gallons of high-octane gasoline. The gasoline would not be delivered that day and Cousin Billy Bob would not make it to the toilet. However, he did learn what it was like to be cremated alive.

Agent West and Doctor Bradshaw were sitting in Chief Evan's office. Both men were nursing sodas as they waited for the chief to appear. The conversation was cordial between the chisel jawed agent and
the sophisticated and charming doctor. They talked about family and
growing up in the south verses growing up in Yankee land. Agent West
talked about J. Edgar Hoover, who was a racist bigot and used his power
to incite fear into politicians, thus getting his budget enlarged to build a
better agency.

Their conversation was interrupted when Chief Evans walked in.
Both men stood, mostly out of respect with a bit of politeness thrown
into the mix. "Agent West, you're not going to believe this," Chief Evans
said, handing him a note.

Agent West took the note from the Chief's hand. Doctor Bradshaw
watched as deep furrows creased West's brow and his mouth tightened.
"Son-of -a-bitch! He cheated us West yelled throwing the note back to
Josiah.

Doctor Bradshaw stood silent. He knew by the expressions both men
were wearing; something had happened to piss them off.

"Well, now our number-one suspect in the killings of all the young
women and perhaps the murders of two FBI agents, is dead. Killed in an
auto accident this morning," Chief Evans announced as he sat down behind his desk and folded his hands, as if in prayer.

Since both men were convinced the man, they were looking for was
dead, Doctor Bradshaw excused himself. Although neither West nor
Evans had handed Bill the note to read, he had quickly glanced at it while
in the agent's hand and been able to see the part that said:

William Robert Lee, killed on Route 85 Sunday morning.

Once on the Interstate, Bill dialed his cousin, Jimmy Ray. He wanted to tell him about Billy Bob. There was no answer.

❧ CHAPTER 36 ❧

Amanda placed her binder on the podium and adjusted the light intensity. Cliff by his years of working with her knew that she was ready. Furthermore, he knew by her subdued manner that this briefing was not going to be good.

The dog and pony show was soon to begin. Doctor Moore walked into the conference room followed by two men. The one on her left was an air force captain. Rumor had it that he was the Surgeon General's representative. By his demeanor Cliff knew he had something to say, and it wasn't going to be good either. The other man was tall, over six feet and wearing an expensive suit. What you noticed first after the suit were his piercing blue eyes, next his thick black curly hair and then his smile. He was a man who exuded charm and confidence. Cliff could tell that Nancy wanted him, as she hung on to the doctor's arm like a three peso hooker.

After introductions were made all around, the lights were dimmed and Amanda took her too-familiar position behind the podium. First, she took a drink of water and then placed her hands on each side of the podium, as if to brace herself against what she was about to say. She nodded her head to the technician who, as if by magic, produced a fact sheet on the large, wall-screen to her left. Then she cleared her throat and began her briefing.

"Perhaps not since the great plague of Europe or the great influenza epidemic of 1917 to 1918, has the world witnessed such a catastrophic pandemic. According to this morning's news reports, the death toll in the United States, alone, stands at approximately six million. The World Health Organization reports the worldwide figure stands at over thirty million and that figure is climbing daily. Please note, we do *not* have the death toll from China and North Korea and probably never will. According to the Surgeon General's office, fifty million doses of influenza vaccine that were destined for the United States had to be destroyed because of mercury contamination. As China has closed its borders to all shipping and air traffic, the anti-viral masks, we need cannot be obtained.

"In the interest of public health and safety, businesses have either curtailed their operations or have simply stopped operating altogether. Oil refineries have also stopped producing. Gasoline and diesel fuels are now so expensive that trucking companies are telling their drivers to park their rigs. This pandemic is having a major impact on our country's economy. The nation's food distribution system is in chaos, leaving those areas hardest hit by the disease without an adequate food supply, further affecting those who most need the nourishment.

"However, what is of greater importance, it that pharmaceutical companies *cannot* ship their medicines. Thus, we are now beginning to see what I have termed "associative deaths." Simply stated, these are deaths are arising out of the effects caused by the influenza pandemic.

"Example: Mr. Ralph Brown, a diabetic from Richmond Virginia, was given a prescription by his doctor for insulin. He was standing in line the next morning at a local pharmacy at 8:30 a.m. A pharmacist's assistant walked the line and checked the prescriptions to see if they had the drug in stock. At the time when the assistant walked the line, Mr. Brown was told they *did* have some insulin. Still in line, two hours later, he was informed they were all out of his needed medication.

"Ralph then went to his local Kroger Pharmacy. Once again, he was turned away when the insulin stock was depleted.

"The next morning Mr. Brown drove to the nearest hospital, where he waited for hours in a long line to see the triage nurse. Later, people thought he was sleeping on the curb and when someone finally bothered to check, it was discovered he had fallen into a diabetic coma. He died shortly thereafter. Ralph Brown, age 78, left behind a wife of 45 years he did nothing wrong: He was but a victim of the circumstances."

Without another word, Amanda closed her binder, picked up her coffee cup and walked out. The room remained silent. Finally, Cliff stood up and walked toward the podium. He knew his words would not be as poignant as Amanda's, nor would they have the same impact. His briefing was scientific, thus boring, but extremely essential.

When Cliff nodded his head to the technician, a most beautiful multi-colored picture appeared on the screen. For the first time death had a shape and a color.

When Cliff had finished outlining each slide and explaining what they represented, he turned out the podium lamp and took his seat. His part of the briefing took less than ten minutes.

Doctor Nancy Moore turned on the room lights and walked over to the podium. Ever the consummate politician, she sensed that the FBI's involvement was a direct result of the Under Secretary passing the buck to Secretary Simon, who in turn had told the President about the alleged terrorist attack, who in turn told the Secretary of Homeland Security or perhaps the National Security Advisor. Anyway, whatever the chain of command, the FBI was now involved.

Nancy knew that the buck passing would eventually lead back to the CDC and the Surgeon General because the bureaucrats needed a scapegoat. She and Paul were nothing more than pawns to be used for the pleasure of the Washingtonians. After all, they were expendable.

"Doctor Bradshaw, we have one more briefing from Captain Jackson. His briefing is why you're here with us this morning. When he is done, the CDC's briefing will be concluded. Then we shall entertain your questions," Nancy said, returning to her seat.

Captain Jackson opened up his brief case and handed each of them a multi-colored map of the United States. Bill was quick to note that except for the lime green and yellow, the captain had used the same color code that CNN had used.

Bradshaw now knew the CDC had determined that many of the deaths were influenced by external sources. Furthermore, he was aware that according to the news reports, this influenza virus was immune to wide-spectrum antibiotics. So the question was, how can anyone tell the difference?

Captain Jackson cleared his throat and began his briefing:

"We know that this influenza virus started in Chicago and Milwaukee. It probably arrived by airplane in or on some innocent and unsuspecting person who traveled business class from Asia. Then he or she took it to work with them the next day. The virus had its carrier and its incubator. When it was ready, the virus began attacking with such ferocity that it quickly overwhelmed its victims, rendering them helpless. Up to this point, the virus was unbiased, striking anyone of opportunity. However, other than killing the infirm, the very old and the very young, which is normal, it was merely incapacitating its victims for three or four days. Then I began to see a steady and alarming increase in deaths between the ages of five through thirty-five.

"I asked myself, 'Why?' My research revealed that the influenza and pneumococcal immunization rates among blacks, Hispanics and Asians significantly trail those of whites, making these populations an easy target for the flu and of course, the secondary effects of pneumonia. Further investigation showed that 90% of the blacks affected, lived in predominately black neighborhoods. Then I noticed the same trend developing in other cities. Next, I realized that the majority of deaths were virtually in a straight line across the country, occurring in predominately black neighborhoods.

"When I started looking at the disease in other parts of the country, I found that the deaths resulting from the virus were within the normal range. Again that sparked my interest, and I asked for permission from the Surgeon General to be allowed to investigate my suspicions. The Surgeon General granted my request and allowed me to talk with Doctor Pfeiffer. I told him of my theory and he in turn put me in contact with Doctor Cecilia Stokes, a geneticist, at John Hopkins. When I told Doctor Stokes of my theory, she agreed with me, except for my premise about a terrorist attack. She is convinced that a hate group has targeted mainly blacks and Hispanics, and I concur with that theory.

"Now when you look over the map I have given you, please take note that the areas shaded in lime green are those neighborhoods directly adjacent to the infected neighborhoods. Hispanic's and poor whites primarily populate the adjacent areas. You will notice the death toll in these adjacent areas are almost negligible or slightly elevated."

Doctor Jackson was finished, and he sat down. Now, all eyes turned to Doctor Bradshaw. Slowly, he pulled himself closer to the table. He was stalling for time, trying to collect his thoughts and at the same time divert suspicion from Jimmy Ray and Billy Bob. His voice was soft and gentle, yet his look and the intensity of his voice showed utter disbelief.

"What I heard you say is that although the pandemic originated in Asia and came into this country by airplane. Which it is now virtually everywhere in the country, and the majority of deaths are in a straight line from the west coast to the east coast and that this should not be happening. Furthermore, Captain Jackson you've stated that a hate group has targeted our country, concentrating mainly on this nations black population.

"Doctor Stokes and Doctor Pfeiffer agree that this influenza strain has somehow been altered. The flu virus is nothing more than a cover-up for mass murder. This substantiates your hate group theory! And this alleged hate group has somehow contaminated our nation's entire food supply system, creating widespread food shortages. Furthermore, this hate group has caused our nation to close its borders, suspend air travel, caused banks and businesses to close, creating extensive economic chaos in this country and around the world. Is this correct Captain Jackson?" Bradshaw asked.

"You have encapsulated everything very well, doctor," Captain Jackson replied.

With disdain in his voice, Doctor Bradshaw blurted out: "I think your theory is ludicrous! I cannot in good conscience buy into such a theory. The FBI has sent me here to get a briefing and perhaps develop a psychological profile of the individuals *supposedly* responsible for committing mass murder. In a nutshell, all you have given me is a map showing the outbreak of the flu epidemic. Then you told me the flu arrived by an airplane from

Asia and it has brought death across the Pacific ocean and entered this country in a straight line.

"You know, Doctor Jackson, every city affected has an airport. Maybe all these deaths occurred because somebody else flew business class from Asia and departed in Saint Louis, Kansas City or Boston. Perhaps the original premise made by the CDC is correct. Maybe we *are* dealing with some sort of mutant virus, and it contains an alkaloid of some sort. I don't know what to think. However, I do know that I cannot help the FBI catch the wind."

With that, Doctor Bradshaw stood up and with his usual dignity, charm and grace, thanked the CDC and the Surgeon General's representative for the briefing and left.

As Bill walked to the parking lot, he tried call Jimmy Ray. Again, there was no answer. Now, he was beginning to get concerned. Removing his jacket, he placed it across the front seat of his BMW. He debated whether to go to Valdosta or head home.

It was just past noon when he walked into the hotel lobby. Bill's eyes scanned the registration desk looking for Kitty and found her. She was reading a textbook and was oblivious to him standing at the counter. As his eyes recorded her beauty; he felt that familiar stirring deep within his loins, which had been dormant for some time. No doubt about it, he wanted her.

∞ CHAPTER 37 ∞

"Yes they were and
I was wondering if the beautiful Kitty would go to dinner with me?" He asked smiling at her, as he signed the hotel registration form.

"Oh, and just what restaurant did you have in mind?" Kitty asked.

"Your choice Kitty" Bill replied, putting his credit card back into his wallet.

"I get off at three this afternoon. I have a class at four. How about picking me up at seven. Here is my phone number and these are the directions to my house." Kitty said handing Bill the slip of paper with the information.

"Your house," Bill asked suprised that someone so young would own a house.

"Yes, I live with my folks, but they're in Florida." Kitty replied.

Bill smiled, picked up his luggage and went to his room.

Kitty had given him the same room he had before. For a brief moment, he imagined Pepper lying nude on the bed, her beautiful body moist from lovemaking, waiting for him to return. This time he would play it safe and smart. Screwing a married woman could get you killed. Even if she did lie to you the husband wouldn't care. All the guy knew was that you had made it with his old lady, and she belonged to him.

He placed his suitcase on the small stand that sat in the alcove and opened it. He pulled out a pair of jeans a clean shirt and from the side pocket, a pair of running shoes.

Pulling out his palm pilot, he called Agent West. He was about to hang up when he heard: "Hello, West here."

"Doctor Bradshaw here, I wanted to know if we could get together sometime this week for a beer and a hamburger."

"Where are you?" Agent West asked in a bemused voice.

"I'm here in Valdosta, staying at the Hotel," Bill replied.

"Well, doctor, I'll have to take a rain check on the beer and hamburger. You see. I have been reassigned to Washington D.C., and I'm here talking with my new boss."

"No kidding" Bill laughed. "Doesn't that beat all? I drove all the way from Atlanta to have a beer and a hamburger and discuss a few things with you, and you have up and flown away!"

"Bullshit, Doc! You drove back because there is a woman you want. I'm not sure, but I would guess either Officer Culpepper or that beautiful lady, Miss Kitty."

In part to conceal his fear, Bill began to laugh. Agent West was no dummy. In fact, he was brilliant. Bill made a special note to himself to stay clear of this man.

Within an hour after his arrival in Valdosta, Bill had checked into the hotel, made a dinner date with Kitty and was driving out of town to see his ancestral home. He hadn't been invited to Jimmy Ray's place, and he was concerned about Jimmy Ray. His gut told him something was wrong. It was worrisome not to know the scope of the problem or even if there was a problem. However, he had to find out for himself why no one answered the phone.

The drive was pleasant. He drove with his window down, and his stereo was playing Verdi. Bill knew none of these red necks would know who Verdi was or much care. For that matter, but Verdi gave him pleasure. His mom and grandmother introduced him to literature, the classics and the great musical composers at a very young age. Back in the eighties it was considered important that the social elite get a proper upbringing.

Slowly, he circled the ruins of his boyhood home, surveying the damage. His mind traveled back in time, remembering a kinder, gentler time during his youth and the grand parties his mother had given. As he got closer to the house he was brought back to reality by the fresh smell of charred wood filling his nostrils. Stepping back, Bill walked around to the far corner of the house.

There, the sweet, sickening odor of death and decay, suddenly assaulted him. He pinched his nostrils together as his eyes, seeming of their own volition, traveled directly to the source. The bodies of Martin and Luther were lying side by side. Their throats were slit.

As Bill headed towards Valdosta, his mind turned momentarily to Kitty. *Wouldn't it be nice if I could buy back my family's farm and start a new practice? Or better still; buy cousin Billy Bob's estate? It is in a much nicer setting and probably cheaper.* Bill smirked. He felt like a carpetbagger feeding on the misfortune of others. *Hell,* he thought. It *would be easier and cheaper to move Kitty to Washington, and have her move in with me.*

He made good time. Less than twenty minutes and he was pulling into the visitor's parking spot in front of the Valdosta police station. As he opened the door, he wondered if Pepper would be working the desk. Taking out his FBI Identification card, he approached the front desk. Thankfully, Pepper was nowhere around.

"May I help you sir." T tall, hawk-nosed sergeant asked.

"Yes, sergeant, you may," Bill said showing the sergeant his credentials.

The sergeant smiled and came around the front of the desk, an extended his hand saying "Sergeant Clyde Davis at your service, sir."

Bill clasped the sergeant's hand. "Bill Bradshaw, Sergeant Davis nice to meet you." Bill replied letting go of Davis's hand. Sergeant Davis I need to find out what happened to my cousin Jimmy Ray and his wife, Sue Ellen."

"What is the last name?" Sergeant Davis asked.

"Houghton," Bill replied.

"Hmm, you say that Jim Houghton was your cousin?"

"That's correct, sergeant. Why do you ask?" Bill inquired, puzzled by the sergeant's question.

"Well, sir, perhaps it would be better if you talked with Chief Evans or Detective Culpepper."

"You're telling me Pepper made detective?" Bill asked, shaking his head.

"Yes, sir, she now carries a gold shield," Sergeant Davis replied, his face displaying no emotion.

Bill did not push the subject. He could tell it was a sore subject with the sergeant. If that was the case, then there was no sense in aggravating or alienating a potential friend or source of information.

"Then may I talk with Chief Evans?" Bill asked.

"I'll check!" Sergeant Davis said.

Bill waited until the sergeant returned, his mind turning to Pepper. He couldn't help but wonder: *Did she earn the promotion, or was she given the job for services rendered?*

His thoughts were interrupted when the sergeant said, "Sir, Chief Evans will see you now."

"Thank you, Sergeant Davis."

"This way, sir," the sergeant said as he took the lead with Bill following dutifully.

Sergeant Davis's strides were long and purposeful. It was obvious to Bill that the sergeant knew what was going on, but had refused to take the responsibility to tell him.

Chief Evans was standing when Bill entered his office. Once again, they shook hands. The chief pointed at a chair and asked Bill to sit down and take a load off.

"Sergeant Davis tells me you're kin to Jim Houghton. Is that correct?"

"Yes, sir, that is correct," Bill answered, already knowing where this conversation was going.

"Then you would also be a cousin to William Robert Lee?" the chief asked, his eyes starting to narrow and his voice becoming deeper and more authoritative.

Bill recognized this immediately for what it was: Posturing—trying to put him on the defensive. *He suspects something but he's not sure,* he thought.

"Yes," Bill replied. "Cousin Jimmy bought my family's home after dad died," Bill added.

"Did you know that your cousin was a member of a racist hate group called: The Sons of White Men?" Chief Evans asked.

"Not that particular group. I knew he was in the Klan, as was his dad and grandfather," Bill replied.

Chief Evans did not believe him. He had no real reason not to believe him, however, he was sure Bradshaw was hiding something. Perhaps shame, maybe fear, but something wasn't adding up. Then on the other hand, his own mother had known that the Bradshaw's, Houghton's and Lee's were members of the Klan. She just hadn't mentioned anything about The Sons of White Men. Perhaps Bradshaw did not know anything about this either.

"Chief, why are you asking me these questions? All I want to know is what happened to Jimmy Ray and his wife," Bill stated. His demeanor became aggressive, putting the chief on the defensive.

"They're both dead!" the chief replied. "Seems there was a dispute over a large sum of money. We think he was involved in some sort of scheme."

"Have you notified the FBI?" Bill asked.

"For what," the chief asked indignantly, "a double murder of members of a hate group?"

"Well, maybe the scheme you referred to has some national security issues," Bill added.

∽ CHAPTER 38 ∾

CAPTAIN JACKSON WAS WAITING IN his boss's outer office where he overheard the Surgeon General on the phone talking to the Under Secretary of Health and Human Services, a Leon somebody or other. All he knew was that depending on whom you talked to, Leon was either an asshole or a shithead.

The conversation was dealing with national security and China. Exactly what was being said, he did not know. However, by the sound of the Surgeon General's voice, the exchange was heated. Which meant that Captain Jackson was walking into the lion's den.

He just knew the probable outcome was not going to be good, as his own news was bad. The FBI had rejected his theory about a hate group, making him look and feel stupid. Doctor Bradshaw had ripped him and the CDC a new ass in the process.

Now, he had to inform the Surgeon General of The United States that the FBI had rejected his theory. Personally, he still maintained he was correct. All the research data and even the CDC's own research agreed that this virus was not a mutant, but merely a disguise to cover up a bigger crime. However, Doctor Bradshaw had been correct with one statement: "It would be like trying to catch the wind."

All of a sudden a rush of anger washed over him. How could a psychiatrist who knows nothing about public health understand the magnitude of despair and fear this flu virus had created? Perhaps the doctor was right. It might be better to keep quiet and let the virus run its course. Then the President can go on national television and tell the country, "We're sorry, it's not the flu that's killing you but some homegrown hate group has contaminated our food supply." *Yeah like that will ever happen. When pigs can fly,* he thought.

"Jackson, you out there?" came the booming voice of power.

"Yes, sir, I'm here," the young captain replied.

"Get your butt in here, doctor."

Jackson walked in to face the wrath of his superior. Out of habit, he rendered the customary salute due a superior officer.

"Jackson, I already heard what happened in Atlanta. Not your fault if the dumb sons-of-bitches rejected your theory. You tried, you can do no more."

"Yes, sir," the amazed young doctor replied.

"What I want you to do is help Lieutenant Adams prepare a letter for my signature to the World Health Organization, giving them the history of this pandemic and its expected cost, in terms of lives and economic devastation to this country, and only this country."

"Yes, sir!" Jackson replied, rendering his salute and with great relief, he walked out of the lion's den.

Meanwhile, across town at the FBI Headquarters Building, Agent West was debriefing the Deputy Director of the FBI, Mr. Harlan Fisher and his new superior, Special Agent Philip Graham, concerning Mr. William Robert Lee. His report was detailed, accurate and concluded with how this number one suspect had died. He was also quick to point out that since Mr. Lee's demise, no new murders of young women had occurred.

"Agent West, in your investigation of Mr. Lee, did you uncover ties to any hate groups?" Mr. Fisher asked.

"No, sir. Of course, I wasn't looking in that direction."

"Why not?" Graham shot back.

Agent West was quick to spot the apple polisher. He thought to himself: *Just what I need is another kiss ass bureaucrat!* Out loud he replied, "Because, sir, I was looking for the murderer of two FBI agents and perhaps a serial killer; not a racist. That's why."

West became contemptuous of his new boss. He hated men like Graham. That was the big drawback of the bureau. They promoted people with little or no field experience. Graham was the perfect example of the Peter Principal in operation: Promote the incompetent.

Graham was just about to rebuke his new agent when the director interjected saying, "West, I want you to do something for me. Personally I think this assignment will be distasteful and for that I'm sorry. Will you go back to Valdosta and learn all you can about Mr. Lee and find out if he is, or was, a member of any hate group. He was killed on a Sunday coming from somewhere. Evidently he was gone for two weeks, maybe longer. Search his computer files, his phone records, his bank account and any other damn thing you can think of. I think this man was more than a serial killer. I think he had help and money to plan one of the biggest mass murders in history!"

"Sir, am I to assume by this assignment that I will not be working here at headquarters?" West asked.

"Mr. West, you're not an ass kisser nor are you a bureaucrat. You are a honest-to-goodness field agent. You, sir, would not do well in this environment. You need the wide-open spaces and the freedom to do your job. Oh, by the way, for this assignment you will report only to me. I will notify Atlanta of your return and your assignment and that you will report directly to me, regardless of what the special agent in charge thinks. Ignore him. Is that understood?"

West stood up and extended his hand, "Thank you, sir."

"Now, go do what you're told," Fisher said, vigorously shaking West's hand.

"Sir, what do I do?" Graham asked.

"You will find yourself an ass kisser and leave the real men in the field where they belong," Fisher said, in what could only be described as a disdainful, if not caustic voice.

∽ CHAPTER 39 ∼

BILL STOOD IN THE SHOWER, letting the hot water hit the back of his neck, easing his tension. Slowly he rubbed his body with the small bar of soap provided by the hotel. He was not really paying attention to what he was doing. Rather, he was lost in thought— *Through no fault of mine, both my cousins are dead. How lucky could I get? Now there is no way to trace me to anything. The telephone calls I made to Cousin Jimmy coincided with official FBI business. The other two trips I made were made at personal expense. I covered my bases with visits to the police and to meet with the agent in charge of the investigation. Earlier this morning I called the Deputy Director to tell him thanks but no thanks, as he was not interested in trying to profile the wind. Mr. Fisher was disappointed but I know he understood. He will just have to pursue another course of action.*

Chief Evans as much as said he was not going to notify the FBI of his suspicions as to why my cousin was murdered. He felt the murders were over money dealing, perhaps marijuana, which is grown in abundance in the area. Jimmy Ray had been busted before for possession and transportation of a controlled substance. However, as it was

*his first time, Jimmy Ray had been let off with a fine and community service. For six
months Jimmy Ray mowed the lawn of the city cemetery and painted curbs. He did such
a great job the mayor had actually written him a thank you letter.*

Leaning toward the bathroom mirror shaving, it suddenly occurred
to Bill what Fisher had meant when he had said he would pursue another
course of action. Since Agent West was in Washington D.C., evidently Fisher was going to brief Agent West about the CDC's and Surgeon
General's suspicions about a hate group. Undoubtedly he would start with
Billy Bob, which would then lead him to Jimmy Ray. As Agent West was
no fool, the trail would eventually lead back to him because of the phone
calls. *I'll be ready for him,* he thought. *Given Agent West's intellect and tenacity,
West should be in contact within two, maybe three weeks before I get a phone call or a
visit. Most likely I'll get a phone call to accept the rain check for a hamburger and beer.
If West gets close, he's dead!*

✦✦✦✦✦

Bill drove his BMW into Kitty's drive with one minute to spare. He
left the car running so the air conditioner could keep the leather seats cool.
Before leaving D.C., he had the car detailed and deodorized.

Kitty's parent's house was a large, sprawling ranch with an attached
garage. Bill thought how lucky he was that he did not have to mow the
lawn. The flower gardens were beautiful. Obviously, Kitty's folks had lots
of time on their hands to be able to handle the yard work.

After ringing the front doorbell, he heard barking followed by the
growling of a very large dog. Then, he heard Kitty's soft voice telling the
dog it was ok and to go lay down. Obviously the dog did not obey as when

she opened the door it was standing behind her with its head down, ears laid back, tail tucked between its legs and eyes focused on Bill's privates. Bill knew that one false move and he would be in deep trouble.

The dinner conversation was light and lively. Bill asked Kitty what her major was and what she was planning on doing for the rest of her life. Kitty informed him she wanted to be a concert pianist. Her goal was to get a degree in music and then a degree from Julliard.

After a while, Bill found he was holding Kitty's hand and talking to her very quietly. Kitty in turn leaned forward and whispered, "This is my third mixed drink and I'm feeling good…"

Deciding to capitalize on her weakened condition, Bill ordered a bottle of wine. After two glasses of red wine and a great dinner, Kitty was feeling very happy. She took off her high heels and began rubbing her foot up and down Bill's leg. Her eyes glazed by drink, Kitty became bolder and raised her foot up just inside Bill's thigh. He grabbed her foot and placed it on his crotch. The size of the table and tablecloth, plus the booth location prevented anyone from seeing them.

Naturally, Bill was becoming aroused as Kitty's foot moved back and forth. When Kitty realized the size and length of Bill's erection she placed it between her big toe and index toe and started rubbing up and down.

Subtly, Bill dropped his hand under the table and adjusted his cock. Kitty dropped her foot back to the floor and slid over next to Bill. She placed her hand on his crotch and rubbed up and down and whispered in his ear, "Can I see it please?"

In response, Bill smiled, kissed her lightly on her lips then leaned back just far enough so he could unzip his pants. Quickly he pulled down his shorts just enough for Kitty to see his monster.

"Oh, can I touch it?" she breathed. Bill took her hand and placed it on his erection.

Her hand was large for a woman and her fingers were long and slender. She had no problem encircling his cock. Very gently, she rubbed the head with her thumb. Bill turned his body towards Kitty and slowly brought his hand up onto her thigh. Under the tablecloth he pushed her dress up, exposing the top of her thigh-high hose and her panties. Kitty said nothing as Bill pushed his hand down between her thighs, opening them up to give him access.

"Can we go now?" Kitty asked abruptly.

"Go where?" Bill asked a little bemused.

"My house!" Kitty replied, adjusting her dress and putting on her shoes.

∞ CHAPTER 40 ∞

CHIEF EVANS SAT IN HIS office with his legs crossed and his feet propped up on the large desk drawer. His head was thrown back and resting in his hands. He was lost in thought, wondering which way to go. Did he investigate Mr. Lee, who died in an auto accident or investigate Mr. and Mrs. Houghton's murders? The conclusion should be obvious: Go after the murderers. However, his instinct was telling him that the murders of the Houghton's, and the death of Mr. Lee were somehow related. Personally, he felt that it involved the distribution of marijuana. The monies earned would finance any number of hate group activities. His gut told him Bradshaw knew more than he was letting on. *He practically told me to notify the FBI, but why? Perhaps he was not at liberty to tell,* he reasoned.

Slowly, he disengaged his feet from the drawer and turned his body towards his desk. He reached across the desk, picked up the phone and dialed three numbers. After glancing at the duty roster. It showed only one detective with no caseload. She was new and this type of investigation would be easy, as it was nothing more than a domicile search and a financial background check. He would call the judge and ask for subpoenas himself.

⚜

Detective Culpepper and Sergeant Davis walked around the perimeter of Mr. Lee's spacious home, checking each door in an attempt to gain access; they were all locked tight. Culpepper noticed that the yard needed to be mowed and the shrubs needed to be watered. Sergeant Davis grabbed the mail and began separating the junk mail from the bills. Specifically, he was looking for credit card bills. There were none.

Walking up to the garage door, Detective Culpepper tried to lift it. Slowly, the door began to slide upwards and she laughed.

Sergeant Davis yelled, "We're in!" as he proceeded to open the unlocked door that led into what used to be Mr. Lee's kitchen.

For some reason, they were surprised the kitchen was immaculate. Pepper started opening up each counter drawer. Davis opened the refrigerator and freezer. The freezer was full and the refrigerator was empty, except for a tub of butter, a dozen eggs and a loaf of bread.

Both officers walked into the dining room. It could have been a show room. Pepper recognized the Ethan Allen furniture and knew it was expensive. The front room was tastefully done in creams and soft blues.

"This guy had money," Pepper said.

"This guy was a neat freak. I don't think we will find much out here," Davis remarked, walking down the hall towards the bedrooms.

"Here's his computer room," Davis said, pointing to the computer.

Pepper walked into the room and pulled out Mr. Lee's chair. She lucked out big time and she knew it—the computer had not been turned off! She slid the cursor to "mail" and clicked, causing the monitor to blink. Then she pointed the little white arrow to "inbox" and clicked. In the blink of an eye, a stranger was reading Mr. Lee's private mail.

Davis walked into the master bedroom to fine it was as neat as the rest of the house. He sat down on the bed next to the nightstand. The telephone was flashing, indicating Lee had received some calls. Taking out his pen and a pad, Davis copied each number.

Then he opened the top drawer of the nightstand. In it he found a fully loaded Browning nine-millimeter. Lying under the pistol, Sergeant Davis found a stack of newspaper clippings. Several were about the brutal murder of Mrs. Lee. The story failed to mention she had been shot while in a compromising situation with her lover. Mrs. Lee had been a good-looking slut. The sergeant should know as he had had her once or twice himself. The other clippings were about the two missing FBI agents. One clipping had a note in the margin that read, "Made her squeal like a pig." Davis knew they had their man.

Next, he opened the second drawer and whistled under his breath. It was filled with porno tapes and four homemade tapes. He pulled the homemade videos out and placed them on the bed. The third drawer was filled with dildos of all shapes and colors. Two tubes of KY jelly, each half used, lay at the bottom of the drawer. Closing the drawer, he chose to ignore the dildos for now.

Picking up the clippings and the videos, Davis turned out the bedroom light and closed the door. He took a quick peek into the other bedroom. It was empty except for some weights and a Bow-flex machine. Sergeant Davis backed out of the weight room when he became distracted by the sound of a printer. Making sure to turn out the light, he closed the door. Quietly, he walked the six feet to the office door and stood watching as Detective Culpepper printed off letters.

Knowing that Pepper's enthusiastic endeavors would take a while, Sergeant Davis walked back down the hall and into the den. There he found what he needed—a large screen television set with a VHS recorder attached. Turning the TV to channel three, he inserted one of the home-made videos into the VHS, hit the "power" button and then the "play" button. Slowly, Davis backed away from the television, taking a seat across the room in Mr. Lee's lounge chair.

While Pepper was busy, he thought to be entertained by a homemade porno movie. How wrong he was! What Sergeant Davis had expected was not what he saw. Instead, it was a tape recording of a college co-ed being brutally raped and murdered. In fascinated horror he watched until he got angry. He heard the young girl plead for her life as the assailant laughed, teased and tormented her. Davis stopped the tape and rewound it. Ejecting the tape, he inserted another.

This time he was emotionally prepared for anything—or so he thought. What he saw was a woman strapped to a gurney. Davis sat awestruck as the man he assumed to be Mr. Lee began cutting the woman's clothing off her body. In the tape, the sound of the scissors could be clearly heard. Since the woman's eyes were closed and she did not move, Davis thought she was already dead. Then he happened to notice there was a tube of some sort sticking out of her arm. *What the hell is that for?* he thought.

The woman was now completely naked. He watched as the woman's assailant took a tube of KY jelly and smeared the lubricant on his fingers. Then slowly he inserted each finger, one at a time, into the woman's vagina, twisting back and forth until he had worked his hand into his quarry. As the man backed away from the gurney, Davis could see the man's penis. It was artificial, large and black. Shocked, Davis realized that Mr. Lee did not have a real cock!

Davis re-focused his attention back to the woman and watched as Mr. Lee grabbed her by her legs and pulled her body to the edge of the gurney, allowing him easy access to his prey. For that's exactly what she had become. His prey.

The woman must have awakened from her sleep as he pulled her down the shiny steel table, aligning her body for his assault. Davis heard the woman's screams and her pleas. It was obvious she was begging for her life. Then Davis became furious as he watched Mr. Lee throw his head back and began to laugh, saying something like, "Hell, bitch, you ain't no real FBI agent. You're just an easy fuck."

She screamed again as she twisted and turned, trying to avoid what she knew was about to happen. Ignoring her pleas, Mr. Lee aligned himself with her and then pushed hard. Davis could hear the woman scream louder, still pleading with her attacker. Then he saw something dark begin to flow into the tube alongside the woman's arm. In horror, Davis suddenly realized what had happened to Doctor Ruth Schwartz. Unable to watch anymore, he stopped the tape. Sick to his stomach, he knew he had just witnessed the rape and murder of a federal agent.

Davis turned off the VHS and ejected the tape. Pepper walked into the room, her face flushed with excitement. Silently, Davis put the video back into the case and picked up the newspaper clippings and the other videos.

"What you got there?" she asked.

"Fuck movies," Sergeant Davis replied.

"Oh, you into that stuff?" Pepper asked.

"Not really, but these are interesting. We will watch them at the station. The Chief will probably want to join us."

"No, way!" Pepper replied.

"We'll see," Davis said, walking towards the kitchen.

They were both rather subdued as they rode back to the police station. Davis sat with his arms folded across his chest, his head bowed. His silver-glazed sunglasses gave him a bug-eyed appearance.

Pepper concentrated on her driving as she thought of the approximately twenty letters she had printed from Mr. Lee's internet that were from various people. Since she had their e-mail addresses, she intended to ask for a subpoena to get their names and addresses. Later in the afternoon, she intended on going to the Bank of Georgia to get a copy of Mr. Lee's bank records.

Millie Stowe had obliged Pepper's request without even waiting to receive the official subpoena. Not only was Millie the banker, but also Pepper's Sunday school teacher and a family friend. She had a personal dislike for Mr. Lee, although you would never have known that Millie detested the man when she had talked with him. "Good riddance," Millie had said when she had heard of Mr. Lee's death.

The ride back to the Toombs went quickly. Pepper chose to use her prerogative and use the red lights. Davis knew this was wrong, however most police officers did it once in awhile for whatever reason. Hell, he had done the same thing himself and chose not to say anything.

Pepper drove the cruiser into the parking lot and parked in her assigned spot. Unlike the officers, detectives rated their own parking spot. Without a word, Davis gathered up the tapes and clippings, then walked into the station. Pepper followed at a respectable distance. She knew something was really bothering Sergeant Davis. Having worked beside him for four years, she knew when he got mysterious on her that he was onto something.

Davis should've been made detective, she thought. They tested at the same time and were interviewed at the same time. Pepper was flabbergasted when she had been selected for detective. Given the circumstances, she understood his coolness towards her. However, it really wasn't her problem and she knew it.

Going directly to the downstairs conference room, Davis selected the tape showing the rape and murder of Doctor Ruth Schwartz and inserted it into the VHS recorder. He did not start the tape. Instead, he dialed Chief Evans' extension and requested his presence, explaining what he had.

Chief Evans had not been alone when he received Sergeant Davis's call. Sitting across from him was Agent James West.

"Agent West, I think we have just broken open your case," Chief said as he stood up. "Follow me!"

The Chief and Agent West were sitting at the conference table in less than a minute after Davis's call. Sergeant Davis nodded at West, acknowledging him. Pepper followed them into the room opting to stand guard at the door.

"Pepper, kill the lights," Davis said as he started the tape.

∽ CHAPTER 41 ∾

DMIRAL ERLICH SAT AT HIS desk with a cup of black coffee in one hand and holding Lieutenant Adams' handwritten note with the other. The note read:

Sir,

Please find attached the rough draft of the letter without salutations that you asked Captain Jackson and me to write to the WHO. Please add or delete at will, as this is our first attempt, sir, and we're trying to get our bearings.

Paul smiled, took a sip of coffee, slipped the paperclip off the page and began to read:

> **The United States of America is currently experiencing the worst epidemic of Influenza in its history. Presently, it is estimated that the death toll stands at Twelve million.**

According to the Center for Disease Control, an additional Sixty-seven million Americans are at risk of contracting this virulent and deadly influenza virus. According to statistical experts, this will result in the deaths of twenty-three million more Americans who succumb to this illness, making it the single worst catastrophe to befall this nation in its history.

The economic impact, according to The United States Department of Commerce, has already cost the United States an estimated 71.3 billion dollars. When the global market is factored in, that figure increases to approximately, 250 billion in lost revenue. Without a large-scale immunization program to combat this virus, the Department of Commerce predicts an overall economic impact in the trillions of dollars, which will affect the United States in such a manner that it will be reduced to the status of a third-world nation.

The epidemiological potential of this current virus tends to unfold in waves, with each subsequent wave more severe than the one before it. Apart from the inherent lethality of this virus, it has a predisposition and capacity to be race specific in non-traditional age groups, chiefly, young adult males and females of childbearing age, which is a major detriment of this pandemic's overall impact.

The World Wide Pharmaceutical Company of Great Britain attempted to send fifty million doses of the influenza vaccine to combat the H2N2A virus. However, by divine providence, that vaccine was found to be contaminated with

excessive mercury and subsequently discarded, avoiding another potential life-threatening catastrophe.

An effective vaccine is not available and will not be developed anytime soon because this virus is constantly mutating itself, making it virtually impossible to develop an effective vaccine.

In closing, the ecology of this virus and its behavioral changes have created multiple opportunities for this pandemic to spread not only in the United States, but in the entire world community.

Paul put down his coffee cup down and picked up his red ink pen. The use of the red ink pen was symbolic; it meant that no one else in the entire agency could use a red pen except the Surgeon General of the United States. When it was used, it meant he was either pissed or very disappointed. In this case, he was disappointed in both the nature and character of the letter.

Just then, Paul's phone rang. A quick look showed it was line three, an outside call. It rang two more times while Paul was exercising his red ink pen. He chose his words carefully, ignoring the phone for the moment. He wanted to admonish his two young officers, but not destroy their initiative. He knew they were winners; they just needed some experience and a few setbacks to toughen them up. Paul found himself actually smiling after he read what he had written. He sounded like a coach and in reality that's what he was: A coach. It was his team versus disease, pestilence, ignorance, malnourishment and violence. He threw the letter back into his out basket and picked up the phone.

"Hello, Admiral Erlich speaking."

"Hello Paul." It was Doctor Moore of the CDC.

"Hello, Nancy. How goes it at your end?" Paul asked.

"Paul, I have some good news to share. I wanted to tell you first, before I called Leon,"

"I'm ready for anything good, Nancy," Paul said, and then he chuckled.

"Well, we have isolated the primary cause of death for most of the black population."

"You have?" Paul asked, excitement beginning to register in his voice.

"Paul, both Cliff and Doctor Stokes were correct. The influenza virus is a mutant, all right. However, depending on what part of the country you live in, the microbial analysis reveals different, but very significant traits, leading us to believe that this virus is constantly mutating itself. In reality, what we found was that the virus that traveled across the mid section of the country was contaminated with an alkaloid, which was masked by the virus."

"Nancy, we knew that!" Paul said, interrupting her.

"Yes, Paul. We knew that there was some sort of alkaloid involved, but now we have identified it. Its nicotine! Nicotine poisoning gives off flu-like symptoms, causing the doctors to misdiagnose and prescribe medicines that could actually exacerbate the situation and cause death. The anti-viral agents prescribed would, in fact, reduce the body's natural immune system, causing the person to be more susceptible to secondary infections like pneumonia."

At first Paul did not respond. He couldn't, as he understood all too well the implications of what he had just been told. His mind going a hundred miles an hour and in several different directions, he was thinking to himself: *Captain Jackson had been right. The FBI had refused to acknowledge the fact the nation's food supply system had been compromised. If word got out, the nation would self-destruct, causing the government to collapse, which would create a domino effect around the world. Countries would cease to exist. Anarchy would replace law and order. Millions of lives would be destroyed.*

Those government bastards had intended to hide the truth and ride out the influenza virus until late spring when the crisis would be over. All the while, burying or burning the country's dead by the hundreds of thousands and telling the populace to stay calm, wash their hands and wear facemasks or bandanas in a vain attempt to try and minimize the spread of the virus. Come late spring, when the threat had run its course, the government, all smiles, would assure us: "We feel your pain," and would return to normal...

"Paul are you still there?" Nancy asked.

"Yes, Nancy, I'm still here," Paul responded. "Nancy?"

"Yes, Paul?"

"Don't tell Leon," Paul said.

∞ CHAPTER 42 ∞

AGENT WEST, EYES were fixated on the television screen. He watched in horror, as a woman strapped to a gurney begged and pleaded for her life. He watched a sadistic, homicidal murderer take his perverse pleasure. Unnoticed, he had actually bitten his thumbnail so hard he had torn his cuticle and it was bleeding.

Chief Josiah Evans became engrossed with the efficiency and creativity of this killing machine. So pure, so diabolical, so methodical and meticulous was this man that if he had not been killed, would probably never have been caught. Truly, this man had a genius for killing.

Mrs. Stowe had called and had left a message for Detective Culpepper that Mr. Lee's and Mr. Houghton's bank statements were ready. Detective Culpepper had slipped away unobserved by the others, choosing to walk the couple of blocks to get the bank records rather than stay and watch anymore of the disturbing video. The murder of helpless women angered her. She was glad the sick son-of-a-bitch was now in hell. Hopefully, he would remain there until the end of time.

The trio of men watched each tape from start to finish. When all the tapes had been reviewed, they counted forty women who this man had obviously killed. Throw in the two FBI agents and one dead wife and you had a maniacal genius.

⁂

Upon her return from the bank, Pepper sat at her desk, quietly going over Mr. Lee's bank statements, a diet cherry Seven-up sitting by her elbow. The records for both men covered a period of two years.

Mr. Lee's statements were monotonous. Perhaps boring would be a better word to describe them. He received one direct deposit each month from General Motors and one from Social Security. All his bills were paid on line, on time and they were always for the same amounts. His debit card expenses were routine: Food and gas, nothing odd about that. Absolutely nothing, no large deposits, no checks, nothing to indicate anything illegal or even the slightest bit immoral. However, she realized one bill was missing. There was no house payment. She made a mental note to check with the bank.

Pepper put Lee's statements aside and picked up Mr. Houghton's bank statements. She knew she was looking for some sort of connection, no matter how remote. Mr. Houghton was anything but thrifty. Where Mr. Lee was prompt with paying his bills, Mr. Houghton was anything but. Then something caught her attention: One very large deposit in December, followed by another in January. Total, the amount was over fifty thousand dollars. Evidently Mr. Houghton's financial affairs had taken a sudden turn for the better. *Too bad his personal life was so fucked up*, she thought. In her gut, Pepper felt reasonably sure the Houghton's deaths were somehow

264

related to the sudden influx of money. *Probably drug money just as Chief Evans surmised,* she figured. Mr. Lee, the murdering son-of-a-bitch, most probably died by circumstances out of his control; a happy circumstance for the young women of Georgia, that was for certain.

Pepper picked up the statements and walked back to the conference room. The lights were on and the guys were sitting around the table discussing the best way of identifying many of the young ladies who had been assassinated at the hands of Mr. Lee and notifying the next of kin.

"Excuse me, Chief Evans, but I may have something concerning the reason the Houghton's were killed," Pepper said, handing the Houghton's bank statements for December and January to the chief.

Taking the statements, Chief Evans looked at Pepper's notations.

"Interesting, very interesting, detective! Let's get another subpoena to see how he deposited the money—by cash or check. Then if we just happen to luck out and he deposited a check, we might be able to find out who issued it."

"I don't think you will find it was a check," came the very soft and commanding voice of Agent West.

"Probably not, but we're going to check anyway," Chief Evans said.

"Yes, sir," Pepper said, turning her back and walking out of the room.

Agent West was beginning to lean in Josiah's favor. That is, he agreed there seemed to be a connection between the two cousins and it did involve money. However, he rejected the drug theory. He wasn't sure, nor could he prove anything, but his instincts told him there was a definite connection and that Doctor Bradshaw was somehow involved...

Later, as Agent West sat in the hotel restaurant drinking his coffee while waiting for his order, he rested his chin in his large right hand and his thoughts were about Doctor Bradshaw and the two cousins. He kept asking questions that his reason and intellect just could not answer. Like: *How did Mr. Lee know that Doctor Schwartz was not a real FBI agent, as he had said on the tape? Who told him? What led Schwartz to Mr. Lee in the first place? How did she get there if her car was supposedly parked and locked in the hotel parking lot? Had Mr. Lee driven the car back to the hotel, parked and locked it without being seen and then gotten help getting back to wherever he went?*

Why would the Deputy Director send me back to Valdosta to investigate hate group activity unless he suspects something of national importance? But what and why, he thought. All he was sure of was that Bradshaw was involved up to his eyebrows.

ᴄᴏ CHAPTER 43 ᴏᴄ

NANCY HUNG UP THE PHONE. Paul was persuasive and she had to agree with his logic. The influenza pandemic would be gone in a few more weeks. In fact, the number of actual deaths and related secondary deaths was declining, not significantly, but declining nevertheless. Rural areas of the country were quickly getting back to normal.

China, at the urging of the United Nations had opened its ports and had started shipping medical supplies, which would help to combat the spread of the virus, although air travel into and out of China was still closed to regular traffic.

Thailand had reported no new influenza cases in the last three days. India and Pakistan had suffered tremendous human losses with the estimated deaths ranging in the neighborhood of 20-25%, similar to the United States. Great Britain, France, Germany and Italy had estimated losses from 5-15% percent of their population, mostly the elderly and very young, just what had been expected.

After some thought, Nancy picked up the phone and called Cliff. She wanted to talk to him about her conversation with Paul and what they had agreed upon. However, she needed Cliff's cooperation and she wasn't exactly sure he would cooperate, as Doctor Bradshaw had pissed him off royally. Also, she wanted to meet with Amanda in order to discuss a press release informing the nation that things were actually starting to get better.

⚜

Sitting in a chair across from his boss, Cliff listened to Doctor Nancy Moor as she explained the political situation, the ramifications of going public with their news and the damage it could cause in this country and around the world. As he listened, Cliff fidgeted in his chair. Nancy could tell Cliff wasn't buying what she was selling. Yet, when she was finished, Nancy politely and ever so succinctly, asked Cliff to remain silent about his findings.

By then Cliff was sitting on the edge of his chair with his hands clasped together and squeezed between his inner thighs. His face, although not purple with rage, was certainly red. Bracing herself, Nancy knew she was going to feel Cliff's wrath once again. She knew the look and recognized his body language. He was going to explode. Nancy pushed herself away from her desk, walked over to the door and closed it. *No need in letting the entire agency know what's going on between us,* she thought. Through the years, some of their arguments had become legendary. This one could determine the creditability of the agency and the reputations of two of its directors.

Choosing his words carefully, his jaw clenched, Cliff began: "Nancy, we have spent thousands of man hours and millions of taxpayer's dollars identifying what was killing people. We know that although deadly, this virus had help in killing millions of Black and Hispanic Americans. We would be derelict in our duty and most seriously culpable to the American people if we did not escalate this criminal act to the responsible authorities."

"Even though the FBI told us that we were chasing the wind; that we had nothing but suspicions with no proof? That we could not prove anything other than that the virus traveled from west to east via airplane? I say we act with prudence and forbearance and say nothing, save our nation from wholesale panic. After all, the damage has been done and cannot be undone. What does it matter?" Nancy asked, raising her voice for emphasis.

Cliff stood up and began walking towards the door, as if he was leaving with the situation still not resolved. But then he turned back towards Nancy, his soft voice trembling with emotion and fatigue. "It matters because millions of innocent men, women and children from California to Virginia lie in mass graves, their bodies bulldozed into a big, dark, cold hole. And then with no more thought than it takes me to spit on the ground, their bodies are covered over and no one will ever know their names." Cliff, the ever so reserved and quiet man, began to tremble. Tears were forming in the corners of his eyes. He began to cry.

Nancy stood and walked over to him. Putting her arms around him, she pulled him close and kissed him on the cheek. Then of their own accord, his lips found hers. A slow, loving, gentle kiss ensued. Nancy could feel Cliff's passion beginning to rise. She did not pull away.

∽ CHAPTER 44 ∾

AGENT JAMES WEST'S HAND WROTE his report detailing the deaths of Doctor Ruth Schwartz and Agent Gallopli. Then he addressed the envelope to his new interim boss: Mr. Fisher, Deputy Director of the Federal Bureau of Investigation, (Eyes Only.) He also sent a video copy of Doctor Schwartz's murder along with copies of the rest of the murder videos to Washington D.C. West wanted the ass-kissing bureaucrats to see life as it really was. He also sent a photocopy of Mr. Lee's death certificate for added measure, but mostly so Mr. Fisher would back off from this hate group theory of duplicity between rival groups doing whatever they were supposed to be doing, or had done.

With that part of his job out of the way, James intended to focus his interest on a certain Doctor of Psychiatry, named Bradshaw, who through his position as a profiler was able to influence and misdirect investigations besides being privy to all classified investigation reports. He felt certain that Bradshaw warranted a much closer look.

Though West wasn't sure about Agent Gallopli, he *was* sure that somehow, some way, it had been Bradshaw who had set up Doctor Schwartz to be murdered. For whatever reason, he wasn't sure at this point. Perhaps, because she had disrupted his plan or maybe she had uncovered his plan, whatever that plan or reason may have been. Two agents were dead and in his gut, he knew that Bradshaw was somehow responsible.

Picking up his cell phone, he dialed Bill Bradshaw. Time to collect on the hamburger and beer—and talk.

The sound of Beethoven's fifth echoed in Bill's sleep-deprived brain as his left hand reached out its fingers and walked them across the night stand, searching for the cause of the noise.

"Hello, Honey," Bill uttered without opening his eyes.

"Honey, your ass!" The booming laugh echoed in Bill's ear, causing his laugh reflex to engage.

The two men chuckled at Bill's subconscious remark.

"What time is it?" Bill asked.

"Almost nine," West replied.

"What can I do for you?" Bill asked.

"I'm calling to collect on the rain check."

"That sounds like a great idea, West. Tell you what. Let me shower and shave and I will meet you at the End Zone Sports Bar, say around eleven-thirty?"

"Sounds great," West replied.

Bill hurried into the shower and let the warm water and soft suds cleanse his body. *So it begins,* he thought. *West is going to be a very difficult and a worthy adversary. I wonder which direction West will take—the direct approach or something subtle? Perhaps the, "Let's be friends" type of approach would work best for a man like Agent West. Whichever direction he comes from, or whatever tact he uses,*

I will be waiting for him. And if need be, he will disappear, never to be seen or heard from again.

Leaving that challenge, he switched his overactive mind to the business of last night and Kitty…

Both Bill and West ordered the house's large hamburger combo, with fries and coleslaw. Bill had an ice tea while West ordered a diet Coke.

Bill decided to take the lead and said, "So, Jim, what brings you back to Valdosta? I thought you had been promoted and were moving to D.C.?"

"I was. I did. Now I'm back," West said with a laugh.

Bill chuckled along with his lunch guest yet, all the while, he was observing Jim's body language, facial expressions and the inflection of his voice. This was the warm up, "Be my buddy," period of this interchange.

"I take it you found D.C. not to your liking…or was it too expensive?" Bill asked, taking a sip of ice tea.

West thanked the young server and took a drink, choosing not to use his straw.

"Well, Bill, I was in D.C. for maybe all of twelve hours. I was in my new surroundings for just about thirty minutes when I met my ass-kissing, bureaucratic, new boss. He and I locked horns. I was about to smash his face into the floor when Mr. Fisher, the Deputy Director, asked me to come back here and investigate the deaths of Doctor Schwartz and Agent Gallopli, to see if their deaths were related to any type of hate group activity. I'm to report directly to him."

Bill knew where this was going. West was on a fishing expedition. He had just baited the hook. Time to go on the offense and re-direct West's focus back to Jimmy Ray and Ruth. He intended to ignore Billy Bob unless he was pressed. If that happened, he would make stuff up. With Billy Bob's reputation, it wouldn't be hard to convince anybody that Cousin Billy Bob was a bit odd.

"Well, Jim, maybe I can shed some light on the situation for you," Bill said, moving his place setting to make room for his elbows. "About a week ago, your Mr. Fisher called me at my office. He asked me to attend a meeting at the headquarters of the CDC to discuss an alleged terrorist plot against blacks. A young captain from the Surgeon General's office had this half-baked theory that this influenza pandemic was nothing more than a huge cover-up for mass murder or perhaps genocide would be a better word.

"Supposedly, the CDC had analyzed three, maybe four different strains of virus and had concluded the virus was a mutant and not responding to antibiotics. Also, that each strain analyzed was different, depending on the part of the country from which it came. Mr. Fisher suspected a hate group and asked me to develop a profile on a hate group.

"Now, Jim, that was an impossible task to begin with. The other thing was that the captain's theory was nothing more than speculation. He maintained that this influenza virus had spread across the country, virtually in a straight line, killing predominantly Blacks, Hispanics and poor Whites. He even went so far as to tell me that the virus landed at an airport on the west coast, arriving on some person or persons from Thailand or China.

"I reminded the good captain that there are a lot of airports positioned in a straight line from California to Boston and *anyone* could have brought the virus into this country. I told the captain and the CDC thanks, but I have better things to do. Besides, I'm surprised that neither the captain who works in the public health sector, nor the CDC knew that Blacks and Hispanics are the two most under-immunized races in this country. So naturally, it would stand to reason that they would be more susceptible to diseases and viruses. Not only because of the immunization issue, but also because they live in such close proximity to one another."

"So that's it?" Jim asked, amazed at the simplicity of Bill's story.

"That's it. Now if you talk with Chief Evans of the Valdosta police, he will tell you that I came to him and asked about the welfare of my cousin, Jim Houghton and his wife. He asked about the activities of both my cousins. I did not know much about Cousin Billy Bob and avoided the issue on purpose. I felt Chief Evans could see that I was hiding something. I was, but not about Billy Bob. I was trying to figure out how a hate group could mutate a virus, then spread the virus across the country. Seems pretty far-fetched to me and I was not buying the captain's theory. So if Chief Evans suspects me of any wrongdoing, please set him straight for me.

"Jim Houghton is, or should I say was, my cousin. He bought my ancestral home when my dad died. I called him from Atlanta, as I wanted to see the house and go fishing. Since I got no answer, I drove down partly to see him, but also as you guessed, to see a young and very sexy woman named Kitty."

"Oh, that was the 'honey'," Jim said chuckling.

"Yes, Jim, I think I'm falling in love with her. I know it is premature and I know she is younger than me by about ten years. But, Jim, I just cannot get enough of her. She's like candy to me. Once I taste it I can't stop eating it."

Jim laughed again. "So was your cousin Jimmy in any hate group?"

Here it comes, Bill thought, *the innocent but direct question to probe the unknown and to satisfy a basic curiosity, trying to get the upper hand.*

"Yes, he was, Jim. He started out in the Klan; that is until they threw him out for not paying his dues and skipping meetings. However, men like Jimmy Ray always have to be around people who share their views both politically and socially. So Cousin Jimmy Ray joined a group I had never heard of before. Some group called the Sons of White Men. I know very little about them. However, of special note, Jimmy was an officer in the group, the treasurer, I think."

That should get his curiosity motor revved up really well, Bill thought before he continued. "When I found out that Jimmy Ray, his wife and even the dogs had been killed, I suspected the murders were over money."

Now if he is the agent I think he is, he will ask me about Ruth or Billy Bob. It would make perfect sense to do it now, Bill thought.

"What can you tell me about Mr. Lee?" Jim asked, his eyes becoming two small pinpoints that tried to bore through Bill's outer persona in a vain, if not translucent attempt to get into his mind and search his soul.

West is good; in fact he's great. He would have made a great psychiatrist, Bill thought. "Not much, really. Cousin Billy was what we would call the black sheep of the family. Everybody knew who he was, but nobody associated with him much. He gave the family a bad name. Cousin Jimmy Ray told me that after he killed his wife, Billy became a real woman-hater. I called him a couple of times just to keep peace in the family and say hello. However, that was the extent of our so-called communications."

"What happened the day Doctor Schwartz disappeared? Where were you?"

"I had gone out to dinner that afternoon before. In fact, it was the very place I had dinner with Jimmy Ray and his wife. I got hammered. In fact, I got so drunk, the management called a cab for me. When I came to, I was lying on the bathroom floor. I got up, took a shower, shaved and knocked on Ruthie's door—we had adjoining rooms—but she did not answer. Anyway, I remembered that she had a meeting with Doctor Regina Furbish, the M.E, and that's the last I know of Doctor Schwartz. Except…it just dawned on me. I had the car and I took a cab home from the restaurant. So…how did she get the car if she did not know where I had gone for dinner? Why are you asking me these questions?" Bill asked in a somewhat perplexed voice.

"Well, that day when Mr. Lee was killed, you never admitted you knew him," Jim asked.

"Well that's because you never told me who was killed. Neither did Chief Evans. I heard 'the son-of- bitch cheated me!' I heard some other things too, but no name was ever mentioned. Chief Evans handed you the slip of paper with the name on it and you passed it back. I got up and left. I think that was last Sunday. Today is Wednesday. Until this very moment, I did not know Cousin Billy Bob was dead," Bill said, making room for the server to place his lunch.

"How did you know Cousin Billy Bob was dead?" Jim asked, "if you weren't in the room with me and the chief?"

"Because, asshole, you just said, '…that day when Mr. Lee was killed!' " Bill said, rolling his eyes up into his head.

Jim began to chuckle. The chuckle became a laugh and then he let go with a deep belly laugh. "So I did at that, Doc," West said between gulps of air.

Truth be told, Billy Bob's name *had* been mentioned. Bill hoped that neither man would remember, what with all the confusion and cursing that had been going on at the time.

"Do you think Mr. Fisher is correct about the terrorist plot?" Jim asked.

"No, I think this country has experienced a terrible catastrophe that was probably long overdue. We have gone through this before, back in 1918 and 1919; again in 1957 and 1967. Those epidemics were bad, but not nearly as bad as what we're going through now. Of course, Europe had the plague, which killed so many people that history refers to it as the Dark Ages. The world has faced this type of dilemma before and survived. We shall survive this also. I know it." Bill took a bite of his sandwich as he watched West.

Agent James West sat still, digesting what he had just been told. *With one exception, the mentioning of Billy Bob's name, which was a maybe at best, Bradshaw had told the truth. Fisher had called Bradshaw first to ask him to check things out, but the doctor had declined. So why was I asked to investigate? Is there something going on that I don't know about? If so, it has to be at a much higher level. Perhaps Fisher is setting me up to be the scapegoat. But Bradshaw had refused to profile a hate group before I was sent to Valdosta. That means I'm the fall guy. After all, I am just a field agent, nobody that important to the bureau. I bet I wasn't supposed to find the murderer of Agent Gallopli and Doctor Schwartz. I'm expendable,* West thought.

The sudden realization of his unimportance rocked him to his very core. *Fuck'em! Fuck'em all in the ass! To those ass-kissing sons-of-bitches, this is all a game. Me and others like me are pawns to be used and abused at the pleasure of whichever ass-kisser is in charge.*

West took a sip of Coke, then a bite of coleslaw and then his shoulders began to roll up and down as he began to cry, his tears openly trailing down his cheeks.

"Fuck'em, I quit!" he said aloud.

Bill looked around the restaurant, observing how many people were witnessing the self-destruction of a very prideful man who had suddenly come to the self-realization that he was a nobody. He was his badge, and nothing else. He had lost his self-identity long ago and had hidden behind the title "Federal Agent," which had given him instant respect and fame that he had not earned. West had no personal life, as the FBI was his life.

Bill had seen this a lot living in D.C.—once important, powerful people reduced to footnotes in history, living in the world of yesterdays, their fragile egos crushed by apathy and loneliness.

Fisher opened the envelope that had already been opened and re-sealed. He read the little yellow sticky note that said, "Case closed-West." He inserted the first tape and began to witness the subordination and sub-jugation of women for the insane pleasure of a homicidal maniac. When he had seen enough, the deputy director stopped the tape and inserted another one. This tape hit home. As he watched his friend and sometime lover, Ruthie Schwartz being humiliated and sexually assaulted by some pervert with a plastic cock, he became nauseated. It was horrible to hear the cackling laugh of the monster over Ruthie's pleas. Seeing enough, he turned off the tape and read the report.

Although hand written, the report described in detail the lengths that West had gone to in order to find the killer of Agent Gallopli and Doctor Ruth Schwartz. He had also solved the murders of forty other women killed by Mr. Lee. Fisher finished reading the report and debated giving Agent James West a letter of accommodation but decided against it. After all, West had not submitted the report through proper channels, nor was it typewritten. West was a dinosaur who refused to die. If you don't adapt to your surroundings you get pushed aside and left behind. *Somebody should tell West to retire and get a life,* he thought.

∾ CHAPTER 45 ∾

THE YOUNG MEDIC ANNOUNCED FROM Paul's office door, "Sir, line three."

Surprised, Paul looked up at the directness of the young man's statement, because that was not the way things were done around there. Paul picked up the phone and said, "Admiral Erlich." Anyone hearing would have said his voice could best be described as warm, soft and reassuring.

"Admiral, can you come to the White House this afternoon at 2:00 p.m.? The President of the United States wants to ask you some questions." It was Secretary Simon himself.

"Yes, sir. 2:00 p.m. at the White House!" Paul replied, looking at his watch.

Placing the phone back in its cradle, Paul began wondering what the hell was going on. He was sure it had to be something dealing with the pandemic and what had been and was being done. He picked up the phone, pushed line one and dialed a one and then a two.

"Office of the United States Surgeon General, Petty Officer York speaking. How may I help you, sir or ma'am?"

The voice was unfamiliar to him, however, it did sound like the young sailor who only a few moments earlier had told him to pick up. "York, drag your sorry excuse for an ass into my office!"

"Excuse me, sir, but who are you and just where in the hell is your office?"

Paul began to crack up, laughing. He put the phone down and walked out of his office. He could see the young man clutching the phone, waiting for the person on the other end to give him directions.

"York is it? Get your ass in here, mister," Paul said as he turned, trying to control his laughter. He sat back down at his desk and waited for the young and very new petty officer to enter.

"Sir, Petty Officer Robert York reporting as ordered!" York's salute was crisp and clean. He stood tall and straight, waiting for Paul to return his salute.

"Just what is it, Petty Officer York, that you do in the Coast Guard?" Paul asked.

"Sir, I'm a medic," York replied, still holding his salute.

"A medic here?" Paul asked in a surprised voice. "What the hell are you doing here?"

"Sir, most of your staff is down sick with the flu. I was tending to the staff that is still able to work. I heard the phone ring, sir. I thought maybe it was important, so I answered it. It was some guy who called himself a secretary, asking for the admiral. Since you were the only person still working and you look kind of like an admiral, I told you to pick up."

"Let me get this straight, York. You are a medic, treating my staff. The phone rings, you answer the phone, some guy says he is a secretary, asks for the admiral and you pick me because I look like an admiral?"

"Yes, sir, that's correct," the young medic responded, still holding his salute.

"York, that guy you called a 'secretary' was Secretary Simon, who happens to be Secretary of Health and Human Services of the United States. He called to ask me to meet with the President of the United States at 2:00 p.m. this afternoon. I need a driver and I need some correspondence files. You're telling me Mrs. Clarke is not here; that she has taken ill?" Paul asked.

"Sir, would you mind returning my salute so I can put my arm down?"

"You keep your arm just where it is, sailor," Paul said, becoming angry because he had not been notified about his own staff. Nobody had thought to tell him that his staff had been decimated by the flu and there was no medicine to treat them except for chicken soup and rest.

"Well, York, guess what? You get to be my driver and you get to carry my brief case to the White House," Paul said, finally returning the young medic's salute. "Now, I want the correspondence files from the CDC and both the Secretary and Under Secretary of Health and Human Services."

"Yes, sir. You need the correspondence files from the CDC and the two secretaries. Will do, sir." York saluted and did an about face before Paul could return the salute.

❧

The correspondence file between Secretary Simon and the Surgeon General's office was small, only twenty pages in the last year. Under Secretary Gonzales' files were hundreds of pages, and almost all of the correspondence was over the past five months. There was the usual routine stuff, a few bullshit requests and then in the last three weeks the request for information had doubled. Paul noticed that Leon, the Under Secretary, had requested information relating to a terrorist attack and asked about national security issues. He read Lieutenant Adams' memo telling Leon to ask the FBI for that type of information, as the Surgeon General's office did not keep such information.

Paul stopped right there and sipped his coffee. Now, why would Leon ask such questions? he wondered. *Nancy's e-mail had just said, "Watch out. Leon is going off the deep end again." Everyone knows that Leon Gonzales is prone to joust at windmills and create problems when there weren't any. On more than one occasion both Nancy and I have told Leon off. But now here is Leon, on a fishing expedition, looking for information concerning a terrorist attack...*

Paul quickly re-read the e-mail Nancy had copied and sent to him. It was dated only two weeks ago and was timed in at 5:58 a.m. In it she had stated the influenza virus was a mutant and it had peculiarities that masked something else. However, up to this point, the CDC did not know what those peculiarities were. She had stated: "We are losing on all fronts..." which was a true statement at the time.

⚜

A gentle spring rain was falling as Paul's young driver headed down Fourth Street, the wipers squeaking across the windshield. He looked out through the raindrop-spattered side window. *The tulips will soon be in bloom. A sure sign that spring is here and another catastrophe will soon be over,* Paul thought as he watched a robin pull a worm out of the ground.

York made the left turn onto Pennsylvania Avenue. Suddenly, Paul's thoughts turned to his wife, Andy. He remembered the two of them walking down this very avenue holding hands, so many years ago. At the time, they had had nothing but each other. They couldn't afford a car or a television. All they had were an electric skillet, a coffee pot, two pans—one small, the other medium—for cooking, two hardback chairs, an old green drop-leaf table and a couch that doubled as a bed. He had been in med school and Andrea was finishing law school.

Right then he though of how much he loved and missed her. However, Andrea was safe in Seattle, taking care of her parents; he had seen to that. Both his sons were safe and Andy would be back with him soon.

Petty Officer York used his turn signal and waited for the security guard to motion to them. Paul said in his ear, "Remember, York, we're the hired help, so when we get through the gate, turn right and go around back. Hopefully we can find a spot close to the rear door."

"Yes, sir," York replied.

The security check was relatively painless: A check of IDs and the secret service agent asked Petty Officer York if they had an appointment and if so, with whom.

"Yes, sir, we're here to see the President of the United States," York said in a raised voice that was clear and rather exaggerated yet showed no signs of hesitation or fear of intimidation.

"You are?" the agent asked wide-eyed.

"Yes, sir, and if you don't believe me, my boss is sitting in the back seat. Ask him!"

The agent stood up and began to laugh, as did Paul. "Go ahead," the agent said, motioning for York to pull forward.

York drove around back, maneuvering the staff car close to the rear entrance. He pulled up and stopped to let the admiral get out. The admiral, although not required by convention or military protocol, waited for the young medic while he parked the car. Perhaps it was his paternal instinct, or that he saw something decent and idealistic in this impertinent young man who possessed more courage than common sense by exposing himself daily to great risk. One who willingly fought an invisible enemy with medicines that had little or no effect and who helped remove the dead by carrying them to body collection points for subsequent cremation.

As York walked up, Paul handed him his brief case. "Are you ready?" Paul asked.

"Yes, admiral, lets kick some ass," York said, opening the door for his boss.

Paul had only been to the White House on one other occasion and that was when he had been selected as the Surgeon General. He happened to see a navy commander walking toward him and asked the way to the oval office. The commander smiled and motioned the admiral and young petty officer to follow. They walked through a maze of cubicles and then down a short hall, finally stopping in front of an open doorway.

"Here you are, sir," the commander said, pointing to the lady across the room.

Paul smiled and nodded to the commander, acknowledging his kindness.

Paul removed his raincoat and handed it to York. He straightened his tie and matted down what little hair he had on his head. Then, he walked across the room and introduced himself to the receptionist.

"Yes, admiral, Secretary Simon and the President, are waiting for you. Please be seated; it will only be a moment."

Paul watched as the woman stood up and walked over to the door. He noticed that she was tall and elegant. After knocking on the door, she opened it and said, "Sir, the Surgeon General of the United States is here."

"Show him in, Mrs. Lincoln."

Paul recognized the voice as the President's. Mrs. Lincoln stepped back, holding the door to allow the admiral and his young companion into the oval office.

"Good to see you, admiral. Who is your young friend?" the President asked, extending his hand to the admiral.

"Mr. President, I would like to introduce you to Petty Officer Robert York, of the United States Coast Guard. He came into my life by answering my phone this morning. Actually, Secretary Simon, he took your call this morning. So I shanghaied him into my service. As Lieutenant Adams and Captain Jackson are out sick, I made him my driver."

"Hello, York, it is nice to meet you," the President said, extending his hand.

"Nice meeting you, Mr. President," York said, shaking his Commander-in-Chief's hand.

"Mrs. Lincoln, I think that we have some left-over chocolate cake. I wonder if you could call the chef and ask him to cut a nice, big slice of my birthday cake for Petty Officer York and a glass of milk? Then call his mom. Make sure you say the call is coming from the White House. Let him tell his mom what's going on."

Then turning to the young man he said, "I'd invite you to the meeting, York, but you're a might shy in the rank department."

"You could promote me to admiral, sir."

The President broke out in a hardy laugh, as did the other two men.

"Get out of here," the President said, shaking York's hand and slapping him on the back.

The President closed the office door, turned and walked to his desk. His face had become sullen, all laughter was now gone. The serious side of the nation was about to speak.

Secretary Simon and Admiral Erlich stood side by side in front of the President of the Untied States like two schoolboys in front of the school principal, waiting to be punished. Both men stood silent, each with their own thoughts.

Paul had already resigned himself to the fact he would be the scapegoat. He, along with the CDC and the nation were victims of circumstance: Lack of vigilance, bad planning, wishful thinking by the World Health Organization, inadequate production techniques leading to vaccine contamination by World Wide Pharmaceuticals, ignorance and poor hygiene by the world's population, fear; self-preservation and of course you couldn't forget, mass murder. All these circumstances had played a critical role in the demise of over twenty million Americans. The flu season would be over in another two, maybe three weeks. Already, according to the CDC reports, the reported influenza cases were down and normalcy was starting to reappear throughout the country. The borders between Mexico and Canada had been reopened and trade was once again flowing between the three countries.

"Gentleman, there is no justice for mediocrity," the President began, "as mediocrity leads to chaos and anarchy, followed by civil war, as our neighbors in Mexico are finding out. CNN will be breaking the story any minute now. Italy's government is also about to fall. There is rioting in Paris and Madrid; fear and panic is spreading across Europe. News reports are saying that this is not the flu, but the work of terrorists who have contaminated not only our water and food with toxins, but other countries as well and we are covering it all up. Our nation, gentlemen, is on the verge of collapsing. I opened the borders in an attempt to quiet the country's nerves and let the people know things are returning to normal.

"Secretary Simon says that terrorists attacked this country using the flu as a mask, in order to kill as many Americans as they could by contaminating our food and water supply system. I asked homeland security to investigate and they can find nothing. In fact, some doctor, whom the FBI sent to Atlanta, told the CDC and the FBI there was nothing to prove that a conspiracy existed at all. This flu entered our country and hop scotched across our nation via airplanes from Asia and who's to say the doctor isn't correct? If I go on national television and announce that we have been victims of a terrorist attack, I know in my heart this country will explode and we will join Mexico, France, Spain and Italy in the downward spiral into anarchy."

"Excuse me, Mr. President. Who told Secretary Simon that we were the victims of a terrorist attack?" Paul interjected.

"Good question! Why didn't I ask that in the first place?" the President remarked. "Simon, who told *you* we were victims of a terrorist attack?"

"I believe sir, that Under Secretary Gonzales told me, Mr. President. If I could have a few moments, sir, I can verify that. If my memory serves me, he e-mailed me, sir. I in turn called you, and you in turn called the National Security Advisor, who in turn asked the FBI to investigate," Simon replied, somewhat dismayed by the sudden turn in events. He had expected to be fired. Instead, he was defending his integrity and his honor.

"Go ahead, Simon, ask Mrs. Lincoln for any help you need," the President said, sitting back in his chair and rubbing his temples, trying to make the pain in his brain go away.

"Mr. President, may I show you something?" Paul asked hesitantly.

"Yes, doctor, what do you have?" the President asked, still massaging his temples.

"Sir, I was copied on this e-mail from Doctor Nancy Moore, who is the Director of the CDC. She sent this to Secretary Gonzales. The e-mail suggests that this strain of the H2N2A virus is a mutant. She also alludes that this virus is masking an alkaloid of some sort. But *nowhere* does she say that this country has been a victim of a terrorist plot. She states that, and please remember, sir, this note was written sometime ago, that '…we are losing on all fronts…' which we were. Sir, is it possible, that Secretary Gonzales is feeding CNN lies to exacerbate the situation, thus directing the news media from him to you?"

"Why would he do that?" the President asked.

"Perhaps, sir, because he is a weak man who waits to see which way the wind blows then stands upwind so he doesn't have to see death, except on CNN. However, sir, we have turned the corner. Spring is almost here and reports are showing fewer influenza cases everyday."

Paul readily understood that what he was telling the President was only half true. The truth would not solve the problems. Nor would the truth bring the dead back to life. However, the truth could and would bring down a presidential administration. It could and probably would destroy the infrastructure of the nation and bring about a worldwide recession. And it would play into the hands of the country's enemies.

"I think, Mr. President that depending on what Secretary Simon finds out, that a national television address would be in order to tell our nation that the worst is behind us. Tell them that by the grace of providence, hard work, cooperation with health officials and trust, we *will* survive. Tell the nation that our enemies started vicious lies to promote fear and mistrust and tried to divert our attention elsewhere while they did their evil around the world. Or, words to that effect, sir."

The President was about to say something when Secretary Simon interrupted him. "Sir, here is the memo and the e-mail I received from Leon." Simon handed both letters to the President.

Quickly the President gave each memo a quick perusal. Then he picked up the memo from Doctor Moore and read it once again.

"Read this, Simon," the President said, anger beginning to register in his voice.

Simon's face flushed as he began to read. Little beads of saliva began forming in the corners of his mouth. "I'll kill the miserable, lying bastard!" he shouted.

"No, Mr. Secretary, please don't kill the son-of-a-bitch. Just fire his lying ass," the President said.

"Yes, Mr. President, I will not kill him and I *will* fire him today."

"I suggest that you find a very competent and trustworthy replacement as soon as possible."

"Yes, Mr. President, I will do that."

"I know someone, gentlemen, who fits that description," Paul interrupted.

"Not Petty Officer York?" the president said hesitantly, a smile forming across his lips. Paul and Simon began to chuckle. "No, sir, not him! How about Doctor Nancy Moore?"

The laughter quickly subsided and the serious tone once again returned to the President's voice. "It is your call, Simon, but she *would* be a good choice and it would be a politically correct choice."

"I agree, Mr. President, she would indeed be a good choice," Simon responded, smiling. "But who would replace Doctor Moore at the CDC Mr. President?"

"We're looking at him, Secretary Simon."

"Yes, we are, Mr. President. I can think of no one better qualified."

"I agree, Simon."

"Will you become the new director of the CDC when asked to do so, admiral?" the President asked as he stood up and extended his hand.

"Yes, sir," Paul replied, answering even before he had thought it through.

"Good! Now both of you get out of here. I have a speech to write, telling our nation we have turned the corner and are on the road to recovery."

Paul walked out of the oval office expecting to see Petty Officer York. When he did not see him, he turned and asked Mrs. Lincoln where York had gone. She began to laugh, as did the other ladies. "Sir, the President's youngest daughter, Electra, stopped by, and well, they looked at one another. He smiled and then she smiled. Well, sir, they left together and we're betting that he is going to ask her out."

"Oh, no!" Paul said, putting on his raincoat and grabbing his brief case.

Paul hurried down the hall, all the while looking for his driver. He found him standing in the lobby, talking to a very attractive young woman.

"If you're done, York, I'd like to leave now," Paul respectfully stated.

"Yes, sir!"

"Ok, Electra, I'll call you," York said, walking towards the admiral.

"Well, Petty Officer York, you sure do not lack balls. First, you ask the President of the United States to make you an admiral. He says no and now you want to marry his daughter!" Paul handed York his brief case. "Let's get out of here while I still have some dignity," Paul said, turning his back on the young petty officer and laughing, as he walked away.

∽ CHAPTER 46 ∾

GENT JAMES WEST WAS DRUNK on his ass and hadn't shaved nor bathed in a week. He liked rotating his alcoholic beverages between beer and whiskey, then to rum and Coke, followed by vodka and then tequila. As he had a lot of thinking to do, he was drunk; because he always thought best when he was drunk. On his kitchen table sat two shoeboxes. To his immediate right was a pad and pencil. To his left were his leave and earnings statements from the past year as well as his bank statements.

West had never married because he just had never found the right woman. It wasn't that he hadn't tried to find the right woman. He had and been hurt in the process. Part of it was that he loved his job and he loved the FBI and a woman would always take second place to his job. No decent woman would stand for that, so he had figured, why marry at all?

Through bloodshot eyes, West looked at his leave and earnings statement, discovering to his surprise, he had over five thousand hours of sick leave. That was almost two years of sick leave that he could take. Some quick figuring told him that would give him over thirty-eight years of service to his country. The shoeboxes contained thirty-six years of savings bonds in denominations of five hundred dollars. That was close to a quarter of a million dollars in cash. His car had been bought and paid for almost ten years ago and it had only thirty three thousand miles on it. In fact, it still had the same tires and brakes.

He had had enough bullshit. It was time to retire; just walk away and leave the safety and security of the country to the younger guys and gals. Through long swigs of vodka he sat at the kitchen table trying to figure out his retirement. But a simple question kept nagging at him. He hated to ask himself the question, but had to: "Then what?"

He owned a seven hundred acre farm in Pennsylvania that his parents had left him. His mom's sister and her husband farmed it. Every year he would get a letter from his aunt and a week later a bank statement showed up informing him what his aunt had already told him. The letter would detail all the expenses and then tell him what his share was and that it had been deposited. Sometimes when his uncle needed a new piece of farm equipment he would ask permission to buy it and they would always go halves on it. In forty years he had over a million dollars in the bank just from farming!

Fuck it, he thought, *I'll get my doctor. to say that I'm depressed and I need lots of rest and relaxation. I'll take my two years of sick leave and go back east to visit my aunt and uncle. Maybe I'll even move back and find a woman—not to marry, but one to enjoy and spoil and travel with.*

West took another deep swig from the tequila bottle, watching the little green worm jump up and down with each gulp. Suddenly, the ring of his cell phone startled him, causing his lower lip to leak and spill the clear, intoxicating liquid down his chest.

"Who is it and why the fuck are you calling me?" West answered, anger registering in his voice. His body tensed, ready for a verbal attack that he knew was to come. He had not called his kiss-ass boss to report off duty.

"West, it's O'Neal."

"O'Neal, how the fuck are you? It's been a while, buddy," West said, slurring his words while trying to focus his eyes and reach for his beer at the same time. Slobber fell from his chin onto his chest and mixed with the tequila.

"I heard through the grapevine that you solved the murders of Agent Gallopli and Doctor Schwartz; also, the murders of over forty women. I just wanted to say good job and how very proud I am to know you."

"O'Neal that is a right nice of you, you know that? You're a good guy O'Neal. Too bad those ass-kissing, butt-fucking bureaucrats shit-canned you and sent your sorry ass to Butt-Fucking Egypt."

"Tell me, Jim, how did you solve the case?" O'Neal asked.

"By accident. In fact, O'Neal, I did not solve it. I was on the hunt for a guy named William Robert Lee, a mortician, who by the way was related to Doctor Bradshaw. Anyway, when I talked to the M.E. in Valdosta, she informed me that morticians were licensed and state law required morticians to have their pictures taken. So I talked with Chief Evans of the Valdosta Police Department. He asked his dad, who happened to be a professional photographer, if he remembered taking a photograph of Mr. Lee. Well his mom did remember and somehow they dug through their files and found a negative.

"Then we had a picture. However, I believe it was on a Sunday, may have been a Saturday, I don't remember exactly, anyway, Chief Evans, Doctor Bradshaw and me were talking about the best way to proceed as we really had nothing on Mr. Lee. At the time he was just a person of interest. Then Chief Evans handed me a note. Mr. Lee, our number one suspect, had been killed in an automobile accident.

"Chief Evans was also working on a double murder. A man and wife named Houghton. They, also, were related to Mr. Lee and also Doctor Bradshaw. The chief was of the opinion that the murder of the Houghtons, was over drugs. He sent a detective and a police officer to Mr. Lee's residence. The garage door was open so, armed with a search warrant, they proceeded to search. The police officer, I think his name was Davis, found four homemade videotapes in a drawer a long with some other porno tapes. Also, he found newspaper clippings and on one of them Mr. Lee had written in the margin, 'made her squeal like a pig.' The article was about Doctor Schwartz.

"So I just happened to be in Chief Evans office, asking questions about Doctor Bradshaw, when he and I were asked to come and see some home-made videotapes. O'Neal, this guy was a sadistic son-of-a-bitch. If he had not been killed we would never have caught him. That is how slick and deadly he was. Then I had Chief Evans make copies of the tapes, I wrote my report by hand and mailed it to Mr. Fisher.

"Fisher, O'Neal, is one, smart, ass-kissing, two-faced, double-crossing mother-fucker! He pretends to be your friend but will sell you down the river. Well, I guess you know, he did it to you.

"Another thing, O'Neal, you and I were up against a diabolical combination. I cannot prove it but I think our Doctor Bradshaw was missdirecting the police and us, while at the same time directing his cousins to do his business in some sort of nefarious scheme. Chief Evans thinks Mr. Lee and Mr. Houghton were trafficking in marijuana to finance their hate group activities. He is of the opinion that Houghton and Lee kept the distribution within the state so in that way it would keep the DEA and other law enforcement agencies out of the picture. They intended to go after the more deadly drugs.

"Trafficking in marijuana doesn't bring the big prison sentences like heroin or cocaine. I could almost agree with that theory, O' Neal, except Mr. Fisher felt that some home-grown hate group had somehow managed to compromise our national security. I had to figure that he knew something I did not know. Then I talked to Bradshaw over a hamburger and beer.

"Bradshaw told me that Fisher had set up a meeting in Atlanta with some big wigs from the CDC and Surgeon General's office. That in the meeting, they had tried to convince him that the United States had become a victim of a hate group, who had contaminated our nations food supply. Fisher wanted Bradshaw to develop a psychological profile of this hate group. Bradshaw refused and well, guess what dumb ass comes walking through the door? You guessed it, O'Neal, me, sweet old gung-ho, self-righteous, gullible, USA-is-number-one me.

"I was being set up and Bradshaw put me wise to Fisher's scheme. In fact, I threw a monkey wrench into Fisher's plan when I supposedly "solved" the murders. You see, the FBI is developing a new counter terrorist program, which is part of homeland security. If Bradshaw or I could have proved that the country had indeed become victims of a terrorist plot, guess who would have gotten a big, fat promotion and millions of dollars to spend all in the name of homeland security? Yes, that moronic, ass kissing, self-serving, everybody's friend, Fisher."

"West, wind down a minute. Have you told anybody else about this?" O'Neal asked.

"No, good buddy, just you!" West replied, taking a long swig on his neglected beer.

"Good! Don't say anything to anybody. You got that?" O'Neal said, raising his voice for emphasis.

"Yeah, O'Neal, I got it! You want me to keep quite about Fisher and Bradshaw."

"What about Bradshaw?" O'Neal asked.

"Bradshaw is nothing more than a smooth talking, lying, son-of-a-bitch, who manipulates the truth, people and events. Bradshaw had Doctor Schwartz executed at the hands of his cousin Billy Bob. I can't prove it, but I know it," West said, staggering to his blue velvet recliner.

"How do you know?" O'Neal asked.

"Because who in Valdosta, besides the M.E., the police and the hotel clerk knew that she was with the FBI? When Ruthie was being raped and tortured, Mr. Lee said that she was not a *real* FBI agent, just a pretender or something like that. Now, how did he know that unless his cousin, Doctor Bradshaw, told him? Five will get you ten Bradshaw sent her to the Silent Home Mortuary to meet his sick perverted cousin. For Christ sakes, O'Neal, the man is a fucking psychiatrist. You're trying to tell me that he did not know that his cousin Billy Bob wasn't a raving psychopath? I'll kiss your ass at five o clock in Times Square if I'm wrong. But I can't prove a damn thing, O'Neal."

"West, let me get this straight. You're saying that Doctor Bradshaw is in some way responsible for the deaths of one, maybe two federal agents? And who, with the help of his two cousins and their hate group allies, somehow master-minded some sinister scheme to contaminate our country's food supply system during a major flu outbreak, killing millions of Americans, mostly black? And all the while Bradshaw has misdirected the police and federal authorities? Then, Doctor Bradshaw was asked by Mr. Fisher, Deputy Director of the FBI, to try and develop a profile of some hate group, concocted by Mr. Fisher in order to set himself up for promotion, based on convoluted scientific data and subjective hearsay and conjecture of some public health doctor? After Bradshaw refused, then Mr. Fisher asked you to investigate. You did and through sheer happenstance you solve the case? That pissed Mr. Fisher off big time and you're still not satisfied with the obvious conclusion? You want to discredit and perhaps destroy a doctor who has done nothing but good things all his life and all he did, through no fault of his own, was to be related to a mass murderer and a man who possibly was killed over drug money? Do I have it correct, West? Well do I?" O'Neal asked in an emphatic voice.

"Yeah, you got it right, asshole," West replied, throwing his head back and killing another long neck.

"Well, I suggest you take some time off, West—lots and lots of time off. Sober your sorry ass up and find your self a woman and you make love to her morning noon and night until you get your head screwed back on right. Then you forget this nonsense." O'Neal had become incensed. West always knew what buttons to push to piss him off and this time was no exception to their friendship.

"You're still an asshole, O'Neal. You can't see the truth for the pussy."

"What do you mean, Jim? Explain that remark!" By now, O'Neal had become livid with rage. "West, you drunk cock sucker, explain that remark!" O' Neal's rage was met only with silence. Then came the steady, soft cadence of snoring. West got what he wanted: The soft, warm, emotional release of a long overdue deep sleep.

"Fuck you, West," O'Neal whispered into his phone.

∽ CHAPTER 47 ∾

O'NEAL HUNG UP HIS PHONE, sat back in his office chair, put his hands behind his head and stared up at the ceiling. His eyes found the small brown water stain caused by a toilet mishap on the floor above. Minot, North Dakota was not what you would call a happening place and O'Neal knew he was in FBI purgatory. The Bureau could have sent him to Juneau or Nome, Alaska. That would have been nice as he liked to hunt, fish and hike. But, no, he drew the short end of the stick and now sat in an office not much bigger than a small bedroom, underneath the women's restroom where he could hear every flush. On a positive note, he could hear all the gossip. That was extremely interesting and figured it could be useful when he felt the need for female companionship.

Regina had visited him in Chicago a few weeks ago. She had told him sweetly, "Thanks, but no thanks. You have a good life here in Minot. Write me when you're through with the FBI."

However, right now his mind was *not* on his personal problems. Instead, he was digesting and seriously analyzing Jim's theory about Doctor Bill Bradshaw— *As ludicrous as it sounds, I have to agree West's theory has merit. No matter how one looked at it, there is no denying that Bradshaw definitely is in a position to influence and direct outcomes. He had said the FBI and police should be looking for a mortician and Bradshaw's cousin was a mortician. Maybe Bradshaw should be evaluated as a person of extreme interest?*

Jim's statement about how Mr. Lee knew Ruthie was with the FBI and how Lee knew she was not a real agent is puzzling. Another thing, how did the rental car end up at the hotel parking lot? Agent Anderson verified Bradshaw's story that he had been too drunk to drive and the restaurant manager did confirm that she had called a cab for the doctor. The cab driver then had also confirmed he had dropped Doctor Bradshaw off at the hotel. So how did Ruthie know where to pick up the car? Bradshaw said he had not told her where he was going to eat. Also, he said he woke up nude. Ruthie must have stripped him and taken the car keys. As they did have adjoining rooms, it is feasible and highly probable that Ruthie went through Bill's pockets and took the car keys.

Ok, that made sense. What if she watched the cabbie pull up and struggle with Bill? Say she went downstairs and helped the cabbie with him. Then she asked the cabbie to wait for her. What if he did that and she told him to take her to where he had picked up Bill? Then she could have gotten the car and used it that morning. At least that scenario makes sense. Also, Agent Anderson never asked the cabbie if anybody else got in the cab at the hotel. Hell, why should he? He was only interested in the doctor's alibi.

Ok, so far so good. But still, how did Ruthie know to go to the Silent Home Mortuary? Who told her to go there and who helped Mr. Lee after Ruthie's murder? Was it the other cousin? And if it was, then was Ruthie killed out of fear because of marijuana trafficking? That would make Chief Evans theory somewhat plausible if the other cousin was murdered over drug money.

But what about agent Gallopli, why was he killed? For the same reason…perhaps fear? And if fear was the reason, then Houghton and Lee must have been shitting bricks. No wonder Mr. Lee left town and no wonder the other cousin and his wife were killed to keep them quite. It all makes sense except for someone telling Mr. Lee about Ruthie and of course the question of why Doctor Bradshaw would do that…

His curiosity now really peaked, O' Neal picked up his phone and called Agent Tyrone Anderson in Atlanta. Slowly, O'Neal went over each of the unanswered questions in detail with Anderson. O'Neal knew he was leading his friend to the river of inquiry, hoping Anderson would take the challenge and investigate Doctor Bradshaw as a person of extreme interest.

∽ CHAPTER 48 ∾

ITTY CONSUMED BILL'S THOUGHTS. SOMEHOW, he had fallen madly in love with the beautiful and talented young woman. It wasn't supposed to happen, but it did. He wasn't sorry though, as Kitty was an accomplished pianist, an excellent chef, a great conversationalist and she had a voracious sexual appetite that matched his own.

Having spent three days and nights with Kitty, Bill was now addicted to her. It seemed he wanted her all the time. He wanted to kiss her softly, taste her skin and gently stroke her face. Then he wanted to hold her close, feel her breath on his neck and feel the softness of her breast as it rested against his chest. He had it bad and he knew it. She was a tonic, a rejuvenating elixir for his tired, worn out body and broken spirit. Not only did he want her, but also his whole being felt the need of her. It wasn't just for sex, but for life—his life. The question was, he had been asking himself: *Does Kitty feel the same way about me?*

Bill looked at his watch. It had only been three hours since he had left Kitty. He was hungry and he had to pee. Knowing Route 85 was only twenty miles up the road, he decided to find a truck stop, fill up and take care of his other needs at the same time. He was cruising the highway going eighty. His fuzz-buster was turned on and he figured at this speed, he would make Washington D.C. around 10:00 p.m.

As he drove, he decided he would call Mary when he got into Richmond in order to make sure she was all right with coming back to work. Also, she could get him caught up on all the news and gossip. Then somewhere in the conversation, whenever the opportunity presented itself, he decided to ask her if she wanted to move to Georgia, telling her he would pay for her move and she could keep the same salary.

His thoughts next jumped to buying Cousin Billy Bob's estate. In his mind, after that, he planned that he and Kitty would marry. It all sounded like a great plan to him. He didn't even consider it might not work out as he planned. He was hyped and his thoughts were on euphoric cloud at the moment.

Speaking of a great plan, he remembered there were still a half million tubes of Black Beauty's shampoo, body lotion and hair gel to dispense. However, that was next year's project. Billy Bob had correctly figured that by not shipping and distributing all of the products at the same time, they could save money and with the money saved they could dispense the rice and gelatin to a larger portion of the country thus being more cost-effective. Then if Operation Bitter Vetch was successful, the Aryan Nation and some other hate groups and quasi-military groups would help pay for the distribution of Black Beauty's beauty products.

However, it had been Jonas Tubbs who had come up with the idea of using the Small Business Administration. Billy Bob had liked that idea even better—having the government help pay for exterminating the nig-gers. They both had laughed so hard, they had had to sit down to catch their breath.

The beautiful part of Tubbs plan was that he would apply for a grant from the Small Business Administration. Knowing the entire process would take at least six months; he and Billy Bob had planned to proceed with Operation Bitter Vetch. Tubbs was to apply for a business license in Richmond; Billy Bob would apply for one in Valdosta. Each would say he was going into the transportation, distribution and warehouse busi-ness. They would file for Department of Transportation permits at both the state and federal levels and then all they needed was the money to get started.

The name of the company was to be Tubbs and Lee Transport. They would buy two used trucks. Then rent warehouse space in Richmond and have the beauty products shipped from California. After that, they would hire a front man, preferably an individual from the Middle East and of the Muslim religion, if possible, an individual with strong ties to a terrorist group.

For this, Billy Bob had asked Bill if he could get information from the FBI on someone meeting this requirement. Bill had thought he could.

It was decided that whoever they got, the poor, dumb, son-of-a-bitch was going to be the fall guy in case the FBI came knocking. What with his ties to a terrorist group and knowing that the government would be quick to blame a terrorist group, why not let him take the fall. That would leave Tubbs and Lee transportation in the clear because they could say, if asked, "We only delivered the product. We did not know what the product was."

When the grant money was received and deposited into the compa-ny's account, it would help fund the business and pay for the distribution of Black Beauty's beauty treatments. The front man would in turn be told to hire young black kids or Muslim males who would distribute the free samples to their own kind, next flu season. However, this time they would start in Washington D.C. then follow a different distribution path—Baltimore, Philadelphia, Raleigh Durham, Selma, Birmingham and Montgomery.

Knowing that the federal government would be starting a massive, nation-wide immunization program, probably in late September or mid October for high-risk individuals, they wanted their attack to commence in late October or early November. Bill felt reasonably certain, based on his recent experience with the CDC, that they would be quicker to respond to any influenza outbreak, as this year's complacency had cost the nation dearly.

Bill had become so engrossed in thought that he had not heard the alarm of the fuzz buster until it was to late. He was scared back to reality when he heard the loud whining sound of the state trooper's siren. Looking to his left, he saw the trooper pointing to him, telling him to pull over. Slowing down, Bill pulled over, angry for being so stupid and embarrassed.

The trooper was courteous and professional. Asked for Bill's driver license, proof of insurance and registration. He informed Bill that his radar had clocked him at a hundred and the trooper was curious if there was an emergency to justify that speed.

"No, officer, there was no emergency," Bill respectfully replied.

Taking the ticket, he paid for it using his debit card. The officer stapled the ticket and receipt together, returned Bill's driver's license, registration and proof of insurance and wished Bill a good day.

Bill looked down and read the ticket. He was in North Carolina. He had been so absorbed in detail and planning that he had failed to comprehend his speed. Disgusted with himself, he decided to pull off at Anderson, North Carolina, find a gas station and rest room. After that, he would buy something to eat. By his calculations, he had traveled more than two hundred miles in two and a half hours. Of course, he had just paid for the privilege.

Pretty soon he had gassed up the beamer, checked the oil and was sitting at a booth in Denny's. He ordered and as he waited his thoughts turned back to Kitty.

Looking at his watch, he knew she would now be at work. She would have her sandwich, apple or maybe an orange packed in her school bag. Her textbooks would be close by, if not opened and ready to be read. He knew she used every spare moment to read; that's why she was an honor student. Though he wanted to call her, he decided against it, as the sound of her voice would only make him long for her all the more, tempting him to turn around and drive back to Valdosta. That was something he could not do at this moment in time.

Other than the speeding ticket, the rest of the trip was uneventful. Bill opened his condo door around 9:00 pm. He smiled to himself, knowing he had set a personal speed record. After he unpacked his bag, he sorted his mail. Most of it he threw in the trash; there were a couple of bills and a personal letter. The letter was post-marked from Richmond. The address had been printed. Each letter was spaced and blocked in perfect sequence. It had been printed on motel stationary with no return address. Instinctively, Bill knew what he was about to read were cousin Billy Bob's last written words.

Dear Cousin,

Tubbs and I have finished your bidding. We have killed millions of niggers, a few spics and some white trash. Must say we enjoyed it and look forward to working with you on Operation Black Beauty next fall. I wanted to tell you in case you get any ideas about betraying me that I videotaped me with that lady doctor you had me kill. It is my insurance policy against you.

Also, Tubbs put you down as a reference on the application for the Small Business Administration. So, cousin, watch your step and guard your ass.

Billy

Bill tore the letter up in tiny pieces and pushed the pieces into the garbage disposal. He turned on the hot water and flipped the switched, listening as the disposal ground the note into pulp and the water flushed the words out of his mind.

Bill walked upstairs and undressed. He needed to take a shower and think.

The water hit Bill square in the face, forcing him to adjust the spray nozzle. As he lathered his body, Bill reminded himself: *Billy Bob is now dead. As for Tubbs, I don't know how to locate him. Cousin Jimmy Ray is also gone. All the brains and manpower were either missing or dead. So how then could anybody connect me to anything?*

As to the video, if it was found, so what! It would show some pervert raping and murdering a woman I just happened to know. As far as Jonas Tubbs is concerned, he was a patient of mine who took liberties with his doctor's address and obviously falsified the application.

Bill smiled; he knew he was in the clear all the way.

∞ CHAPTER 49 ∞

LYING IN BED, HER HEAD resting on that special place a man has for holding a woman, Nancy could feel Cliff's chest slowing rising, then lowering has he slept.

Unable to sleep, Nancy was marveling that she had found something that for her had never existed—Love! She guessed it was love, as she had never been in love before. Yes, she had had infatuations and flirtations and two very serious relationships, but that was eons ago. Now she had met the man who loved her for herself. A man who ignited her latent passion so long repressed, because she had lost her femininity and had become a corporate machine, displaying no emotion. She had deliberately suppressed her true feelings, so as not to reveal any weaknesses for her rivals to capitalize on and exploit for their personal gain or profit.

This man, with his raw sexuality and simple, straightforward manner, had told her how he had always felt about her. In no uncertain terms he had told her that she belonged to him. In simple, direct, almost Neanderthal terms he had said, "I have loved you for years. But you were always too busy to notice me." It had taken a national catastrophe to bring them to-gether. Now, only death would keep them apart.

Pulling the blanket up over her shoulder, Nancy felt sleep returning to her now very relaxed and sated body. Cliff had taken care of all her ten-sion.

Not wanting to waste any more time, she and Cliff had decided to fly to Las Vegas the coming Friday afternoon and they would be married on Saturday. Yes, she knew it was stupid, but Cliff was very serious. So seri-ous in fact that after dinner last night he had taken her to a jeweler and bought her two rings. A beautiful matching set of diamond rings. Cliff was very serious about marrying her. Forget they both worked for the CDC.

So why not? Nancy thought. It was the best offer she had ever had!

ᦕ CHAPTER 50 ᦖ

P AUL WAS SITTING IN HIS leather lounge chair that Andy had
bought him for his fortieth birthday. Though that had been only
fifteen years ago, it seemed like a lifetime. He was sipping at
a bourbon and ginger while his eyes were glued to the television. The
President of the United States was about to address the nation. He wanted
to discuss the past events and predict future events,—as only a president
seemed able to do.

He was unable to speak for the nation. However, Paul could speak for
himself and his office. What he could say was that it was real and fun, but
not real fun. Under his leadership, over twenty million Americans were
dead. Under his guidance, the nation was close to anarchy and bankruptcy.
And for his leadership skills, he would be named the new head of the
CDC. *The Peter Principal is alive and well in the good old U.S. of A.,* he thought.

After that thought zipped through his mind, Paul came to the realization that he was drunk. He missed Andy. Fuck the president. Paul picked
up the phone. It was time to bring his wife home so he could take care

of her. That was a laugh; take care of her. The woman took care of the Surgeon General so he could take care of the nation. Andy, the woman who had raised two sons while working full-time and who cleaned and ironed and did charity work. Yeah, right! Take care of Andy that was a hoot.

Paul did not listen to the president. He called his wife and asked her to come home, telling her he loved and needed her. All she said was, "Yes, honey, I'll leave tomorrow. I love you."

After he hung up the phone, Paul broke down in tears. The stress had finally taken its toll. He was nothing without his wife and he knew that.

CHAPTER 51

MARY LOOKED RADIANT AS SHE sat across from Bill. Her eyes seemed brighter and her face seemed to actually shine. "Tell me, Mary, how are you doing?" Bill asked.

"Oh, doctor, you won't believe it but I found a man. He's in the military, a major. He is so cute. I can't believe my good fortune," Mary said, gushing like a schoolgirl after her first kiss.

"Really, Mary, that's wonderful! I'm so happy for you," Bill said, smiling at her. "So, Mary, back to the local news. How bad was it here in the city with the flu and all?" Bill's voice became serious like he really cared.

"Not good, doctor. D.C. and the surrounding areas have been devastated. Whole families and neighborhoods have been wiped out. On the local news, yesterday, they showed all the new graves at one of the local cemeteries. It looked like a war zone with the ground all piled up like slit trenches. In Bowie, Maryland, the state has dug a huge mass grave. They showed guys with facemasks grabbing the dead out of every kind of truck you can think of and they were throwing the bodies into the hole. No body bags, as there are none. Some were wrapped in sheets or blankets, but most were not.

"When you go shopping the stores are virtually empty. Streets are deserted. The rush hour is a joke. Maybe two hundred cars, like early Sunday morning traffic."

"How about the crime rate. Has it gone down at all?" Bill asked, taking a sip of coffee.

"What crime?" Mary retorted. "Last night they showed the 911 operators knitting or playing solitaire. They showed traffic cops giving out parking tickets instead of roping off crime scenes."

"How many have died so far?"

"They estimate about seventy-five thousand in D.C. and around the same amount in the surrounding suburbs," Mary responded. "So, doctor, how was Atlanta?"

"Atlanta was a very somber and sobering experience."

"In other words, it sucked," Mary said.

Bill laughed. She could always make him laugh.

"Let's say, Mary, it was informative and I learned a lot about our government," Bill said, smiling at Mary's inquisitive look. "Mary, the CDC, the Surgeon General's office and the FBI think that our country has been attacked by either a terrorist group or a hate group, who supposedly has contaminated our country's food supply system from California to Boston.

"Some captain from the surgeon's office even showed me a map detailing the progression of the influenza from California eastward. He said he had never seen an epidemic travel in a straight line. The captain stated that this influenza came by commercial air from Asia to the United States by someone who was infected with the virus and that this influenza virus was killing only Blacks, Hispanics and poor Whites.

"I told him that the blacks and Hispanics were not big believers in immunization shots. Then the CDC threw in some kind of wild-ass theory about the virus strain being contaminated with an alkaloid of some sort that could only be introduced by man.

"Fisher, the Deputy Director of the FBI, asked me to develop a profile on hate groups that could or would do such a terrible thing. I told him, 'No.' " Bill took a large gulp of coffee as his throat was dry from so much talking.

Mary sat silent; her smile gone; her face pale. Bill had badly scared her. That had not been his intention but that's what he had done.

"So, doctor, all these innocent people are dying because some crazy group of hate-filled, godless men decided to kill all the Blacks because they could? They want to exterminate them because there skin is different and as a way to reduce crime or perhaps it's to make room for new condos, or maybe it's because there isn't enough work for White folks so they decided to kill all the Blacks so the Whites can have jobs?" Mary's eyes were tearing up and her once pale face was now red.

"Now, Mary, please don't get all worked up over this. It was only a theory. Perhaps speculation would be a better word. They're just trying to cover their asses, Mary, because they were not prepared to deal with this catastrophe." Bill was talking fast and he knew his voice was raised for emphasis as he tried to reassure Mary.

"I also met a woman, Mary! Her name is Kitty. She is younger than me by about ten years, I think. It is my desire for her to be my wife. Also, I want to close this office and move back to Georgia. I intended to ask you if you wanted to move with me. Your salary will not change and I will pay for your move. Plus, I will pay for your first month's rent."

Mary did not respond to his offer. Instead, she sat quietly for a moment, then turned her body sideways, her posture suddenly changing as her head slumped down to her chest. Bill could see the crying before he heard it. Reaching out, he handed her a box of tissues. He did not know if the tears were of joy or anger. So Bill did what all men do. He waited!

ᕤ CHAPTER 52 ᕤ

A GENT TYRONE ANDERSON SAT AT his desk in Atlanta with his head bent and his fingers playing with the NFL tie clip that he had bought on a visit to the Football Hall of Fame. He was thinking about Agent O'Neal's theory concerning Doctor Bill Bradshaw. Tyrone knew that what the doctor had said was all true because he had verified everything himself. In fact, he had even told O'Neal he had verified everything.

Now, based on nothing but a hunch, O'Neal had asked him to make Doctor Bradshaw a "person of interest" in the murder or murders of one, possibly two FBI agents. Because some homicidal maniac says, "You ain't no real agent" as he is killing her. And O'Neal wanted him to ruin a man over that? *Hell, if I didn't know better I'd think O'Neal had talked to Agent West,* he thought.

Tyrone decided to kick fate in the butt. Picking up the phone, he dialed Doctor Bradshaw's number. He wanted to ask the doctor a few questions, more for clarification than investigation. Based on the doctor's responses, he would decide which way he wanted to go. The phone rang once, then twice. "Hello, Doctor Bradshaw's office," the voice was sweet and clear.

"Yes, this is Agent Tyrone Anderson of the FBI. I would like to talk with Doctor Bradshaw, if I may."

"Yes, Agent Anderson. The doctor is not in session, yet. I'll ask him if he can talk with you," Mary said, putting him on hold.

"Doctor, there is an Agent Anderson of the FBI on line one. He wants to talk with you. I also want to remind you that you have a session in fifteen minutes."

"Thank you Mary, put Agent Anderson through, please," Bill said sweetly, trying to get back in Mary's favor. Evidently a move to Georgia would wreck her love life.

"Hello, Agent Anderson. How are you this morning, sir?" Bill's enthusiasm took the agent aback for a second.

"I'm fine, doctor. I'm calling you because I have some unanswered questions and that just annoys the hell out of me. Doctor, I'm hoping you can help me."

"Ok, sir, ask your questions," Bill said, purposefully sounding up beat and very positive.

"Well, doctor, they are rather personal and perhaps a bit insensitive, but they would clear things up for me," Tyrone said, as he adjusted the note pad on his desk and clicked his government issued black ink pen.

"Doctor, were you and Doctor Schwartz romantically involved?"

The tone of the question, the person who was asking it and the simple fact that agent Anderson was a co-worker of Agent West's, made Bill suspect danger. *West had suspected me as well. Maybe I didn't sell West on my innocence after all. I can tell something is not right. Be convincing and be forceful,* he thought, *the FBI is only fishing.*

"Yes, sir, Ruth and I had become lovers," Bill replied, his voice soft and serene.

"Well, then, doctor, that would answer my next question, which was: If you were drunk and lying on the bathroom floor, how did you wake up naked? In other words, who undressed you? But that is now obvious."

"Oh, I see what you're looking for now," Bill interjected. "How did Ruthie get the car when she did not know where I had gone to eat?" Bill asked.

"Yes, doctor, that is one of the big questions," Agent Anderson replied doodling on his note pad.

"You know, sir, and this is just speculation on my part, but knowing how you guy's work, I know you have already checked out my cab ride story. But my question to you is: Have you asked the cabbie if a woman got into cab after he dropped me off? In other words, could Ruth have asked the cabbie to wait on her while she helped me to my room, stripped me, took the keys, then let me lie in my own vomit on the bathroom floor while she ran down the back stairs? And then had the cabbie take her back to where the car was? Is that possible, Agent Anderson? If not, sir, then I cannot answer any more of your questions, because I don't know what happened."

"No, sir, I did not do that but I will call the cab company and ask that question," Tyrone replied, looking back over his notes and trying to find the name and number of the cab company.

"What is the other big question, Anderson?" Bill asked.

"What do you mean, doctor? What *other* question?" Tyrone said, momentarily caught off guard.

"You said that was one of the big questions. I'm asking what your other question is?" Bill asked.

"Oh, yes, doctor, I remember now. Sorry for my confusion but I was looking for the cab company and number in Valdosta," Tyrone replied. "The question is, doctor, other than yourself, the hotel staff and Doctor Regina Furbish, who else knew that Doctor Schwartz was working for the FBI?"

"Well, Agent Anderson, I think I may have told my cousin Jimmy Ray, because at dinner he asked me what I was doing back in Valdosta. I'm not certain…but I may have told him that Doctor Schwartz and I were profiling a serial killer. So other than those you mentioned, I'd have to say my cousin and his wife," Bill replied.

Bill knew that response would end it all. *How could the FBI investigate when all the principals involved are dead? Logically it makes perfect sense. I told Jimmy Ray, Jimmy Ray told Cousin Billy Bob, Billy Bob got scared, lured Ruth to the Silent Home Mortuary and killed her.*

"Hello, are you there, sir?" Bill asked.

"Yes, doctor, I'm here," Tyrone replied.

"Agent Anderson, my patient is here, sir. I must now go. I hope I cleared things up for you. And tell Agent West I said, hello. Will you do that for me?"

"Yes, sir, I will and thank you. You have helped me tremendously," Tyrone replied.

Agent Anderson decided O'Neal was wrong. *If Doctor Bradshaw had told his cousin and he probably did, then his cousin Jimmy Ray probably told his cousin Billy Bob, who then laid a trap for the inexperienced and much too naïve Doctor Schwartz. Then he had killed her.*

Just to be sure he, called the cab company in Valdosta and asked the dispatcher to check the cabbie's log. The total time spent on the phone was less than five minutes. Total time saved in a worthless investigation, probably weeks.

O'Neal, now I know why you are in Minot. You're an arrogant dumb ass. The dispatcher verified there had been another fare from the hotel back to the End Zone Restaurant.

Case closed.

⚜

Bill sat in his very quiet office. His head was beginning to hurt. He felt that old familiar throbbing at the base of the occipital lobe and knew from experience that a migraine headache was not too far away. It had been months since he had had one. Though he had medication for the migraines, it was at home. His only recourse was to try and drink hot black coffee. The caffeine acted as a stimulant, constricting the capillaries, thus staving off a potential migraine. However, all caffeine ever seemed to do for him was make him jittery and cause him to urinate a lot. *Although, a migraine would be worth it if it stopped West cold in his tracks. I know West is behind Agent Anderson's questions. So throwing a dead cousin at the FBI makes everything credible. Besides, what could they prove? Nothing that's what!*

∾ CHAPTER 53 ∾

NANCY WAS BUSY TRYING TO clear up some last minute details and make some job assignments for the staff. Cliff he was doing the same thing. Nobody knew what was about to happen and keeping a secret at the CDC was near impossible. Looking at her watch, Nancy saw she had only two hours to wrap everything up and be at the airport. What with the distance and road construction it would take about an hour. So she gave herself thirty more minutes.

She was about to call Cliff when Carol walked into her office. "Doctor Moore, you have Secretary Simon on line one. He says it's urgent!"

"Thank you, Carol," Nancy smiled and picked up. "Morning, sir, how may the CDC help you today?' Nancy said.

"Good Morning, doctor. I have a special request for you and it comes from both me and the President of the United States."

"Yes, Mr. Secretary, what is the request?" Nancy asked, her voice becoming serious and very business-like.

"Doctor, on behalf of the President of the United States I am requesting that you take the Under Secretary of Health and Human Services position."

Nancy had heard rumors that Leon was gone, but nothing official. She guessed it was now official.

"Sir, can I call you back on Monday. I need some time to think about this?" Nancy said trying not to let her enthusiasm and shock get in the way of her professional demeanor.

"I was going to suggest that very thing, doctor. I think that is a good idea. I trust I can rely on your silence until you decide."

"Yes, Mr. Secretary, you can rely on my silence, and thank you, sir. No matter what decision I make, it is a great honor." Nancy replied.

Damn it! Wouldn't you know it? Just when things are happening for the better, I get selected to become the next Under Secretary of Health and Human Services. This decision I must talk over with my future husband. Nancy thought as she smiled and then giggled to herself. She liked the sound of it. "My husband…"

⚜

Nancy and Cliff were on their way to the airport when Nancy finally shared her news. "Cliff, we are not even married yet and there is a dilemma that can and possibly will, affect us." Nancy said.

"Yes, Nancy, I know. I have made the correct and logical decision for us," Cliff said, smiling at his bride to be.

"Oh? And who told you? It was supposed to be a secret." Nancy replied, surprise registering in her voice.

"Nancy, the rules of employment say that a husband and wife cannot work with or for one another. Thus, after we are married, I will retire and become a house hubby. Then I can start taking care of you and support you. It is the only logical thing to do," Cliff said, reaching over and taking Nancy's hand and kissing it.

"You would do that for me? You would retire so I can move on and do other things" Nancy asked.

"Yes, honey, I will do that for you. I will sell my house, and then we can buy a bigger house to accommodate all our belongings."

"Cliff, not more than one hour ago I received a call from Secretary Simon. I have been offered Leon's job," Nancy said.

Nancy smiled, took Cliff's hand in hers, reached up and kissed him on his cheek. She definitely had found the right man and he, without a doubt, loved her. How lucky could a girl get?

∽ CHAPTER 54 ∾

BILL WAS LONELY AND VERY horny. He needed Kitty. Over the past six weeks, they had chatted and sent funny cards and Bill had even written what he considered a love letter. However, chatting on the telephone and sending e- mails did not take the place of holding the woman you loved in your arms.

He was just about to get on-line and make a plane and hotel reservation to Valdosta when Mary walked into his office. She had the usual: Correspondence that needed to be signed, plus the checks and a hot cup of coffee for him.

Since he had been back she had not mentioned the move to Georgia, nor had she said another thing about her cute major. So Bill decided to leave well enough alone for now.

He already contacted a real estate agent about Billy Bob's property and of course Jimmy Ray's land. As both men died in testate, the court had to make the final decision. Nevertheless, Bill had gone to high school and college with the judge, and they had killed many brain cells together.

Therefore, he decided to call his old friend and see if the judge could help him.

"Mary, what does my schedule look like today and Friday?" Bill asked, sitting back in his chair.

"You have three sessions this morning, and this afternoon you have your group therapy session. On Friday, I think you have only two sessions, and then we were to go over the office finances. You were to decide on renewing the lease for the office," Mary responded, getting up from the chair and walking out with all the checks and letters.

So much for a Friday morning flight to Georgia, he thought. Mary would not allow him to take off until everything was done. Though he was the boss, Mary ran the show and that's the way it was. He picked up the file of the patient he was about to see. It was Sally Pritchard's file. Quickly, he scanned it and reviewed his notes. He liked Sally, not only as a patient but also as a person. She was what his grandma would have called "good people." Yes, she was just that: A very good person. All she needed was a man to love her, someone to help her through the tough emotional times, and give her moral support.

Bill decided to go to the rest r before Sally arrived. Mary had flushed his kidneys with t cups in an hour and a half that was a lot of coffee for Bill's urinary and nervous systems to take.

He decided to call Kitty between his sessions and fly her up to Washington. The Japanese cherry trees were in full bloom now and the dogwoods, making the "Monument Valley" a sight to be seen. Monument Valley is what Bill called it. It was the area around all the major national monuments. Kitty and he could stroll the walkway holding hands enjoying the beauty of the national capital.

Sally had the most interesting dreams. They always seemed to be in a logical sequence of events. Never about sex or money though at least she had never confided to him of those dreams. This time the dream was about animals, specifically about dogs.

After six months of intensive psychotherapy, she had a breakthrough! From the second session on, Bill had felt Sally was repressing her own primitive desires and sexual nature. Depending on the particular animal, Sally dreamed about, it could be the key to unlocking her subconscious and freeing her fears. Animals symbolized the untamed and uncivilized aspects of each person. Thus, to dream that you are fighting an animal signifies that you are trying to push back and reject a hidden part of yourself into your subconscious. To dream that your particular animal can talk, represents superior knowledge. Often the animal gives a message that comes in the form of some sort of wisdom.

To see a dog in your dream could indicate several things that Sally might be experiencing. The most frequent was the loss of a skill that had been long ignored. Furthermore, seeing or talking to a dog in your dream can symbolize intuition, loyalty, generosity and fidelity. If the dog is vicious, it signifies inner conflict. It could also signify betrayal or untrustworthiness on the part of someone you held in trust or high esteem. Now that Bill had identified Sally's inner conflicts and issues that she needed to address and resolve, effective meaning and long lasting treatment could begin.

Sally had been gone only a short time. Bill was still writing his notes in her file when Mary walked in with the next patient's folder. Bill took one look at the purple color and knew that this was a new patient. He looked at the name, and something clicked in the deepest recesses of his brain. He was in trouble, and he knew it. H read the patient's bio, and knew this was the person who could destroy him. And now patient was now waiting in his outer office. Bill's thoughts were interrupted when Mary buzzed him on the intercom.

"Doctor, you have a long-distance call on line one. She says her name is Kitty."

Bill forgot his terror, for the moment, and picked up the phone. "Hello. I have been thinking about you all day," Bill said.

"I hope they were good thoughts, daddy!"

"What did you just call me?" Bill asked.

"I called you, daddy, for that's what you will become this October," Kitty said, her voice quaking, as she feared her one-time lover would deny her. And in truth, Kitty had fallen madly in love with him.

"Kitty, do you want to fly up to Washington? It is beautiful this time of year," Bill said softly.

"Yes, I would like that very much. I miss you terribly," Kitty answered, her voice starting to tighten, as she held back her tears.

"I will wire you the money, today. I will see you tomorrow. And Kitty, I'm madly in love with you. Please don't cry and don't be afraid. I will protect you."

THE END

www.ingramcontent.com/pod-product-compliance
Lightning Source LLC
Chambersburg PA
CBHW020332180626
46812CB00001B/164